I0633543

Moving is Murder

Joan Havelange

Published by Brown Wolf Publishing, 2025.

Also by Joan Havelange

Mabel and Violet Mysteries
Wayward Shot
Death and Denial
The Trouble with Funerals
The Suspects
Murder Exit Stage Right

Standalone
Moving is Murder

Published by Brown Wolf Publishing
Saskatchewan, Canada

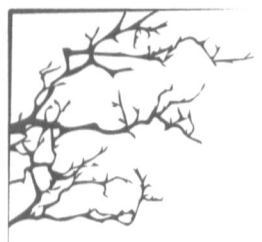

Dedication

To my readers.
Thank you for allowing me to share my stories with you.

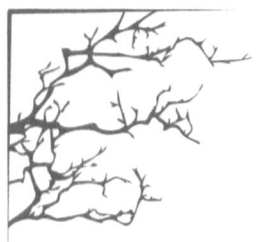

Chapter One

"Gertrude," Linda Burton hollered for the third time. The petite, freckle-face woman with auburn hair stood on a wooden veranda overlooking the backyard. Linda rested her forearms on the railing, her brown eyes searching for movement. Was the cat prowling in the yard? Or had it wandered away? A warm spring breeze rustled the lilac bushes that lined one side of Mabel Havelock's backyard. Linda took a deep breath, enjoying the floral aroma of the lilacs. Overhead, a half-moon shone. The moonlight filtered through green leafy trees onto Mabel's newly planted garden. There was no sign of Gertrude, Mabel's cat.

Linda was house-sitting for Mabel Havelock. Mabel had broken her foot; the woman was a good friend of Violet Ficher, Linda's aunt. Her Aunt Violet explained that she had to get Mabel out of town and away from her garden because, broken foot or not, Mabel would be out in the garden, hoeing and weeding. So, her aunt took Mabel to Calgary, where they both had daughters. Linda, who was newly divorced, had been a kindergarten teacher at a school in Regina for ten years and had just quit her job. Now, she was between jobs and at loose ends, and the peace and quiet of house-sitting appealed to her. City life was fine while she was working, but now the country life was calling.

Maybe not only a change of jobs but also a change of location was what she needed. She was still young at thirty. She'd find a job. Her ex-husband Howard's gift to her on her thirtieth birthday was the announcement he was leaving her for a younger woman. Linda took in a deep breath of the fragrant, fresh air, yes, this friendly, peaceful community of Glenhaven looked inviting. It might be time to move.

"Gertrude," Linda called again. She wanted the cat in the house. If something happened to Gertrude while she was house-sitting, she would never forgive herself. Linda had grown very fond of the tabby cat. Her ex said having a pet in an apartment was unfair to the animal to be alone all day. And as always, she'd been compliant. It was time to make decisions for herself. If she did move to Glenhaven, she would get a cat. She had fallen in love with Gertrude.

A small furry animal shot across the lawn. The animal stopped and crouched. Looking down from the porch, Linda couldn't tell if it was the cat, a gopher, or a squirrel. The animal darted across the grass into the lilac bushes. "Kitty, kitty," Linda called in the high-pitched voice one used for calling cats. She padded down the porch steps and across the lawn. Linda sat on her heels, peered under the shrub, and called again. She pressed her lips together and sighed. There was no answering meow.

Linda scrambled to her feet and brushed the grass off her knees. It would be a fabulous evening for a stroll down the back lane. Something she would never consider in the city, but she might find Gertrude, who was probably a frequent visitor down the alley. The alleyway, lined with trees and hedges, was undoubtedly good hunting for the errant cat. But Mabel's cat was old, and Linda suspected Gertrude was unsuccessful in her hunts.

A brilliant streak of light shot across the night sky, leaving a long, shimmering white tail. Linda tilted her head back and watched the path of the meteor. The meteor disappeared as quickly as it came. Didn't people make a wish on a shooting star? If she had, what would she want to wish for? Maybe good health? She was already healthy. Good fortune? She was fortunate. A safe and happy life? Linda smiled. The shooting star was long gone. Too late to make a wish.

Linda trod across the lawn. Dew was already forming, making the grass damp. Her feet, encased in red rubber flip-flops, felt squishy. "Gertrude," she called as she ducked under a branch from a low-hanging tree. A leafy twig brushed her head. Combing the leaves from her hair, Linda continued down the back alley, calling for the cat. She listened. But there was no answering meow, just rustling in the grass as some small rodent scurried away.

Continuing her trek down the laneway, Linda pursed her lips and shook her head. Many of the backyards had overgrown hedges, which was in contrast to the neighbour's front yards. The yards along the street were well-maintained. With green-mowed lawns and neat, well-tended flowerbeds. If she could see past the shrubs and trees, would she also see untidy backyards?

As she passed a tall wooden-planked backyard fence, Linda chuckled to herself. Who were Mabel's neighbours trying to keep out? After all, this was little Glenhaven, Saskatchewan. Linda lived in Regina and never walked down a back alley alone at night. But Linda felt at ease in Glenhaven, a friendly little community in the middle of the Canadian prairies. She had nothing to fear as she walked down the dark alley, even though she had only the moon and the stars to guide her.

A low, menacing growl sent the hairs on the back of Linda's neck to stand. She sucked in her breath and froze. The threatening growl came from behind a tall chain-link fence. Ferocious barking followed. Linda's heart leapt as she darted to the far side of the lane, falling on her hands and knees. Scrambling to her feet, she looked across the narrow gravel road. A massive rottweiler charged at the metal fence. The fence shook. Linda recoiled, backing up even farther from the raging beast. The enormous rottweiler bared its teeth, viciously growling and barking. The angry animal, snarling and growling, lunged repeatedly at the fence; the chain-link fence rattled, swaying with each leap. The enraged rottweiler stood on its hind legs, pawing to get out. Linda turned and fled. Her short legs pumped as her flip-flops slapped on the gravelled laneway. She raced down the alley away from the chain-link monster. When the barking stopped, Linda stopped running and bent over. She put her hands on her knees, her breath coming in gulps. Who the heck lived there? And what did they have that needed a rottweiler to protect?

Linda's breath eased. She stood, brushed off her hands and knees, peering down the dark alley toward the chain-link monster. She would walk down to the other end of the alleyway and return home via the sidewalk. There was no way she was going back near that crazy dog. Sure, the dog was behind the chain-link fence. But what if somehow it escaped? She was not going to take that chance.

Calling again for the cat, Linda waited and listened. Again, no answering meows, only the cries of a far-off hoot owl. After her heart returned to its regular beat, Linda resumed the trek down the lane. She slowed her pace. It was a beautiful night. Linda wasn't going to let some mangy hound spoil her walk. The owl hooted again as she passed by more backyards with tall wooden fences. Linda stepped into a pothole and stumbled. She shook the gravel from her flip-flop. In her opinion, the alleyway had more than its fair share of potholes. But still, walking down this alley was a treat. It was something she would never do in her city neighbourhood at night.

A light gust of wind whistling through the leaves in the trees blew Linda's short auburn hair. The warm breeze felt wonderful on her bare arms. Overhead, the stars twinkled, and a sliver of the moon appeared now and again through the clouds. *Country living was the best*, Linda thought as she continued her stroll. Everyone here would know everyone on the block. In the city, you were lucky if you knew who lived in the next apartment. And you minded your own business. She heard that people in a small town were a little nosey. But maybe that was the price you paid for living in a caring community. Someone would always be ready to offer a helping hand. The idea of moving to Glenhaven was growing. She was house-sitting for Mabel for a week. She'd see at the end of the week if she still thought that moving was a good idea.

Strange high-pitched chirping sounds made Linda stop in her tracks. Her eyes darted, searching in the darkness for the source of the weird chattering. It definitely didn't sound like crickets or birds. Uttering a small, frightened cry, Linda ducked. A flock of chirping, bird-like creatures flew straight at her from across the alley. She sucked in her breath, whimpering as she felt the flutter of wings inches above her head. The hoard of small black, clicking creatures beat their wings, circling. Linda covered her head with her hands. Were these bats? Did bats get in your hair? Or was that an old wives' tale? It was never an old husband's tale. Giggling nervously, Linda hunkered close to the ground.

The strange fluttering hoard flew off into the night. Linda rose to her feet, brushing the dirt from her hands on her denim shorts. She looked at the night sky, only the moon and the stars. No flying, nocturnal creatures. Linda blew out a breath. Whatever they were, they had disappeared. Satisfied, Linda resumed her walk. Her feet crunched on the gravel. It was quiet. The only sounds now were the crickets, no high-pitched chirping bats. A dog barked in the distance, not the ferocious barking monster dog. This was more of a yapping. Was Gertrude in the dog's yard?

Linda hurried down the rutted alley, listening for a cat and dog fight. Her flip-flop twisted, coming off her foot, and she stepped on a stone. Linda grimaced. She ought to have worn runners. Linda picked up her sandal and hopped on one foot to an old, weathered wooden garbage stand. She sat on the edge of the structure, rubbing her foot. Examining her flip-flop, she pondered the name. Flip-flops were an apt name for the sandal. The darn thing flipped off her foot.

Linda wrinkled her nose at an unpleasant odour, and it wasn't the garbage stand. Her Aunt Violet told her the town had stopped the garbage pickup in the back alley four years ago. No, the tall hedge behind the garbage stand was the source of the peculiar stinky odour. Linda decided the hedgerow must be boxwood. It was a beautiful hedge, but it had an odd smell. She remembered the odour from her childhood. Her mother had a boxwood border in her yard.

"Son of a bitch," swore a man from the other side of the hedge.

Linda stopped shaking her flip-flop and froze. Was that digging? What an odd time to be gardening. The man swore again. Linda dropped her sandal and tried to peer through the thick hedge behind the old garbage stand.

"Son of a bitch, first I dig the damn grave, then I have to fill the damn thing up."

Linda's eyes widened. She sucked in her breath. What had she heard? Was someone digging? Whose yard was this? Did he say grave? She couldn't see through the hedge. And did she want to? No. The hair on the nape of her neck stood up. The man could be coming to the garbage stand. She slid off the wooden frame into the tall weeds, shaking. Elbows pressed to her side, she crouched, trying to make herself small. Would he see her?

The man grunted, and the sound of digging continued. "Damn it, all to hell. Where else am I supposed to hide the damn body?"

A chill ran down Linda's spine. Her heart thumped in her chest. She held her breath, afraid to make a sound. A man was digging a grave on the other side of the hedge!

A small furry creature scrambled up beside her. The furball was Gertrude. The orange tabby cat climbed onto her lap, angrily meowing in a high-pitched wail. Linda hugged the cat. Her eyes darted to the hedge. Would the man come out to investigate?

A large barking dog came charging down the back lane. Gertrude's back arched. She hissed, jumped out of Linda's arms, and shot into the nearby hedge. The dog closed in on Linda. The big, shaggy sheepdog stopped, sniffed her, then licked her face. Still stunned at what she'd heard, Linda, her hands shaking, patted the friendly dog's head. Who was that man? And who was he talking to? Were there two men?

Across the alleyway, an outside light turned on, and a door slammed. "Bongo, Bongo, get back here. Bongo, Bongo. Here, boy." The dog gave Linda one last lick, shook his furry coat, and loped back up the lane. "Here, boy. Good boy," a man's voice said. The door banged shut, and the outside light shut off.

Linda sat very still, her head cocked, listening for the ominous voice. All was quiet. There were no voices. Menacing or otherwise, only the breeze rustling the leaves in the shrubbery. Her heart leapt. Was the man peeking out at her through the hedge? She scrambled to her feet. And bending low to the ground, Linda hastened a retreat. Her heart pounded as fast as her feet, back down the alley, unmindful of the ruts and potholes. She ran with one sandal on her foot, the other abandoned in the weeds by the garbage stand. The chain-link monster greeted her by charging the fence. The ferocious barking gave her more reason to run. The backyard light was a welcoming sight. Her breath came in big gulps as she plowed straight through the garden. The other flip-flop flew off, and Linda's bare feet sunk into the soft soil. Sitting at the top of the porch steps was Gertrude. The cat greeted her with an impatient meow.

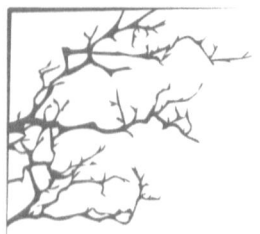

Chapter Two

Linda's bare feet slipped, and she fell onto her belly. She crawled through the lush, tall, green grass. Parted the reeds and peered out. Yes, there he was. She couldn't see the man's face, but she was sure he was old. He was leaning on a stick. She crawled closer. The stick became a shovel. The hunched man turned. There was a machete in his hand. Linda felt a crushing pressure on her chest as he uttered a strange yowling sound. A hoard of insects was attacking her face.

Her eyes flew open to find Gertrude standing on her chest. Linda's breath came in big gulps, and she laid her head back on the pillow, laughing with relief. She'd had a nightmare.

Gertrude's rough, raspy tongue licked Linda's face. She elbowed herself to a sitting position and scratched Gertrude behind the ear. The cat purred, rolling over to present her tummy. Linda rubbed Gertrude's furry belly. The purring increased. Linda yawned, trying to remember her dream that was fading. Something about a jungle, a machete, and a threatening man. The cat rolled over again, dislodging the book Linda had been reading. A Mystery by M. C. Beaton slid to the floor. Gently moving Gertrude out of the way, Linda picked up her book. Yawning again, she smiled.

The book and the voice behind the hedge had led to her dream. Linda was a big fan of Agatha Raisin. "Wouldn't being a detective be a fabulous, fun career move?" she asked Gertrude as she petted the cat's furry back. Gertrude arched, stretched, sauntered to the end of the bed, looked at her and meowed.

"Yes, I guess you're right. There isn't much call for a lady detective." Linda laughed, then became thoughtful. She'd heard stories from her

Aunt Violet about how she and Mabel Havelock had solved murders. Linda sat the book on the night table. What if she investigated the weird voice from the other side of the hedge? But in the light of day, she wondered if she had mistaken what the man said. Maybe it was her overactive imagination. Linda swung her legs out of bed, tucking her feet into her fuzzy pink slippers. No, she was sure he said grave. And something about hiding a body.

Gertrude mewed pitifully.

"You faker." Linda grinned, ruffling the tabby cat's fur before slipping on her robe. "I know there is food in your dish." Yawning, she followed the cat to the kitchen. Linda's fluffy pink slippers made a soft swooshing sound as she walked across the black and white tiled kitchen floor to the old white porcelain sink.

Linda loved the comfy feel of Mabel's old-fashioned kitchen with worn oak cupboards and red laminated countertops. A gray chrome table with padded red vinyl chairs stood in the middle of the room. The early morning May sun streamed through the floral curtains. She drew back the cheery red and white gingham curtains and peeked out the window. It was going to be a glorious day. Spotting her flip-flop in the garden, she remembered her mad dash down the alley. She dropped the curtains and turned on the water tap, filling the coffeepot.

Gertrude brushed up against Linda's legs and meowed. Linda looked down at the cat. "Yes, I know. I was scared of my own shadow. Your mistress would have laughed at me." Recalling the man's voice from the other side of the hedge, Linda spooned coffee grounds into the filter. It was probably an innocent comment about a TV program or something. Wasn't it? She paused, holding the spoon in the air, her brow wrinkled. She hadn't heard anyone answer the man. Of course, the man could have been talking on his phone. Linda resumed spooning coffee into the pot. But he was digging. She'd heard the sounds of digging. The man couldn't be on his phone and digging at the same time. Darn, she'd lost count of the spoons of coffee she'd added to the pot. She dumped the grounds back into the can and recounted.

Gertrude looked up at her and meowed. "Seriously?" Linda asked, looking down at the cat's food dish. There was a tiny bare spot. "Fine, I'll get you some more. You're spoiled, you know that?" Shaking her head, she grinned, scooping more dry cat food into Gertrude's dish. Plopping down on one of the red chrome chairs, Linda waited for the coffee to drip.

Gertrude finished chowing down. Stretching, she strolled to the door and meowed. "Don't go teasing poor Bongo," Linda cautioned the cat as she opened the back door.

Clad in her pyjamas and robe, Linda stood on the porch steps. She lifted her chin, enjoying the warm sunshine on her face. Gertrude sprinted across the grass to the garden. Daintily picking up her paws, she sauntered between the rows of newly planted potatoes; tips of green plants were peeking through the black soil. Linda grinned as the cat stopped to inspect her flip-flop. She could see her footprints in the dirt, where she'd run through the garden from the alleyway. She shook her head. Yes, in the light of day, her race from danger was almost laughable. After all, this was a friendly little country town.

Or was it? Linda's eyes became thoughtful. She recalled the stories Mabel told her about the murders in Gravenhurst Manor. The senior's apartments where Mabel's mother lived. She had listened with rapt attention to how Mabel and her Aunt Violet had solved the murders and brought the criminals to justice.

But that was a one-off. It was hardly likely there was another killer here in Glenhaven. Or was it? Linda's imagination took over. How exciting it would be if she solved a mystery. Her aunt would be impressed. And, after all, she was good at solving puzzles.

Her excitement grew. Yes, she was sure of what she'd heard. *First, I dig the grave, and then I have to fill the damn thing up.* Did this man bury someone in the garden? And if he did, whose yard was it? She knew for sure the yard was past the angry dog. And she remembered the old wooden garbage stand and the high boxwood hedge. Her eyes sparkled. She'd stroll down the back alley after getting dressed and see if she could find the yard. She was curious. Besides, she'd lost a perfectly good sandal. It couldn't hurt to take a look.

Linda tightened the belt on her pink flannel bathrobe, tromped down the porch steps, and crossed the lawn to the front yard. On the sidewalk lay the weekly newspaper. The Glenhaven Herald was damp from the early morning dew. That darn kid, how hard was it to put the newspaper on the back porch? She leaned down to pick up the damp newspaper from the pavement.

"Good morning," called a cheery voice.

The cheery voice came from Mabel's neighbour, Wanda. In Wanda's hand was the Glenhaven newspaper, which she was waving in Linda's direction.

Wanda made a striking figure as she strode across the driveway. The tall, sturdy woman had her hair wrapped in a green-gold and blue turban. She dressed in a multi-coloured bathrobe and wore scarlet plastic clogs. Her robe reminded Linda of Joseph's coat of many colours from the bible.

Linda grinned. She loved the friendliness of this small town. "Good morning. Looks like a great day," she said.

"It does, indeed," agreed Wanda.

"Come on over for a cup of coffee," invited Linda.

"Thanks. But not this morning. I've got a lot on. The town-wide garage sale is today."

"Are you having a garage sale?"

"No, but I plan on taking in a few. How about you?" Wanda waved the newspaper at a wasp circling overhead.

"I don't know. I'm not sure. I'm thinking of moving, so I should probably be getting rid of stuff instead of buying."

"Moving?" Wanda swatted again at the wasp. "Where are you thinking of moving to? I could suggest a nice little town. Namely, here."

"I'm thinking about it."

"I hope so. You'd like it here. The townsfolk are warm and open-hearted. And I'd love it if you did."

"Thanks." Linda's face lit up. Moving to this friendly little town was very appealing.

"Think about it. Glenhaven is a great place to live."

"I will," promised Linda.

"Good. Well, I better get dressed so I can take in those garage sales. I'm a bargain hunter. I never know what treasure I might find."

"True, you never know." Laughing, Linda waved goodbye. She returned to the kitchen and kicked off her damp pink slippers. Padding to the counter, she poured herself a mug of coffee and spread the moist newspaper on the kitchen table. Linda glanced at the clock on the wall, wondering what time it was in Alberta. Should she phone her aunt? Or phone Mabel? Linda could hardly wait to tell her aunt about the crazy, weird voice she'd heard. Her excitement grew as she punched the number on her cell phone. Linda waited, but no one answered. Instead, she got a '*The number you have reached is unavailable*' message. Linda looked at the number she'd keyed and rolled her eyes. She'd punched in Mabel's cell phone number by mistake. Her finger was about to tap her aunt's number when her cell phone rang. "Hello."

"Hi Linda, I'm just calling to see how you are doing."

Chuckling, Linda set her coffee cup on the table and moved the newspaper to the side. It was her Aunt Violet. Her aunt was checking up on her. "I'm fine. And yourself?"

"I'm fine too. I thought maybe you might still be in bed."

"No, I'm up having coffee."

"Oh, that's good. I didn't want to wake you."

"You didn't. How's the visit going?" Linda shifted in her chair. She could hardly wait to tell her aunt about the guy behind the hedge.

"Wonderful. Susan and the boys and I went to the zoo yesterday."

"The boys are at the best age to enjoy the zoo."

"Yes, they are. But caged animals are not my thing. Mind you, the zoo does have big areas for all the animals."

"I'm glad you're enjoying a lovely family holiday," Linda said. "Oh, by the way, I accidentally phoned Mabel instead of you. Anyway, she didn't answer."

"She has probably forgotten to charge her phone. Mabel is a bit of a Luddite."

Linda giggled. "I don't understand why she does that. I always have my phone charged and on. Why else have a cell phone?"

"Me too. Anyway, the reason I'm calling so early is to give you a heads-up."

"What's happened?"

"Mabel's daughter Melina has made an appointment with an orthopedic surgeon for her mother."

"Oh, no, poor Mabel."

"Poor Mabel is right. Melina doesn't trust Mabel's doctor and has decided her mother should get her foot looked at. Mabel, I can tell you is not happy. Strong-minded women run in the Havelock family. And this time, Melina has won out."

Linda chuckled. "I'm glad I'm not there for that confrontation."

"Me either," agreed Violet. "Anyway, I'll be home on Monday. But Mabel will be delayed. I just wanted to let you know in case you have to go back home. And if you do, no worries, I'll look after Gertrude."

"No problem, I can stay. I have nothing else to do. And Gertrude and I are good buddies."

"Great, and when I get home, we can get together. We never got to visit long enough when you came to house sit."

"Sounds great." Linda took a sip of her coffee.

"And you? What are you doing to keep busy? Anything new happening in town?"

Linda's eyes flashed with excitement. "Well, last night, I went out to look for Gertrude and heard the weirdest thing."

"Is Gertrude lost?"

"No, she's fine." Linda blew out a breath, fidgeting with the newspaper. Anxious to get to the story about the man behind the hedge. "That isn't the weird part. The weird part was I heard a man's voice. This guy said: *First, I dig the grave, and then I have to fill the damn thing up.*"

"Really! Dig a grave? Are you sure?"

"And then the man said, *'Damn it, all to hell. Where else do you hide a body?'* I'm absolutely sure that is what I heard."

"Exactly where was this?"

Detecting the incredulous tone of her aunt's voice, Linda screwed up her lips. "In the back alley."

"Good God, someone was burying a body in the back alley?"

"No, no," assured Linda. "I was sitting in the back alley, and I heard this voice say—"

"What were you doing sitting in the back alley at night?"

Linda frowned. "I wasn't sitting. I was running down the alley looking for Gertrude."

"You just said you were sitting."

"Let me explain." Linda sighed, drumming her fingers on the table. "First, I was running."

"Seriously. You were running up and down the back alley at night?"

"Not up and down." Linda furrowed her brow. She rubbed her forehead with the tips of her fingers. "Forget the running. Let me explain. I thought Gertrude was getting into a cat-and-dog fight, so I ran to stop it. But she wasn't."

"So, why were you sitting in the alley?"

Linda took a deep breath and continued, "As I said, I ran down the alley because of Gertrude. That's when my sandal twisted on my foot. I stepped on some stones and hurt my foot. And I looked for a spot to sit down."

"How's your foot?"

"Fine, thanks."

"Good, we don't want another broken foot."

"Anyway, as I said, my sandal twisted, and I went to have a sit-down. So, I did. And the next thing I know, I hear this guy swearing. And I hear the sound of digging. And before you say anything, I know what the sound of digging is."

"Okay, you heard digging and some guy swearing."

This was more like it. Her Aunt Violet was beginning to believe her. "Yes, and this man says *I dig the grave, and then I have to fill the damn thing up.*"

"This man was in the back alley with you?" Violet asked.

Linda could hear the worried tone in her aunt's voice. "No, I was sitting on a wooden thingy when I heard the voice from the other side of the hedge."

"A wood thingy?"

"A wooden garbage stand."

"Eew, a garbage stand."

Linda grinned. She knew her aunt was a bit of a clean freak bordering on OCD. Her Aunt Violet, however, explained it as obsessive-compulsive tendencies.

"You shouldn't sit on one of those things. It's not clean, you know."

Linda drummed her fingers on the table. Her aunt was more concerned with germs than someone digging a grave. Didn't she believe her? "Yes, I know. Please let me get on with my story."

"All right, just be careful of what you sit on."

"Okay, where was I?"

"You were sitting on a wooden thingy, a garbage stand. A stand you should never sit on. And you heard a man swearing."

"Right. The man was on the other side of the hedge. And–"

"There was a hedge behind this wooden garbage stand thingy?"

"Yes. And then the guy said, '*Where else am I supposed to hide the body?*' Then he swore some more."

"*Where else am I supposed to hide a body?*" Violet asked.

"No, the man didn't say a body. He said the body," Linda stressed 'the.'

"That is very odd, to say the least. You didn't see who it was?"

"No, it was dark, and he, whoever this man was, this guy was on the other side of a hedge. That back alley is overgrown with hedges. And the fences, some of the yards have really high fences. Anyway, I don't have a clue which yard the voice came from. But it's ominous, don't you think?" Linda asked, warming to her tale.

"The man could be burying a pet."

"The guy said, hide the body. I guess it could be a pet. But you don't hide a dead pet. Do you?"

"Maybe it's the town bylaw? Maybe we can't bury a pet in our backyard?"

"Well, I don't think he was talking about hiding a pet's body," Linda said, lifting her chin. The more she tried to convince her Aunt Violet that something nefarious had happened, the more she convinced herself of it.

"But you don't know who said it?"

"No." Linda sighed. "Remember the hedge?"

"Yes, of course, the hedge. You really think this man is contemplating committing a murder?" Violet asked.

"I don't know. But I heard the sound of digging. Why dig a grave if the victim isn't dead?"

"What does digging sound like?"

Linda rolled her eyes. She knew her aunt wasn't going to let that pass. "I can't describe it, but when you hear it, you know it."

"Maybe this guy is getting ready for a victim. Maybe there is no dead body."

The corners of Linda's lips lifted. Her aunt was finally taking her concerns seriously. "And if the guy is getting a grave ready for someone, don't you think it would be a good idea for me to find out whose house this is?" There was a long pause. Linda waited and then asked, "What do you think?" She wanted her aunt to say yes. She wanted to prove that just like Mabel and her aunt, she could solve the mystery of the complaining, grave-digging man.

"Fine. If you are going to snoop, oh, pardon me, investigate, tell me, what's your next step?"

Linda, taken aback, said, "I'm not going to snoop."

"Oh, sorry, of course not. It's just you remind me of Mabel. She is always bent on going into an investigation headfirst. And that is not always a good idea."

Linda's face lit up with a big smile. She felt a swell of pride. She reminded her Aunt Violet of Mabel. She would investigate. All her life, people had underestimated her. Her husband would pat her on the head, which she hated, and he'd pretend to take her concerns seriously. But then he would ignore any suggestions she made. Yes, she was a tiny five-foot woman with a sunny disposition. Her nickname at work was Mary Sunshine. Of course, she was a Mary Sunshine at work. She'd taught kindergarten. And the children were a delight. But that didn't mean she wasn't a strong, capable woman. She would show everyone she was as skilled as any detective, male or female. "I'm going to go back down the alley and see if I can recognize the hedge I was sitting behind when I heard this guy's voice. It won't be hard to find. I lost a flip-flop nearby. When I find it, I'll find the hedge." "I'm not even going to ask about your flip-flop. And if you find your sandal and the hedge, what then?"

"I don't know. I haven't figured that far ahead." Linda guessed her aunt was right. Even if she found the yard, she wasn't planning on searching the garden for a grave. Linda grew thoughtful as she flipped another newspaper page. But there might be a hole or a mound. It couldn't hurt to look.

"Are you going to report what you heard to the RCMP?"

Linda, feeling unsure, bit her bottom lip. "I have no proof that anyone is dead. Or that anyone is going to die. I might come off sounding like a loon."

Violet chuckled. "Yes, maybe hold back on the police. And tramping down the back lane and sneaking into people's backyard is a bit creepy."

Nibbling again on her bottom lip, Linda sighed. Aunt Violet was putting a damper on her investigation. "Yeah, I guess." She frowned, wet her lips, and flipped another newspaper page. But wasn't that what detectives did? They investigated.

"And you don't want to get on the bad side of Mabel's neighbours."

"Oh, no, for sure," agreed Linda.

"The last thing you want to do is accuse one of Mabel's neighbours of murdering someone. Or planning to," cautioned Violet.

"Planning to?"

"Yes, remember, your victim could still be alive."

"Please don't say that. Not my victim. That sounds creepy."

"Yes, okay, sorry. But this grave could be for someone still living."

"I guess so. But maybe I should find out if someone has disappeared," Linda suggested.

"And how are you going to do that?"

Linda's eyes caught an ad in the paper. The ad promoted the town-wide garage sale that Wanda had told her about. "There is a town-wide garage sale today. I could go to that."

"That's a good idea. Searching for bargains is way better than searching for bodies."

"I wasn't planning to look for bodies," Linda denied. She shuddered in revulsion. "That would be weird."

"Good to hear."

"I'm hoping Mabel's neighbours are participating in the yard sales. I will look for bargains, which will give me an excuse to ask around and see if anyone is missing. I can be discreet."

"I hope so. It will be a nice change. Mabel tends to barge right in."

Linda felt another surge of pride. *Better than Mabel.* She smiled. "I could have misunderstood what that man said, although I don't think so. But I sure hope I did."

"Yes, it's likely nothing. And the more I think about it, the more farfetched the idea of a backyard grave digger is. A murderer living in Mabel's neighbourhood is unbelievable."

"Oh, right, like you haven't encountered a crazy neighbour before."

"Pardon me?"

"Sorry, maybe not a neighbour. But you and Mabel have encountered a few weirdos who thought nothing of doing away with someone. Remember Gravenhurst Manor? Mabel's mother's condo? Mabel told me those guys were nuts."

"That was a one-off. And that reminds me. Would you mind taking Mabel's mom to bingo? I'm not sure of the day."

Linda had met Sophie, Mabel's mother, and found the little lady charming. She was like a second grandmother. "Sure, no problem. Bingo with Sophie sounds like fun. Maybe I'll be lucky."

"Great, and about this mystery of yours. I hope you will forget about this and take my advice. Cool your jets. This voice you heard could be nothing."

Linda preened. *This mystery of yours,* she had caught her aunt's words. Excitement shot through her, imagining how proud her aunt and Mabel would be when she solved it. "I'll take your advice. And I promise you, I won't do anything rash."

"I really hope so. Please remember these people are Mabel's neighbours."

"Don't worry. I'll be cautious. I'm just curious. And as you say, it was likely nothing. I'll go to the garage sales and see what is what."

"All right. And take someone with you. And don't go stirring up a hornet's nest."

"A hornet's nest?"

"Don't go poking into people's homes."

"I will."

"Will what? Go into their houses?"

Linda laughed. "I didn't say that."

"Please be careful. I'll be home in a few days."

"No worries, I'll just do the garage sales. Talk to a few people, learn what I can, and maybe pick up a few bargains. I'll keep you in the loop." Linda grinned. She could hardly wait to start. She'd show Aunt Violet she could solve mysteries. How hard could it be?

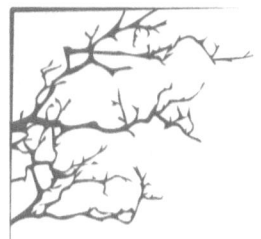

Chapter Three

C ars and trucks jammed the street. The sidewalks were crowded with bargain hunters searching for treasures.

Squinting in the bright morning sun, Linda wished she wore sunglasses or a hat. She shielded her eyes with a hand, watching a blue SUV pull to the curb. Linda hitched her tote bag over her shoulder and started down the sidewalk. A short, plump woman with rosy cheeks and curly salt-and-pepper hair climbed out of the SUV. It was Mary Woodhouse. Linda waved a welcome. Her Aunt Violet had introduced her to Mary at Coffee Row. Mary was another reason she thought about moving to Glenhaven. The kindly little woman was so friendly. It took time in the city to make friends, but it was so much easier in this little prairie town.

Linda waited on the sidewalk for Mary. "Good morning," she said.

Mary wore a big straw hat with small pink and white flowers woven into the brim. She took a creamed-coloured cloth bag from her car. "Good morning. Isn't this a great day for the town-wide garage sale?"

"It is." Linda smiled back at Mary.

"Busy place, this street," commented Mary. "I was lucky I found this place to park."

Linda nodded, feeling guilty that she had parked on the street-side. She should have left her car in Mabel's driveway.

"I've been all over the town."

"Have you picked up much?"

"Not much. A lot of the sales are for kids' toys and clothes. Not for me. This is my last street. May I join you?" asked Mary. "I always think it's more fun to shop with someone."

"Me too." Linda was more than happy to accompany Mary. While Mary hunted for bargains at the garage sales, she would investigate. Linda was more interested in the sellers than what they were selling. She was on a mission to find out if anyone was missing from the neighbourhood.

LINDA'S RED AND WHITE cloth bag, with the name of the local grocery store, held a potato masher and two green Tupperware containers; Mary's bag was weighted down with colourful plaster of Paris yard ornaments. The neighbourhood had a festive air. Garage sale enthusiasts were out in full force, and almost everyone on the street was having a garage sale. The neighbours were only too happy to get rid of their unneeded items. And the bargain hunters were just as happy to buy them. In front of one house, three little girls had set up a lemonade stand. Linda smiled. They, too, were doing a booming business. Mary and Linda each bought a glass of lemonade.

The sun was hot, and they had stopped at a lot of the sales, crossing back and forth to each side of the street, looking, and sometimes buying. Next to the lemonade stand was a neat little white cottage with a black shingled rooftop.

"This is Elsie Pinquist's house. Are you ready to do more shopping?" asked Mary, tossing her paper cup into a small bin beside the lemonade stand.

Linda noted that Elsie's lawn needed mowing. And the flowerbeds on either side of the front steps were empty except for the blooming dandelions.

"This is odd. This isn't like Elsie. This is very strange. Elsie has neglected her yard," exclaimed Mary. "Elsie is known for her beautiful flowerbeds."

Linda's eyes narrowed. Was this where she heard the ominous hiding-the-body voice? She dodged around two white-haired women with shopping bags over their arms. The women were standing beside a rack of women's clothes that hung on a stand at the entrance to the garage. The pros and cons of buying used garments seemed to be the topic of their discussion.

Mary also slipped past the women. She sped to a table displaying china dishes. Picking up a set of figurines, a blue and white shepherd boy and a shepherdess with three small lambs. "Hi, Elsie," Mary called.

Linda watched Mary chat with Elsie, a thin, elderly, bird-like lady. So, Elsie wasn't the victim. If there was a victim?

She'd asked Mary about the inhabitants at each yard sale they visited. So far, everyone who lived in the houses they visited was still living. Linda felt foolish. What the voice had said behind the hedge must have been a product of her overactive imagination.

But then maybe her aunt was right. Elsie could be a potential victim. Perhaps the man digging in the garden was plotting? Linda bypassed the tables displaying dishes, handy craft items, and books. A young teenage girl with blue and red streaked white, blonde hair was minding the cash box. The young girl looked up from her phone. "What are you buying?" she asked. The rhinestone studs in her nose sparkled.

"I'm just looking. Elsie has a lot of beautiful things. Is she your grandmother?" Linda asked.

"Yeah, she sure has a lot of stuff. Grandma is downsizing."

"Oh, she is moving?"

"Yeah, she is. Grandma lives alone, so my mom has convinced Grandma to move. She's moving to Gravenhurst Manor. You know, the senior's condos," the girl said, looking down at her phone.

Mabel's mother's name popped into Linda's mind. Sophie wanted to go to bingo. And she still hadn't found out what day or time the bingo was.

Linda moved aside. A woman stepped forward. The young woman carried a basket of colourful yarns. Tucked under her arm was a needlepoint picture of a little girl with blonde ringlets and a basset hound. The teenager sighed, put down her phone, and looked at the hand-printed price tags on the items. "Six dollars," she said.

The move explained Elsie's neglected yard. And Elsie lived alone, and no one was missing from the house. So, no victim, potential or otherwise. But Linda's eyes sparkled. Elsie Pinquist was moving. The house looked small, but there was only her. She would have to see how much the listed cost of the house was on the local real estate site.

"I hate to look and not buy," Mary said as they left Elsie's garage sale. The cloth shopping bag over Mary's shoulder was laden with bric-à-brac. "I'll have to find a place for these shepherd ornaments. I know Alvin will raise an eyebrow at all the things I've bought. But I think our place needs an old-fashioned, comfy look." Mary and her husband, Alvin, owned a bed-and-breakfast. "I see you bought something too. That is lovely," Mary said, admiring the white crocheted lap blanket draped over Linda's arm.

"I couldn't resist. I wish I could crochet like Elsie," Linda said, shifting her bag on her shoulder. Her bag held the treasures she'd purchased: two Tupperware containers and a potato masher. They stopped at Mary's blue SUV. Mary pressed the button, the hatch opened, and they emptied their bags. Linda neatly folded her crochet blanket on top of the green Tupperware.

"I think walking to each yard sale is better, don't you?" asked Mary as she closed the hatch. "Parking on this street is a real problem today."

"Yes, it is," agreed Linda, thinking of her car parked in front of Mabel's house. "This way, we can do the rest of the block and come back to your car and dump."

"I wouldn't say dump. That sounds like we are collecting trash."

"You know what they say. One man's trash is another man's treasure."

Mary smiled. "I suppose you're right."

The women left the car and trotted down the sidewalk, stopping in front of a white house with a blue tin roof and a wraparound deck.

"This is Nick and Charmaine Barstow's house. I bet they have some good stuff. Nick is a bit of a packrat," explained Mary.

The garage door was open. And Nick, a large pot-belly man with beefy arms, sat in the shade of his garage at a small card table. A gray metal cash box was near at hand. Behind Nick set three rows of tables constructed from sawhorses with sheets of plywood lying on top. One table displayed garden tools, electric cords, and old plant pots, some with soil inside. Another laden with baskets, mismatched household dishes, and Christmas decorations. The third held old boots and fishing gear.

Mary sped ahead of Linda, picking up a Barbie doll in a bright green hand crochet dress. Under the dress was a toilet tissue roll. As Mary set the doll back on the table, a small blonde-haired girl snatched it up. "Can I have this, Mommy?" she asked.

Her mother chuckled. "Sure, I remember my grandmother had one of these."

"Granny played with dolls?"

"No, dear." The mother chuckled again as she and her daughter moved down the row between the tables, stopping to look at a dusty red vase with artificial flowers.

Linda followed a rather severe-looking man and a stout but attractive woman. The man sped off to inspect a fish net. The plump woman paused, rummaging through the Christmas decorations. Linda stopped in front of the card table where Nick was sitting. "It's a good day for the garage sales," she said.

"Yep, it is, for sure," replied the big man as he handed change to a tall, young woman holding a floor lamp.

Linda stepped to the side, allowing the woman to carry the floor lamp out of the garage to her waiting car. A bearded man dressed in faded blue patched coveralls stepped between Linda and Nick. The man had a roll of twine and a box of screws in his hands.

As the man paid for his items, Linda watched the woman struggle to put the tall lamp in the backseat of her sedan. She hoped the young girl would get the lamp home in one piece. She had shoved the lamp through an open car window. The pedestal of the lamp was now sticking out of the car.

The coverall man left, and her attention switched from the lamp woman to Nick.

"Where's Charmaine? I haven't seen her in ages," asked a woman in tight-fitting jeans and a bright green T-shirt.

"Charmaine is inside, resting. She has a cold or something."

Linda's eyebrows rose. The woman was under the weather, with a cold. Really? In May?

"Please step aside," he told the bright green T-shirt lady. "Frank here has a purchase." Frank was dragging an old grass-incrusted lawn mower across the garage floor.

"Five bucks," Frank offered, pulling a five-dollar bill from his jeans pocket. "I want twenty bucks for the mower. It works good."

"Ten dollars and not a penny more."

"Fifteen, and I'll throw in a litre of oil."

"Fine, it's a deal." Frank dug back into his pocket.

"I'll just pop in and say hi to Charmaine," Linda said, mounting the garage steps leading into the house.

"She's sleeping," Nick said, taking a dirty, old oil can from an oiled-stained cardboard box and handing it to Frank.

"I'll just peek in and see if she needs anything," Linda said.

"Hey, don't go in there," Nick growled. Opening his cash box, he accepted Frank's fifteen dollars. "I'm telling you. Leave her alone. She's not well. Charmaine needs her sleep."

Hoping he'd be too busy to stop her, Linda slipped into the house, shutting the door on Nick's warning. She was glad he didn't ask who she was and how she knew Charmaine. Linda felt bold. It was pretty gutsy and pretty nosey of her to barge into their house, but this was what detectives did. Not that she expected to find a body. At least, she hoped not. But she might find a clue.

The house had a sour smell. The odour was coming from the kitchen. A pile of dirty dishes filled the sink. Linda paused in the living room, where a big-screen TV dominated. Two large white framed pictures hung on the wall over a long gray sectional sofa. The pictures' green, white, and blue splashes reminded her of hotel art.

But she wasn't here to critique Charmaine and Nick's taste in art. Her mission was to see if Charmaine was alive and well. Tipped-toeing down the hallway, she passed the laundry room. Clothes were spilling out of the laundry basket. She continued down the hallway, peeking into each room as she passed. The window blind was closed in the last bedroom, and the room was dim, but she could see a mound in the bed.

Linda paused in the doorway. She bit her bottom lip. Was there a body under the quilt? She held her breath as she crept toward the bed. Charmaine's head was lying on a pillow. In the dim light, her face looked yellow. Her mouth was hanging open. Linda crept closer. And with a shaky hand, she reached out and touched Charmaine's shoulder.

"Eek," shrieked Charmaine. Coughing and sputtering, she shot up in bed.

"Oh, I'm so sorry." Linda jumped back from the bed, her face flushed in embarrassment.

"Who the heck are you, and what are you doing here?" croaked Charmaine, her mousy blonde hair matted. She coughed and elbowed herself in a sitting position.

"I'm so sorry I startled you. Your husband said you were sick. So, I thought I would see if you needed anything. Ah, how are you feeling?"

Sighing, Charmaine threw off her quilt. The dumpy woman dressed in a gray tracksuit swung her feet off the bed. Coughing, she grabbed a tissue from a box on her night table and coughed into the tissue. She grabbed another tissue and blew her nose. "I've got a heck of a head cold. Who did you say you are?"

"Linda Burton, I'm Violet Ficher's niece. I'm so sorry I woke you," Linda apologized, back-peddling toward the door.

"Oh yeah, I think I remember you. Violet said you are a nurse."

Charmaine had mixed her up with someone else. "Ah, yes, Violet is my aunt." Linda, unable to meet Charmaine's gaze, told herself. She wasn't really lying, but she wasn't telling the truth either.

"Well, it's nice you are concerned. But it could be just my sinuses acting up. Maybe I have an allergy." Charmaine blew her nose again and tossed the used tissue toward an overflowing white plastic bin of crumpled tissues. Her tissue fell to the floor, adding to the pile scattered by her bedside. "I'm probably allergic to all that crap Nick's selling out in the garage." Charmaine stuck her feet into a pair of worn green slippers. "Anyway, I'm not spending my day in that garage. I hate haggling with my neighbours." She chuckled and added, "But Nick, that man loves to haggle. He's a sweet man, but I think haggling must be in his blood."

"Well, good to know you aren't sick. I'll let you rest," Linda said, backing out of the bedroom.

"I can make us a cup of tea if you like," offered Charmaine. She stood, hitching up her track pants and pulling down her sweatshirt.

"No, but thanks. You should rest. I'm so sorry I woke you." Linda smiled. This small town was the best. They even offered a cup of tea to an intruder.

"Are you sure you don't want a cup of tea?"

"No, you go back to bed, and I'll go back to the garage. I'm here with Mary Woodhouse. We're taking in the town-wide garage sale. I just thought I'd check on you. I'm really sorry I disturbed you," Linda apologized again.

Her instinct was to flee. But Charmaine accompanied her, shuffling along in her slippers.

Linda descended the steps to the garage. Charmaine stuck her head out the door and croaked, "Nick, I'm locking this darn door. Don't let anyone else in."

"Okay, sweetie," answered Nick as the door closed.

Standing in line and holding a floppy green and red elf, Mary turned. "Oh, Linda, there you are," she said. "I was wondering where you went."

"What did I tell you?" Nick looked up at Linda as he took Mary's money. "Going in the house and bothering Charmaine. That dear woman is the lid to my pot. I don't know what I would do without her. She has been running her feet off helping me get this garage sale off the ground. Actually, I think that's why she's a little under the weather."

"Yes, I know. I'm very sorry," Linda said. She'd been an idiot, jumping to a silly conclusion because the woman wasn't in the garage. But still, she had to investigate. That's what detectives did. After all, last night, she had heard a man's voice grumbling about digging a grave and asking where to hide the body.

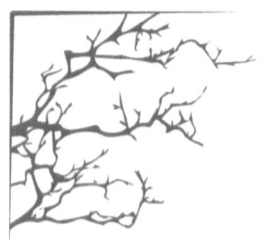

Chapter Four

"There is another yard sale two doors down," Mary said. "It's the Hutchins' place. They have furniture on the lawn. Come on," she said, cramming the green and red elf into her bag.

Linda followed Mary down the sidewalk to the sturdy two-story bungalow built back from the street. Wide wooden steps led up to a white-trimmed, covered veranda and a big, heavy wooden door. White-framed windows on the second story looked down at the large, well-manicured front lawn.

"Alfred and Faith really look like they are downsizing. This is a lot of furniture. Some of it looks vintage." Mary marvelled, joining the large crowd that was inspecting the furniture. "They must be moving."

"I think they would be better off having an auction. Some of this furniture looks new. Look at that TV," Linda said. "Oh, I like the coffee table and the matching end tables. And that recliner chair looks new, too. Unfortunately, I'm not in the market for furniture."

"I am. I need antique furniture for my bed and breakfast. The new stuff won't do." Mary stopped to admire a brown brocade sofa. "I do like this couch. It's not antique, but it is old-fashioned." She leaned over and whispered, "The sofa needs a good cleaning. I'll think about it."

Linda trailed behind Mary as she moved on to look at a cherry wood dining room table and chairs. "I don't need the table or chairs. But, oh, just look at this china cabinet," Mary gushed. "It's cherry wood, too. This would look good in the dining room at my B&B. All this dining room furniture is made from genuine wood, not that pressed-board stuff. I wonder what they want for it?"

Mary and Linda waited as a man wearing a green and yellow baseball cap advertising John Deere equipment. Pulled a wad of money from his jeans pocket. He counted out the money to a tall, handsome, twenty-something man with tousled blond curly hair. The young athletic man recounted the cash, shook hands, and pocketed the money.

Linda raised an eyebrow. That was a lot of cash. Maybe a yard sale is a good idea.

Mary tapped on the blond-haired man's arm. "How much is that china cabinet?"

The boyish-looking man looked down at Mary and sighed. "I'm so sorry. This nice gentleman just bought it."

"Yep, my wife will be thrilled. I'll go and let the tailgate down so we can load it into my truck," the man said and sprinted across the lawn to the street.

"Oh, darn. I'm Mary Woodhouse, and I run a B&B. That china cabinet would have been perfect."

"Do you need any beds?" asked the young man, his blue eyes sparkling as he smiled down at Mary. "Aunt Faith has a four-poster bed in the master bedroom. It's too heavy for Uncle Alfred and me to lug down. Would you like to see it? It even has a canopy."

"Yes indeed," replied Mary, rubbing her hands in anticipation. "Is it okay if my friend Linda Burton comes too?"

"Sure, no problem." The blond-haired man tilted his head and flashed Mary an infectious grin. "Would you mind waiting for a few minutes? I want to help the gentleman carry this china cabinet to his truck."

"Not at all," assured Mary, smiling back.

Linda strolled across the lawn with her friend toward the garage. Mary stopped to exchange pleasantries with friends and neighbours drawn to the sale. The hip-roofed garage stood back from the house. Linda thought the garage might have been a horse barn in a bygone age. Inside the open garage, crowds of bargain hunters walked between trestle tables. Rows of tables lined each side of the garage, with a long row down the middle. The tables on one side of the garage were loaded with gardening implements and garden hoses. Dishes of all sorts filled the table down the middle. Another table had books, ornaments, and various electric appliances and bowls. Against the back garage wall, a table had electric cords and Christmas decorations. Near the garage door, a table was covered with bedding plants: pansies, marigolds, petunias, and tomatoes.

Alfred Hutchins, a sixty-plus, raw-boned man with sparse gray hair, sat at the front of the garage, minding the cash box. His thin lips smiled as he accepted the money from the people lined up with purchases in their arms.

Following their fellow bargain hunters, the women slowly snaked past the tables piled with household items. Linda selected a cat ornament and a blue bud vase. The orange cat ornament reminded her of Gertrude and would be a nice memento from Glenhaven. And the bud vase because it took her fancy. Linda stopped at the table with the bedding plants and picked up six small pots of pansies, a gift for Mabel. She'd plant them as soon as she got back to the house. Mary, carrying an assortment of tablecloths, joined her and selected pots of tomato plants. They waited in line to pay Alfred.

Alfred's thin, graying hair flopped down on his bony forehead. Brushing it back with his liver-spotted hands, he sorted through Linda's items. "Twenty bucks," he said. "You new in town?"

"I'm visiting," Linda said, pressing her lips together. Twenty dollars was a lot of money for stuff they didn't want. But she didn't want to be a piker, so she dug into her pocket and gave him the money. Spotting a pile of cardboard boxes, she asked, "May I have one of these boxes to put the bedding plants in?"

"Yeah, sure, that's what they're there for. What's your handle?" Alfred asked.

"Handle?"

Alfred's blue eyes twinkled. He chuckled. "What's your name?"

"Oh, I'm Linda Burton." Linda smiled back. The man was a nosey old guy, but maybe in a small town, new people were an oddity.

"You sure have a great variety of bedding plants," Mary said, setting her items on the table.

"Yeah, Faith has a green thumb. Every year, the house is full of these darn plants. I had a greenhouse built for the darn things. But there is never enough room for her. If you're interested, grow lights are on one of those tables at the back."

"Not me," replied Linda. "I like plants that are ready to put into the ground. You guys are really getting rid of a lot of stuff. You must be moving."

"Yep, we're selling everything. We have a brand-new motorhome. We are going to tour across Canada and the USA. Go where we like and stop when we want."

"That sounds wonderful," Mary said.

Linda's ears picked up at the mention of moving. If the Hutchins were moving, this house would be for sale. She'd love to have a look inside.

"Yep, selling the house and moving on. A new adventure, and about bloody time. We aren't getting any younger. Thirty bucks, Mary."

"Where is Faith?" Mary asked, putting the bedding plants in a small cardboard box. Alfred closed the lid on the cash box and grinned. "She's around here somewhere."

The blond-haired man with a friendly winsome smile bounded into the garage. "So, ladies, do you want to see the bed I was telling you about?"

"Yes, please," answered Mary.

"You can leave that box of bedding plants here," he said. "I promise Uncle Alfred won't sell them on you." He laughed as he placed a hand on his uncle's shoulder, giving the older man's shoulder a gentle squeeze.

"You're taking these women into the house?" Alfred asked, a frown appearing on his face.

"I am, don't worry. I've taken care of everything. Uncle Alfred here is a worrier," he said, winking at Linda and Mary. "I won't be long. If someone needs help to carry anything, tell them to wait, and I'll be right back to help them."

"You stay here, Richie, and mind the store. I'll show Mary and this lady the bedroom furniture. It's the four-poster bed you're interested in?" Alfred asked, rising.

Richie shrugged and took Alfred's place behind the small table.

"Well, it's me who is interested," explained Mary. "Alvin and I run a bed and breakfast. "

"Yeah, I know."

Mary smiled. "We find people from the city expect a rustic look. Well, maybe not rustic, but they like to see old-fashioned things. If you know what I mean."

"Then the four-poster will fit that bill. The bed was a wedding gift from Faith's grandmother. Her grandmother told us it had been a wedding gift to her. So, it really is more of an antique. But lucky for you, we want to downsize," said the stooped man, leading them out of the garage, across the lawn, and up the steps to the big wooden door. Alfred stopped at the door, took a key from his pocket, and unlocked the door. "We have to be careful. People sometimes think they have free range to go into your house when you're having a garage sale."

Linda, looking sheepish, lowered her eyes. She had done just that at the Barstow's garage sale. She followed Alfred and Mary into the house. The aroma of freshly baked homemade bread greeted them.

"Put your bags here. The master bedroom is on the second floor. It's a bit of a climb. One more reason I'm happy to move."

The women set their tote bags beside a white-slatted closet door. Nearby, a green leafy plant grew in a large, square black pot.

Alfred led the way past the living room. The room looked sad. Only a curtain rod remained on the window. Indentations in the brown shag rug indicated where the furniture had set. The beige walls were bare. Nail holes showed where the paintings or perhaps mirrors once hung. The next room was also empty. A large chandelier with tiny glass globes hung from a white embossed ceiling. "You have a nice dining room," Linda said.

"Yeah, we never used it much," muttered Alfred, leading them by the kitchen.

Linda poked her head in the doorway. The kitchen was neat and tidy. The walls were pale yellow lined with white painted cupboards. Linda screwed her lips. If she did buy this house, the olive-green appliances would be the first things to go. Four shabby, worn, black chrome chairs and a small wooden table sat in the middle of the kitchen floor. The table seemed too small for the size of the kitchen. On the gray countertop. A wire rack with two freshly baked loaves of bread and a crock-pot set beside a glass mortar and pestle.

"This way, ladies." Alfred led them down a hallway to a flight of stairs. The thin rail of a man plodded up the steps. He turned at the top of the staircase, watching Linda and Mary continue their climb. "What did I tell you? These stairs are a bit steep."

"So, when are you putting your house up for sale?" Linda asked as she reached the top of the carpeted stairs. A multi-coloured purple, blue, and green carpet lined the dark hallway.

"The sign should be up already. Maybe you didn't notice it with the furniture all over the lawn. The sooner this place gets sold, the better. I just want to get out on the road and enjoy the summer."

"I gather that nice young man we met is your nephew," Mary said, puffing as she climbed the last step.

"Yep, Richie is the son of my younger brother. The boy lives in Toronto. Since he's here visiting, I put him to work. He's been very helpful." Alfred chuckled.

"He seems like a nice guy," Linda said politely.

"Yep, he'll do." Alfred passed a sturdy oak door and said, "This room on your left is the bathroom. I can tell you it was a lot of work to get that darn plumbing in."

Further along the hallway were three more rooms with sturdy wooden doors.

Alfred stopped at the next room and opened the heavy oak door with a flourish. "Ta- da, the master bedroom in all its glory," he said, stepping aside so the ladies could enter. An old-fashioned cream-coloured globe chandelier hung from the high white ceiling.

The wallpaper was blue with faded pink roses on faded green vines. Wide white baseboards lined the gold and brown linoleum that covered the floor.

The room had an odd antiseptic smell. A large four-poster bed with walnut legs dominated the room. The canopy matched the rose and gold comforter covering the bed. An assortment of pillows piled up at the head of the bed made Linda grin. You'd have to harvest all the pillows before crawling into bed. Across from the bed was a walnut armoire with a long mirror.

As Mary examined the bed, Linda strolled to the window, pulled back the ivory lace curtains, and looked out at the backyard. A big silver motorhome was parked in front of the greenhouse. Linda couldn't imagine driving that big rig, let alone parking it. The motorhome was longer than a school bus. Next to the greenhouse was a garden. A high boxwood hedge encircled the backyard. Was this where she heard that voice? *Hard to hide a body.* Linda's eyes glinted. Where was Faith?

"Sold," Alfred said, shaking Mary's hand.

"Don't you want to ask your wife if the price is okay with her?" asked Linda. "Sorry, Mary, I shouldn't have intruded."

"No, that's fine, Linda. I don't want to take advantage."

"Faith leaves everything up to me. I'm the man of the house. Faith just wants to be gone on our road trip. We've been planning this all winter. Next winter, we will be down south enjoying the sunshine while you guys dig yourselves out of the snow." Alfred threw back his head and laughed.

"Where is Faith?" asked Linda. "I'd like to wish her a bon voyage."

"She can't be too far. The bread is out of the oven. She must be in the attic looking for more stuff to sell. Anything else in here you would like, Mary? How about this old walnut cupboard? Faith called calls it an armoire. It's just a darn closet. But it was Faith's grandmother's armoire," Alfred scoffed as he said the word 'armoire.'

"The darn thing came with the bed. So, it's a real antique." He opened the door. Inside, women's clothing hung on wire hangers. "Faith," he yelled. "If you want me to sell this armoire of yours, you'll have to get your clothes out of here." There was no answer. "Yep, she's probably in the attic. You can't hear a thing up there."

"I'd love to buy the armoire. How much?"

Linda wandered to the window as Mary and Alfred haggled on a price. Linda grinned. Mary was a sweet lady, but she was also a savvy businesswoman. Linda pulled back the curtain. And looked out the window at the backyard. Rows of plants were already poking up through the well-worked soil. Alfred had just told them the decision to travel across the country was made in the winter. So why did they plant a garden? Her thoughts were interrupted. Mary and Alfred had agreed on a price.

Still puzzling over the garden, Linda followed them downstairs.

"It was a pleasure to do business with you," Alfred said, shaking Mary's hand. "I'll get Richie and some guys to carry the bed and that closet down and deliver it to your house."

"Thank you, and I'll write you a check when they deliver," Mary replied, picking up her bag. She looked at the potted plant and said, "I hope you don't have a dog or a cat. The seeds from this caster bean plant are poisonous. I think even the leaves would make them sick."

"No worries, we don't have any pets," Alfred said. Smiling, he winked and added. "Now."

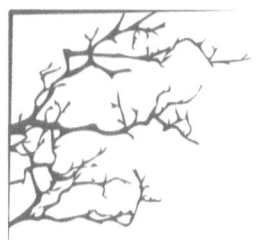

Chapter Five

L inda draped the white crochet blanket over the back of the
kitchen chair and set her tote bag on the table. She took the potato
masher and the green Tupperware containers from the bag. With a
sheepish smile, she held up the cat figurine. The little orange cat
clutched a white wool ball in its paws. She set it beside the blue bud
vase. Linda knew she didn't need either. But who didn't need more
Tupperware containers? Okay, maybe not the potato masher. Linda
looked at the box of bedding plants she bought at the Hutchins' garage
sale. The bedding plants were her best buy. Linda loved pansies. She had
small planters on the balcony of her apartment and had tried
germinating pansies from seed. First, you had to start them in a dark
place. And she knew from experience that she had always forgotten
about them. Out of sight, out of mind, and the pansies never
germinated. She always ended up buying bedding plants.

She picked up the seedlings and carried the plants to the porch.
Gertrude was sunning herself on the railing. The orange tabby cat
jumped down, rolling over on its back. Linda knelt, scratching the
cat's belly. Stretching, Gertrude rewarded her with purrs. "Enough,
you spoiled cat. I have work to do." Giving the tabby cat one last pet,
she continued down the steps to Mabel's flower bed, setting the box
of plants on the ground. "Where does Mabel keep her trowel," she
muttered, trotting back up the steps. She stopped to scratch Gertrude's
belly again, grabbed a trowel off a shelf, returned to the flower bed, and
began to dig holes for the pansies.

Gertrude stretched and ambled down the steps, joining her. The cat
curled up in a ball and watched Linda as she planted the seedlings.

"What do you think, inspector? Do you think your mistress will like them?" Linda asked as she patted the dirt around the last pansy. "You don't care, do you? You just want to be fed."

Gertrude meowed in agreement.

Linda stood and looked at her handy work with satisfaction. Maybe she should have bought more pansy plants. There was still more space in Mabel's flower bed. Faith sure had a green thumb. Linda frowned as she stretched her back. There were a heck of a lot of bedding plants for sale. Starting any plant from seed was a lot of work, especially pansies. She cupped her chin, her eyes thoughtful. Alfred said they had been planning their getaway all winter. So why did Faith start all those bedding plants? The table was full. It didn't make sense.

Was Faith the victim the man on the other side of the hedge was talking about? Linda closed her eyes and rubbed her forehead, remembering what the man in the alley had said. He'd said it was hard to hide a body. If the victim was dead, it couldn't be Faith. There was fresh homemade bread on the kitchen counter. She doubted Alfred and his nephew had baked the bread. But where was Faith? Alfred said she was in the attic. She remembered he hollered up to her, but there had been no answer.

Linda's imagination kicked into high gear. Maybe the man was talking about planning to do away with someone? That was precisely what her aunt had suggested. Could Alfred be holding his wife a prisoner in the attic? No, she was being silly. Just because Alfred called to his wife and Faith didn't answer, there was no reason to suspect foul play. Or was there?

As Linda looked down at Gertrude, rolling in the dirt, she remembered Mary pointing out that the caster bean plant was poisonous. And Alfred's odd remark, '*We don't have any pets now.*' Was Alfred trying to be funny? A strange sense of humour, if he was. But what if Alfred wasn't trying to be funny? Did a pet of theirs die from eating a leaf from the plant? And if a pet died from eating the plant, you wouldn't think it was funny. Linda bit her bottom lip. Would you?

Linda picked up the trowel and the empty pots off the ground; she stuck the plastic pots one into the other. Walked to the porch and dumped the pots in a pile by the steps.

Gertrude rushed ahead of her and pawed at the door, meowing.

Linda paused, looked skyward, and shook her head. She was letting her overactive imagination run away with her. Why would Alfred imprison his wife, let alone kill her? What would Aunt Violet and Mabel do? Would they investigate? The garden and the bedding plants. Were these clues? She thought they were.

Following the cat into the kitchen, Linda opened the cupboard. She took out the box of dry cat food and filled Gertrude's bowl.

Turning on the water tap, Linda washed her hands, filled the cat's water dish, and watched Gertrude lap up the water. She pulled out a chair and sat at the table, turning the little cat ornament in her hands. Would Aunt Violet tell her she was jumping to conclusions? Linda sighed. She'd probably tell her to go and play bingo. Her brow wrinkled. Aunt Violet asked her to take Mabel's mom to bingo. What day was the bingo? Linda went to the counter and ripped off a small leaf of paper from Mabel's notepad. She'd make a note to remind her to ask Mabel's mother where and what time the bingo was. She returned to the table. And wrote the word '*bingo*' on the paper, followed by a big question mark, and set the cat ornament on top.

Linda's thoughts went back to the Hutchins. The yard did have a boxwood hedge. What if what she heard in the alley was a murder plot? She'd never forgive herself if something happened to Faith, and she hadn't done anything to prevent it. It couldn't hurt to have a peek into the Hutchins' backyard.

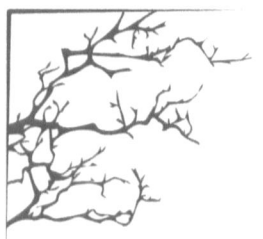

Chapter Six

A mosquito buzzed around Linda's ear; she swatted at the insect but missed it. She was sitting on an old wooden Adirondack chair on the back porch, waiting for dusk, mentally counting how many houses down the block to the Hutchins' yard. Gertrude was on the prowl looking for little furry creatures. If Alfred caught her peering through their hedge, she'd say she was looking for her cat. Linda nibbled her bottom lip. She hoped that excuse would work. Looking in their yard wasn't snooping. Okay, maybe it was. But she wasn't sneaking into their house. Not like she did at Nick and Charmaine's. She wouldn't make that mistake again.

Yes, she'd just take a look in the Hutchins' backyard and see if there was a newly dug hole, a grave in waiting. She hadn't seen one from their bedroom window, but she hadn't been looking for one. And Linda hoped she wouldn't see one now.

Would Aunt Violet tell her she was being snoopy or applaud her detective instincts? The pesky mosquito was back. Linda waved her hands above her head. She rose, stomping to the shelf where Mabel kept her garden tools and the mosquito repellant. Linda held her breath, sprayed, and padded back to the deck chair. She sat again, watching the brilliant shades of pink and purple fade into darkness.

Linda sighed. Country life was the best. She lived in a good neighbourhood in Regina. But the city was always noisy, and she never saw sunrises or sunsets, too many tall buildings. In Glenhaven, nature was on your doorstep.

She stood. It was dark enough to trek down the alley. This time, she was armed with a flashlight and came prepared for the chain-link monster with a plastic bag containing wieners. Linda told herself that the dog could not get through the fence but decided it was better to be safe than sorry. She'd watched a movie where the intruders distracted a dog with steaks. Wieners would have to do.

A breeze sprang up. Branches creaked as the gentle wind whistled through the new green leafy trees. The red eyes of some animal peeked out from under a hedge. The little animal scurried down the lane ahead of her and disappeared under a fence. In the distance, she heard an owl hoot. The moon vanished behind low-hanging clouds. Was it going to rain?

She could hear music, voices, and laughter as she passed a yard with a high board fence. She smelt a BBQ. Linda only had soup and a sandwich for supper. The smell of BBQ steak made her hungry. She plodded ahead, keeping the flashlight focused on the rutted alley.

This time, Linda wore her new white runners as she trotted down the lane, wondering about her shoes. They were called runners in Canada, although most people wearing them didn't run, and called trainers in Britain, but training for what? In the USA, the same shoes were sneakers. Why sneakers? A low growl followed by snarling and barking halted Linda's musing. Her heart leapt as she backed away from the angry animal.

Linda shone her flashlight at the huge black dog as it charged the chain-link fence. She dug in the plastic bag, grabbed a wiener, and tossed it over the fence. The dog immediately stopped barking and leapt into the air. The wiener sailed past the dog. The animal raced after it, snatched it off the ground, and gulped it down. Linda didn't think the dog could have even tasted it. The animal returned to the fence, but this time, it didn't snarl or bark but wagged its tail. She threw another wiener over the enclosure. The big dog jumped in the air, catching the wiener, gulped it down, and trotted back to the fence, wagging its tail. I made a friend, Linda told herself as she left the dog behind, counting the yards as she went.

When Linda smelt the pungent odour of the boxwood hedge, she stopped counting and shone her flashlight at the old wooden weathered garbage stand. Her heart picked up a beat. Nearby, her flip-flop lay in the weeds. Yes, it was the same stand she had sat on last evening.

Spotting a small iron gate nearby, Linda opened the gate, cringing as the gate creaked. Maybe tramping around in someone's backyard in the dark wasn't a good idea. She paused, listening. No one was about. She crept into the yard. Her flashlight momentarily lit the silver motorhome parked in front of the greenhouse. She'd gotten the right place. This was the Hutchins' backyard. Linda lowered the flashlight. There were butterflies in her stomach. She was here.

Playing the light over the garden, Linda looked for a hole in the ground or, worse, a mound. She shone the light up and down the rows of plants in the garden. All the rows had little wooden stakes, denoting what was planted where. Linda saw row upon row of potato plants poking up from the black soil. Faith had indeed planted a garden. Linda stepped over the rows of potatoes. At the back of the garden, nothing had gotten planted. But to Linda's relief, there was no suspicious mound. She was on a fool's errand. Her aunt would have a good laugh when she told her. As Linda turned, retracing her steps back over the potato plants, her suspicious nature kicked into gear. What if Alfred had Faith tied up in the attic?

A tall, dark figure stepped out of the greenhouse. "Hey, you," called the man.

Linda's hand shook as she shone her flashlight at the dark figure that was striding towards her. She sagged in relief. The man tramping across the yard was Richie. He held up a hand, shielding his eyes from the light.

"Sorry." Linda lowered her flashlight, thankful the man was Richie and not Alfred. But she'd been caught snooping. She'd have to bluff her way out. "I'm searching for Gertrude. Have you seen a tabby cat?"

"No, but I heard a dog down the alley barking. Maybe your cat is there."

"Oh no," Linda said. "The dog was barking at me. I think its bark is worse than its bite. But I'm not in any hurry to find out."

The young man chuckled.

Linda's tense shoulders relaxed. He was curious but not upset that she was in the backyard. "Do you remember me? I'm Linda Burton. My friend Mary and I were at your uncle's garage sale. I live down the alley, past the barking dog. I'm sort of a neighbour."

"Oh, yeah, sure. I think your friend bought the four-poster bed and the armoire."

"Yes, she did. Beautiful pieces of furniture."

"By the way, my name is Richie Hutchins."

"Yes, I know. And you're visiting from Toronto."

Richie laughed again. "You have to love small towns. Everyone knows everyone."

Linda joined in his laughter. "Your uncle told me who you were when I went with Mary to see the furniture. Your aunt and uncle have a nice home."

"Not for long. Uncle Alfred and Aunt Faith are moving. Or rather, they're taking up travelling. So, I guess it's moving." Richie grinned.

"That's what your uncle said, selling up, taking the camper, and touring Canada and the USA."

Richie shrugged. "Yeah, not my idea of fun, living in a camper."

"I gather it's an adventure they are both looking forward to."

"Yeah, retirement on wheels." He chuckled, then cocked his head. "I don't see any sign of your cat."

"Yes, I know. I'm sorry about the trespassing. Gertrude doesn't always come when I call."

"No worries. Are you more of a cat person or a dog lover?" he asked.

"Both, but cats are easier to look after."

"Your cat is called Gertrude?" Richie asked.

Linda debated: should she correct him? "Well, Gertrude isn't really my cat. I'm looking after him. I mean her. I guess I shouldn't let her run loose. I hope Gertrude doesn't come into your garden."

"Oh, no worries. Aunt Faith likes cats, too. And cats...what can you do? They are so independent."

"Yes, true, except when they want food."

The young man threw back his head and chuckled.

Linda liked the sound of his good-natured laughter. "I don't usually go into people's yards," she assured him.

"No problem. I'm sure my aunt and uncle don't mind."

Linda shone the flashlight on the garden. "This sure is a well-tended garden. Everything seems to be coming up well. I think maybe it's your aunt's handy work. I bought some of her bedding plants at the garage sale."

Richie stepped over a tomato plant to stand three rows closer to Linda. "Yeah, Aunt Faith has a green thumb."

"Did the garage sale go well?"

"Yeah, a lot of stuff went. We'll keep it going for another day. They need to get rid of a lot of stuff before they leave on their camping adventure."

"Yes, the camping adventure. It's funny that your aunt planted a garden. A garden she won't be here to harvest."

Richie was silent for a moment. He stepped over a row of potatoes. "Yeah. A force of habit, I guess."

"How's your aunt? This was a busy day for her."

"She's fine, I guess. Why?"

"Have you seen your aunt today?"

"Why are you asking about Aunt Faith?" Richie stepped over the last row to stand in the same row as Linda. His foot crushed a potato plant.

"I just wondered if your aunt was ill or something. She wasn't outside in the garage or on the lawn with the furniture. And we didn't see her when we went into the house. It seemed a little strange, especially when Mary and I were in the bedroom. Your uncle told us the beautiful antique furniture in the bedroom was a wedding gift from Faith's grandmother. That four-poster bed and armoire must have meant a lot to your aunt."

Richie drew a little circle in the soil with the toe of his runner, then looked at Linda. "Aunt Faith is not ill. Uncle Alfred told me she was too emotional. Seeing the bed and armoire being sold would have probably been too much for her to witness."

"Well, your uncle did say Faith left the selling up to him."

"Did he? Well, that's Uncle Alfred for you."

Had Richie seen his aunt? He didn't actually say he had. But how was she going to broach the subject of his aunt without rousing suspicions? Undoubtedly, he would take offence if he thought she was laying aspersions on his uncle. "A hard worker, your aunt."

"Yeah, she sure is. Before we even had breakfast, Aunt Faith had the bread baked. A busy woman, my aunt. And I have to confess, I went outside to organize things for the garage sale. And didn't offer to help with the breakfast dishes."

"I expect your uncle helped."

Richie chuckled. "No, Uncle Alfred likes to cook, but washing dishes is not his thing."

"Do you think she's busy now?"

"Why?"

"I'd like to wish your aunt and uncle a happy retirement. Travelling across Canada in a camper is quite an adventure."

Richie took a step closer to Linda. "Aunt Faith isn't home."

"Oh."

"After breakfast, she went out somewhere. And she's not back yet."

"Your aunt went away the day of their garage sale?"

"Yeah. The garage sale is up to Uncle Alfred and me to organize. I haven't seen Aunt Faith since breakfast."

"Not since breakfast?"

"Yeah, I went out to start hauling furniture and things onto the lawn. Uncle Alfred told me she left before the sale started. She didn't want to see her stuff sold. He said she was too sentimental." Richie dug a small hole in the garden soil with the toe of his shoe.

"You didn't see her leave."

"No. As I said, I was out in the backyard, getting the lawn chairs, barbeque, and other stuff out to the front lawn for the garage sale."

"When did you arrive here in Glenhaven?" Linda asked.

Richie stepped closer to Linda. She saw a frown on his face. "Last week, why?"

"Do your aunt and uncle get along?" Linda felt bold asking. But then, wasn't that what detectives did? Gather background information.

He rubbed his forehead with the tips of his fingers, dropped his hand, and looked narrowly at Linda. "Yeah, sort of," he said.

If anyone knew what was happening in the Hutchins household, it would be Richie. "I hear that your aunt and uncle are always arguing," lied Linda. "And yet they are taking a road trip across Canada. Close quarters in a motorhome. Not a happy way to spend your retirement if you're always at loggerheads with your spouse."

Richie was silent for a moment. He sighed and said, "Yeah, my aunt is kind of a nagger and a perfectionist. And the two of them are always arguing." He shook his head and chuckled. "Sometimes I wonder why they even stay married. But they have been married forever. So, I suppose they are used to how things are between them."

So, there was strife, thought Linda proudly. Her instincts were bang on. She was right; something wasn't adding up.

Richie crossed his arms and asked, "Why are you asking about Uncle Alfred and Aunt Faith?"

Linda took in a deep breath. "Well, because your uncle told you your aunt left before the sale began. And yet he told us your aunt was in the attic."

"Did he?" Richie squared his shoulders and looked down at her.

"Yes, it might mean nothing. But it does make me wonder why your uncle told you one thing and told us another."

Richie stood still, tilted his head toward the night sky, then looked down at Linda. "That is weird," he said.

Linda debated whether she should tell Richie about the 'digging the grave voice?' But it wouldn't do to cast aspersions without evidence. She needed proof. But how? Linda straightened her shoulders. She would find the truth of it one way or another. She just didn't know how yet.

Richie leaned closer to Linda, his face inches from hers. He whispered, "Do you think something has happened to Aunt Faith?"

"I don't want to worry you." Linda fiddled with the flashlight, turning it off and on.

Richie placed his hand on Linda's, preventing her from pressing the flashlight button again. He looked back at the house and said in a low voice, "Yeah, but now you've got me worried. Why hasn't Aunt Faith come home?"

Linda shone the light on the ground. Unsure what to say. She'd alarmed the nephew. Maybe she should have kept quiet.

Richie wrapped his arm around Linda's shoulder, guiding her toward the backyard gate. "Maybe we shouldn't be talking here in the garden. Uncle Alfred might see or hear us. Not that I think anything is wrong with Aunt Faith," Richie said, hustling her into the alleyway.

Did he believe what he was saying? She flashed her flashlight up at him and saw the concerned look on his face.

Richie grabbed her arm, pushing the light downward. "Please don't do that."

"Oh, sorry."

Closing the gate, he stood beside Linda.

Feeling guilty about voicing her suspicions about his uncle, Linda said, "I'm sure your aunt will be home soon. And I should go home.

Gertrude is most likely back by now. I'll say good night." She started down the back alley.

"I'm sure she will," agreed Richie. His hand under Linda's elbow, he began walking beside her.

"You don't have to come with me. I can find my way back." Linda pulled her arm from his grasp.

"Oh, I know you can. I just want to make sure you're safely home. I always like to be helpful. My dad brought me up to be thoughtful."

Linda smiled at him. She bet he was a hit with the girls. Good looking and good manners.

"You know what?" Richie stopped walking and grabbed Linda's arm. "I bet they had an argument, and Aunt Faith left in a huff."

"Yes, that's most likely it," agreed Linda. She hoped that was the case.

"Uncle Alfred would never harm Aunt Faith," the young man said earnestly.

Linda pressed her lips together and resumed walking. Did Richie believe what he was saying? Or was he trying to convince himself?

"Yeah. I can't be thinking Uncle Alfred would do anything to Aunt Faith. That's just too weird and creepy for me."

"Oh, I'm sure everything is just fine," Linda said, her voice had a worried note.

Richie strode beside her, his head down and his hands in his pockets. "Do you think my uncle has tied my aunt up somewhere? Like in the attic? To teach her a lesson or something."

"I don't know, most likely not. I'm being silly, is all." Linda shone her flashlight on the rutted back alley. Why did Richie use the phrase, '*Teach her a lesson*'?

Did Richie hear Alfred threaten his aunt? If he did, should she ask or let sleeping dogs lie?

"Yeah, that's just silly. This is Uncle Alfred we're talking about," Richie said, slowing his steps to match Linda's. "Sure, he's kind of an odd old dude. But you would be too if you had to live with Aunt Faith."

Linda glanced up at Richie. His face was shadowed so that she couldn't see his expression. But he said his uncle was odd. Odd enough to harm his wife? "I'm most likely wrong, and your aunt is fine."

"Yeah, I'm sure she is. You had me worried there for a minute."

Thoughts churned in Linda's mind. Something wasn't adding up. "Something is not right," she blurted. "Your uncle told Mary and me that he and your aunt have been making plans all winter. Plans to sell up and go travelling in that motorhome. Spend the summer touring Canada and the winter in the USA. Yet, it looks like your aunt intended to spend the summer here. She has bedding plants, and she's planted a big garden."

"Yeah, I guess it is odd."

Linda wished she could see Richie's face. "What do you think?"

"I don't know what to make of it. I—"

Snarling, growling, and sharp barking from the chain-link monster stopped Richie mid-sentence. The large dog, baring its teeth, charged the chain-link fence. The fence swayed.

"Shut the hell up," Richie yelled.

Linda reached into her pocket and grabbed the plastic bag with the wiener, tossing the frankfurter over the fence. It landed on the ground a few feet from the ferocious dog. The dog barked once, then loped over to the wiener, gulping it down.

"You're prepared. Way to go. Good thinking."

Linda chuckled. "Last night, that big brute scared the heck out of me. So tonight, I was ready. I always try to think on my feet." Pleased with Richie's praise. She grinned as she trotted beside him past the chain-link fence.

Richie stopped and put his hand on her arm. "You came down the alley last night?"

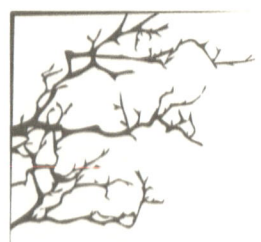

Chapter Seven

Linda looked up at him and chuckled again. "Yes, looking for Gertrude."

"Like you were tonight?" Richie slowly nodded his head, released her arm, and resumed walking.

"Yes. And I'm sorry. I shouldn't have said anything about my suspicions. They are your aunt and uncle. I'm a worrywart. I'm being silly."

Richie sighed. "I have a feeling you don't believe you are being silly. I think you are worried about my aunt. And hey, maybe this getaway is all Uncle Alfred's idea. Now that I think about it, Aunt Faith didn't seem to know anything about the motorhome when they delivered it yesterday. She might be getting Alzheimer's. Because Uncle Alfred swore up and down, she was there when he bought the motorhome. And now, when I think back, Aunt Faith got upset when we started getting the garage sale ready. And when Uncle Alfred said we were selling the furniture, Aunt Faith got even more upset. You know, if Aunt Faith has Alzheimer's, she might have wandered off somewhere."

"Maybe. But why did your uncle say your aunt was in the attic?"

Richie jammed his hands into his pockets and remained silent as they continued down the back lane.

Linda went silent, too. She wished Aunt Violet was home. Her aunt would know what to do. Should she wait for her aunt before investigating? Linda mauled over the possibility of Richie's aunt having Alzheimer's. Yes, Faith might have dementia, and she might have wandered off. But if Faith did, why wouldn't Alfred look for his wife instead of lying about her being in the attic? Linda stopped walking.

They were in Mabel's backyard. "Thanks for walking me home," she said.

"No problem. I like to be helpful. Is your husband waiting for you?"

"No, I'm not married." Linda opened her mouth to add she was divorced, then changed her mind and pressed her lips shut. She was not going to get into a dialogue about her ex.

Richie walked with her to the back porch. "It sounds lonely. Do you have family and friends close by?"

"Oh. I don't live here in Glenhaven. I'm from Regina. I'm house-sitting for Mabel Havelock. This is her house. She's a friend of my aunt. And I'm looking after Gertrude, Mabel's cat." She laughed. "Well, trying to look after her. Gertrude goes where she likes."

"When is this friend of your aunt coming home?"

"Not for a bit. My aunt has taken Mabel to Calgary. Mabel broke her foot, and her daughter is taking her to see an orthopedic surgeon. So, Gertrude is stuck with me." Linda chuckled again.

"That's good. I mean, it's a good thing your friend has a daughter to look after her," Richie said. He cupped his hand under her elbow as she mounted the stairs to the porch.

"Thanks, Richie, but I'm quite capable of climbing stairs." Linda giggled nervously.

Somehow, his helping hand made her feel uncomfortable. She crossed the deck and turned on the outside light.

Richie flashed her a big, wide smile. "I always like to be helpful to my elders."

Linda's brow knitted. Richie thought she was a senior. She didn't think she was that much older than Richie. Linda prided herself on her appearance and thought she looked younger than her thirty years. But she guessed one should never fault someone for their good manners. Manners were something her ex-husband Howard lacked. Linda couldn't remember the last time Howard held a door open for her or took her arm.

"I appreciate your good manners. And about what I said tonight, please forget it. It was all a lot of nonsense," Linda said. She definitely wasn't going to forget. But he didn't need to know that. She couldn't imagine how awful it would be to suspect your uncle had done something terrible to your aunt.

"Yeah, we should both forget about it," Richie said eagerly. "And I sure have no intention of going home and accusing my uncle of, well, you know..." his voice trailed off.

"Good."

"And please, Miss Burton, don't say anything to anyone about what we talked about tonight," he pleaded. "If people found out about your wild suspicions, it would ruin poor Uncle Alfred's reputation."

Wild suspicions? Linda guessed Richie would think her suspicions were wild. After all, it was his uncle. "Oh, no worries. I won't say a thing until I have proof."

"Until you have proof?" Richie asked, his eyes studying her.

Linda shifted in her chair, bit her lip, and said, "Well, until I know why your uncle lied. Or who he lied to. Did he lie to Mary and me when he told us your aunt was in the attic? Or did he lie to you when he said your aunt left before the yard sale even started?"

"You don't think Aunt Faith just wandered off?"

She rubbed her brow with the tips of her fingers, sighed, looked up at Richie and said, "If your aunt did wander away. Why did your uncle say she was in the attic? And why has your aunt gone to the bother of raising all those bedding plants? And why has she planted that big garden?"

"Maybe she planted all that stuff because she has Alzheimer's. And forgot they were moving out of town."

"Maybe, but until I know where your aunt is. I'm going to continue my investigation."

"Continue your investigation?" Richie guffawed.

Linda's hackles rose. She clenched her jaw. Richie sounded just like her ex, always downplaying anything she said. She remembered one of the last arguments they'd had. And the tone Howard used when he said, '*Stick to your kindergarten kids. That's your level.*' Linda crossed her arms over her chest.

Richie leaned back on the porch railing, his blue eyes crinkling. "You're going to investigate. What, like that old lady on the TV show? Jessica, something?"

Linda straightened in her deckchair. "Jessica Fletcher. I'm surprised you have even heard of that program?"

"My mom watched it. Sorry, I guess I sounded a little rude," he apologized, giving her a lopsided grin.

"I'm no Jessica Fletcher. But my Aunt Violet and I have solved crimes," Linda lied. She didn't know why she wanted to impress Richie. Maybe it was because he seemed to think she was a doddery old lady. And maybe because his taunting tone reminded her of Howard.

"You. Really." Richie chuckled. His eyes twinkled with amusement.

Linda pressed her lips together. He thought she was a joke. She was sick of being underestimated. "I know it's hard to believe. But it's true." She squared her shoulders and spread her hands. "Of course, Aunt Violet and I aren't famous. But you will find that we are pretty good investigators. We have a knack for spotting inconsistencies."

A lock of wavy blond hair fell over Richie's eyes. Brushing his hair from his eyes, he chuckled and asked, "What kind of things have you and your Aunt Violet figured out?"

Linda perched on the edge of her chair and said, "I don't like to brag. But we have solved murders. And believe it or not, some of the murders have happened in this very town."

"I thought you lived in Regina. And yet you solve crimes here in Glenhaven." His tone was skeptical.

Linda cleared her throat and licked her lips. Why, oh why, did she lie? "Yes, my aunt calls me, and I come out to Glenhaven and help her."

"And you and this aunt of yours solved a murder?"

"Murders."

"Seriously. You two have solved murders and brought these murderers to justice?"

It was too late to back out now. Linda sat back in her deckchair, folded her hands, and said, "Yes, we have."

Richie leaned forward, his hands on his knees. "Are you going to tell this aunt of yours about your suspicions about Uncle Alfred? I sure hope you're discreet. I'd hate to ruin Uncle Alfred's reputation, especially since we don't know if anything has happened to Aunt Faith."

"I will be very discreet. I promise you."

"And your aunt? Can you say the same for her?"

"I told you Aunt Violet isn't here. She took Mabel to Calgary. She's visiting family, too."

Richie sat back on the railing. He bent his head, scuffing the toe of his shoe on the deck. He stood, looked at Linda, smiled briefly, and crossed the deck to sit beside her. "I could help. Your aunt isn't here, but I am."

Linda pressed her lips together as she looked at Richie. Now that he decided to take her seriously, she felt a little queasy. It was all well and fine to say she was going to investigate. But should she? What did she know about being a detective? Not much. The fact was, she didn't know squat about investigating. However, maybe with Richie's help, she could muddle through. Should she let him help her? But it wasn't fair to Richie. "Richie, I don't know. I shouldn't have even told you about my suspicions. I don't want to put you in the middle. It's not right."

Richie took her hands in his and looked gravely into her eyes. "You already have. And now it's all I'll think about until I find out for sure what has happened to Aunt Faith. Like maybe she is tied up somewhere, waiting for me to help her."

Linda looked into his solemn eyes. He wanted to help. So why not? He would be the perfect person to find out if Alfred had done something. Should she tell him about the voice she heard from his backyard? No, that might freak him out. "Okay, maybe it's best if you scout around and see what is what. That way, no one will know we are investigating. Least of all, your uncle."

"Right. How do we do this without alerting Uncle Alfred?"

"Well, I can't, but you can. You have free rein. You can search the house to look for your aunt. If he catches you, say you're looking for more stuff to sell."

"You mean spy on my uncle?"

"You're not spying. You're searching. Do you think you can do that?"

"Okay, I guess. But maybe Aunt Faith is home already, and I don't have to do anything. But do you want me to tell you if she doesn't return home?"

"Yes, I think that's a good idea." Linda knew she should tell him to phone the police, but she was curious. It couldn't hurt to know first. Aunt Violet, of course, would probably tell her that curiosity killed the cat.

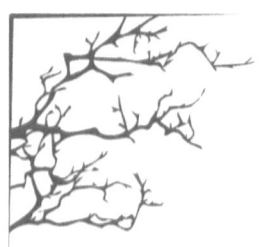

Chapter Eight

Linda sat on her deck chair, sipped her morning coffee, and stretched her legs. She grinned. Gertrude had chased a squirrel up a tree. The squirrel, leaping from tree to tree, left the cat far behind. The furry, chattering rodent eyed Gertrude from its tree. The cat was sitting on a branch, three trees from her prey. Linda giggled. The squirrel was either scolding or bragging. Gertrude scampered down the tree trunk and crept low on her belly. Switching her tail back and forth, she sat below the squirrel.

"Give it up, Gertrude. That squirrel is much faster than you." Linda took another sip of her coffee. In the distance, a dog barked. The barking was from the back alley. She cradled her coffee mug in her hands. At least it wasn't Gertrude annoying some poor dog like Bongo. The bark sounded more like her nemesis, the chain-link monster. Her thoughts went back to Faith. Did Richie's aunt come home? She hoped so.

Linda set her coffee mug on the porch railing and took her phone from her pocket. She'd text her aunt. Looking up at the cloudless sky, she squinted, then looked back at her phone. What to say? Should she tell her aunt her suspicions about Faith and Alfred? No, she'd phone her tonight and explain. By then, she'd know if her suspicions were right or not. She texted. *'I hope you are having fun with your grandsons. I've been busy,'* She grinned, used the fingers-crossed icon and added. *'I may have a lead'.*

"Miss Burton," called Richie. Smiling and waving, he jogged across Mabel's Garden. Leaping over the little green plants, Richie kicked her sandal. He bent down, picked up the flip-flop, and continued across the garden.

Linda pressed the send button and stuck the phone in her pocket. "Good morning."

Richie held up the dirty sandal and asked, "Is this yours?"

"Yes, thanks." Linda smiled. "I have another one somewhere." She wasn't ready to tell Richie she'd been poking around their hedge at night. He might think she was some kind of old busybody.

Richie grinned, tossed the sandal on top of the piled plant pots, and wiped his hands on the seat of his jeans. "Oh, sorry, Miss Burton. I should have said good morning first," apologized the young, muscular, fair-haired man.

Linda smiled. "No formalities needed. And please call me Linda."

"Oh no, I couldn't do that," he said, mounting the steps to the porch. "My dad always made sure I used proper titles when addressing an elder. It's a sign of respect."

Linda sighed. How old did he think she was? But what the heck, he meant well. "I see. Well, I'm not in my dotage just yet, but I appreciate the sentiment. Anyway, would you like a cup of coffee? It's fresh."

Richie brushed a lock of hair off his forehead. "No, but thank you. I just dropped by to tell you not to worry about Aunt Faith."

"I gather you have good news."

"Yeah." Richie hoisted himself up on the porch railing, and with a broad smile on his tanned face, he said, "The best."

"Great, your aunt has come home?"

"No, she hasn't. But we don't have to worry about Aunt Faith anymore."

"Your aunt isn't home?"

"No, but don't worry, Aunt Faith is fine. She doesn't have Alzheimer's. And she hasn't wandered off."

"That's good to hear. So where is your aunt?"

Richie, perched on the porch railing, swinging one leg back and forth, said, "She's visiting." Richie grinned a friendly, lopsided grin. "When I got home last night, Uncle Alfred was at the kitchen table counting the days' take from the garage sale."

"I see."

"Yep. Everything is fine. I asked Uncle Alfred where Aunt Faith was."

"You asked where your aunt was." Linda bit her lip. That wasn't very smart if his uncle had tied his aunt up, or worse. Richie had just alerted his uncle that he was concerned about his aunt's well-being.

"Yeah, there was no reason not to ask about Aunt Faith. Uncle Alfred doesn't know you suspect him of...well, you know."

"That's good. I wouldn't want your uncle to think I was thinking bad things about him."

"Even though you were."

"Well, yes, I was." Linda's face flushed.

"Anyway, it's all good. While we were having tea, I asked where Aunt Faith was."

"What did he say?"

Richie's eyes twinkled. "Uncle Alfred told me he and Aunt Faith did have a big argument." Chuckling, he brushed another stray lock of hair from his forehead. "Which isn't a surprise, as they are always at each other over one thing or another. Anyway, I guess this yard sale was all Uncle Alfred's idea. And Aunt Faith was mad as heck. She stormed off to stay with her sister."

"Your aunt didn't know your uncle was having a yard sale? There was furniture on the front lawn."

Richie slid off the railing. His eyes narrowed. "Well, yeah, I guess she did. I think the argument was more about the new motorhome. She doesn't like the motorhome and isn't happy about camping across Canada. Anyway, I guess the two of them had a screaming match, and off she went to her sister, Lana."

"Where does your aunt live? Does she live in town?"

"I don't know. I don't think so. I never asked."

"Did you phone her?"

"No, why would I do that?"

Linda threw up her hands. "Because your uncle might be lying to you."

"I don't think so."

"You believe his explanation?"

"Yeah, why not?" Richie widened his stance, jamming his fists into his pockets.

"If it was a screaming match, don't you think it's odd you didn't hear this argument?"

"I guess I was outside getting stuff ready for the sale."

"And don't you find it odd that your aunt didn't say goodbye to you?"

Richie ran a hand through his hair, another strand falling onto his forehead. Pacing, he shook the hair from his eyes. "Well, it's not that odd. Aunt Faith probably blames me for helping with the yard sale. I helped carry furniture and stuff out to the lawn."

"But would she be mad at you? You said she knew about the yard sale."

"Yeah, she did. I guess she was so mad about the motorhome and the trip. She just up and left in a big huff."

"I'm sorry, Richie, this just doesn't add up. Your uncle told you she didn't want to go on this cross-Canada camping trip. Yet he told Mary and me that your aunt couldn't wait to go on the road trip. And think about it. He said they'd been planning this camping trip all winter. And if your aunt doesn't have Alzheimer's. Why the bedding plants and that big garden? Did she know your uncle planned to sell the house?"

"How'd you know about that?"

"Your uncle told me. When Mary bought the bed and the wardrobe."

Richie rubbed the back of his neck, shut his eyes, pressing his lips together in a frown.

"And your uncle told you this argument happened before the sale started. And your aunt took off in a huff. But remember, he told Mary and me another story. There are too many contradictions. Something is wrong."

Richie put his hands in his pocket and bent his head, scuffing his toe on the porch floor. After a moment, he looked worriedly up at Linda. "So, you don't believe what Uncle Alfred told me? You really think something is wrong?"

"Unfortunately, I do."

Richie looked down at his feet, sighed, and looked back up at Linda with a crooked smile. "You told me you have a knack for ferreting out inconsistencies. I did doubt you. But now I believe you."

"You believe me about things not adding up?"

"Yes, I guess I do." Richie dropped his head again, drawing little circles on the porch floor with the toe of his runner. When he looked up, his eyes were full of concern. "I hope you're wrong. I love them both. I want to help. But I don't know how. What do you think we should do?"

Linda bit her bottom lip. No matter how the investigation ended, it wouldn't end well for Richie. If his aunt is unharmed, his uncle will be furious with him for thinking he'd harm his wife. And the other outcome would be even worse. "I think I should call the RCMP."

Richie's back stiffened, his hands clenched by his side. "You are kind of jumping the gun. You said last night that you would be discreet. Informing the RCMP of a crime you don't even know is committed. That isn't very discreet. Think of my uncle's reputation."

Linda lowered her head, closed her eyes, and thought. Richie was right. She had no proof that Alfred was responsible for his wife's disappearance. "Yes, you're right. We must not rush into things. I still don't have proof anything is amiss. Yet."

Richie sagged onto the railing.

Gertrude, meowing, sauntered up the steps. "Hey, kitty," Richie said, bending to pet the cat. Gertrude bristled, her back arched. Hissing, she shot past him, sidestepping toward the door to the house.

"Gertrude, where are your manners?"

"So, what do we do?" Richie asked, eyeing the cat.

Linda set her mug on the railing and hastened to the tabby cat. Gertrude stopped hissing and rolled onto her back. "Honestly, I don't know what to do," she said, rubbing the cat's tummy. "I'm going to think about it. I don't have a plan yet. If I don't come up with one and Faith doesn't turn up, I'm afraid my only option is to call the RCMP and tell them my concerns. I'm sure they will be discreet."

Richie leaned back on the railing, his eyes thoughtful. The toe of his foot made a little circle on the porch floor. "I think I have an idea," Richie said. He stood looking down at Linda, who was crouching beside the cat.

Giving Gertrude one last pet, Linda stood. "Tell me your idea."

Shaking his head, he backed away. "No, this is definitely a bad idea." He hesitated for a moment, then started toward the step.

"A bad idea?" Linda followed, putting a hand on his arm. "What is it? I'm open to any suggestion you have."

Richie gave Linda's hand a gentle squeeze. "I'm sure my idea would work. But this is my family." He turned his head, started for the steps again, and turned back. Sadness clouded his features. "I know you want to help. But I shouldn't get you involved."

"It's fine. Just tell me your idea."

"You're sure?"

"Yes," Linda said with conviction. This was her chance to prove she was as good a detective as Aunt Violet and Mabel.

"Thank you. You don't know how much I appreciate you helping." Richie wrapped his arms around her, hugging her.

Linda, embarrassed, shrugged off his hug. "I want to help. This has been my idea from the get-go."

Richie gave her a sad smile. "Yes, it was."

"What is your idea?"

"We are having another day of the garage sale. So, my idea is that while Uncle Alfred is busy in the garage with the bargain hunters. You sneak in the back door and search the house. And see if Aunt Faith is in the attic."

"The attic? Well, I guess. But why don't you search while your uncle is in the garage?"

"I could, I suppose. But I don't want Uncle Alfred to catch me in the act. My idea is that while you search, I'll make sure Uncle Alfred stays in the garage."

"This does sound like a good plan, except the house is locked. Yesterday, your uncle had to unlock the door so Mary and I could go into the house."

"Yeah, but I have a key. I'll unlock the back door and let you in. Then I'll beat it to the garage and keep Uncle Alfred busy."

"Okay. I'm game. First, I'll put Grumpy in the house and meet you whenever you say." Linda opened the back door, and Gertrude raced inside.

"I think we should go now."

"Now?"

"When I left the house. Uncle Alfred went out to the garage to open the garage door to start the sale. We should be able to sneak in the back door without him noticing."

"Good idea," agreed Linda. "It's always busiest with shoppers at the start of the sale."

"Good. That is, if you're sure you want to do this?"

"Like I said, I'm game." Linda started down the steps.

"Wait, aren't you going to lock your door?"

"Here in Glenhaven, I was told they hardly ever lock their doors, especially the back doors."

"I'd feel better if you did."

"Big city boy," joked Linda. "But being a city girl myself. I agree. You can't be too careful." She reached under a small green and white gnome. Took the house key, locked the door, and replaced the key under the gnome.

"A gnome." Richie laughed. "Cute little guy."

"He's a Rider gnome." Linda joined in his friendly laughter.

"A rider gnome?"

"The gnome is a nod to Mabel's football team. Not that they have gnomes playing for them, of course." Laughing, she joined Richie, waiting at the bottom of the steps.

He chuckled and took Linda's arm, ushering her toward the back alley.

Linda pulled her arm from his. "I can walk on my own steam. I know I look old to you, but I don't need any help."

"Oh, sorry, Miss Burton. I'm just trying to be helpful."

She shrugged and smiled warmly. "Linda, please."

"Oh no, Miss Burton. As I told you, I was raised to respect my elders. And my dad made damn sure. Sorry. Darn sure, I never forgot my lessons."

Linda sighed. She didn't like being classed as an oldster. But it seemed Richie was bent on classifying her as one. "That's so sweet. You are a gentleman. Your parents have brought you up well."

"Thank you." Richie flashed her a winsome smile.

"What about your mom? Was she a stickler for proper titles, too?"

"My mom was a mouse," scoffed Richie. "She agreed with whatever my dad said."

Linda frowned. Richie didn't seem to have much respect for his mother. She pushed the thought away as they approached the chain-link fence. Linda's nemesis, the chain-link monster, lay on the grass, panting. There were white speckles on the rottweiler's muzzle, the dog's mouth was open, and his tongue hung out as it heaved.

"There is something wrong. This dog is sick," Linda said. She wasn't fond of the monster leaping at the fence, but the dog wasn't even moving.

"The stupid dog is probably played out from barking."

"I think I should tell the owners there's something wrong with their dog."

"I thought you hated that animal?"

"No, not hated. I was alarmed." Linda took a step toward the gate.

"What if the dog gets up? Are you fast enough to get to the door before that rottweiler gets you?"

Linda stopped, warily looking at the panting dog. The dog briefly lifted its head, then dropped his head on the grass. It didn't look all that big lying down, but Richie could be right. She remembered how it charged the fence. The animal was strong and fast.

Richie tugged on her arm. "Come on, the owners will check on it. We need to find out about Aunt Faith."

"Okay, I guess you're right," agreed Linda reluctantly.

"Good." Richie placed his hand on Linda's back and urged her down the alleyway. Smiling down at her, he began whistling a tune.

Puzzled, Linda looked up at him. They were on a serious mission to find his Aunt Faith. They didn't know if she was alive or dead. And Richie was whistling a cheery tune? "You're whistling?"

"Am I?" Richie ducked his head. "Sorry, when I'm nervous, I tend to hum or whistle," he said, giving her a sheepish grin.

Linda offered a bemused smile. "That tune sounds familiar. Isn't that from Mr. Rogers? My brother and I watched that show when we were little kids. I think the song goes, *It's a beautiful day in the neighbourhood.*"

"Yeah." Richie chuckled. "I don't know why it popped into my head."

"I'm surprised you know the theme song of Mr. Rogers."

Richie smiled. "I saw the movie on TV, and I guess it just stuck in my head."

Linda looked sadly at Richie. She guessed a song from the feel-good movie, like Mr. Rogers, would be comforting. Linda couldn't imagine the conflicting emotions going through his mind. How awful was it for Richie to suspect his uncle of doing something nefarious to his aunt? It had to be too terrible for words.

As they neared the Hutchins' backyard, Richie's steps slowed. He paused at the gate and took in a deep breath. "You know, my aunt is probably home, and she's bustling around the kitchen. I'm sure Uncle Alfred wouldn't harm Aunt Faith over a disagreement about a motorhome and the travel plans."

"Put like that. It does seem a little far-fetched," Linda said. Should she stop now? What would Mabel and her Aunt Violet do? Would they continue investigating? The motorhome and the trip might not be the reason for Faith's disappearance.

Richie looked down at the weeds by the garbage stand and then back up at Linda. He leaned down and picked up her sandal. "I think I have found your other flip-flop."

"Ah. That's where it went. That darn dog must have picked it up and run away with it. I hope it's not chewed up," Linda said, feeling proud of herself. She was thinking on her feet. It wouldn't do for Richie to think she was a busybody snoop.

Richie arched an eyebrow. "Yeah, that explains it." He tossed the sandal back into the weeds and swung the gate open. "Here goes," he said, placing a hand on Linda's back and guiding her into the yard.

Linda's eyes darted, taking in the Hutchins' backyard. The sun was reflecting off the shiny silver motorhome. The back of the two-story house was a simple affair. The upper story had two tall windows and another on the ground floor. The ground floor window was open, and checkered white and yellow curtains fluttered. There was a small white wooden back door with an old screen door that needed a paintbrush. The only spot of colour was two big orange urns on either side of the cement steps. The petunias inside the pots drooped. The plants needed watering.

Linda heaved a sigh of relief. There was no sign of Alfred. Richie was right. His uncle was out in the garage.

Richie was silent, his face set as they walked past the garden toward the house; he stopped at the bottom of the steps. Running a hand through his hair, he turned to Linda. "I don't think I can do this."

Feeling guilty, Linda chewed her bottom lip. She should have kept her suspicions to herself and never involved him. But what if Alfred had his wife tied up, and she could rescue her? This was her chance to find out once and for all. "It will be fine. You just go out to the garage as we planned. I'll nip upstairs and have a look in the attic."

"Right, and if Aunt Faith is not there, we can forget all about this." Richie laughed nervously. "And Uncle Alfred will never know anything about our silly suspicions."

"If your Aunt Faith is not in the attic, I'll search elsewhere. I'm very good at finding clues," Linda bragged. "And you don't have to worry. If I find something, I'll phone The RCMP immediately. I promise you won't be involved. You just stay in the garage with your uncle. It will be fine, and if I don't find anything, I'll pop around to the garage sale and wave. Then you'll know everything is okay."

Richie rubbed the back of his neck, sighed, and slowly shook his head. Then, looking down at Linda, his mouth curved into a crooked smile. "You have it all figured out," he said, wrapping his arms around her.

Linda returned the hug, looking up into his friendly, smiling face. "Leave it up to me. I'll look after everything. Don't worry. It will be fine."

"I know it will," Richie said as he unlocked the back door and stood to the side, ushering Linda into the house.

Linda felt the house had a lonely, empty feeling.

"Please wait here," instructed Richie. He sped to the kitchen, returning seconds later. "No, Aunt Faith is not there."

"Did you really think she would be?"

"No, I guess not." His face was sullen.

Linda gently squeezed his arm and then started to go up the stairs.

Richie's eyes lit up. "You know, Aunt Faith could have gone to her sister Lana's place, just like Uncle Alfred told me. We should check in Aunt Faith's wardrobe to see if her clothes and suitcase are gone. She must have packed some clothes if she went to stay with her."

"Good idea. That's a great place to start. Is the armoire still in the bedroom?"

"Oh, yeah, everything is still there. I think we should look now, don't you? I sure don't want to accuse Uncle Alfred of some horrific crime of murdering his wife. If it's just some silly spat, and she's gone off to visit her sister Lana."

"Have you ever met this Lana?" asked Linda as she ascended the stairs.

"You know, now that you ask, I'm not even sure Aunt Faith has a sister. I've never met or heard of her until last night."

"You don't know who your aunt's relatives are?"

"Uncle Alfred is my dad's brother." Richie chuckled. "And you know, I don't know anything about Aunt Faith's side of the family." Richie placed a hand under Linda's elbow. "Here, let me help you. These stairs are steep. I don't want you to fall."

Linda chuckled. "I appreciate you want to help this little old lady, namely me, but as I told you, I'm not helpless yet. And shouldn't you go to the garage? That was the plan, remember? You stand guard and make sure your uncle stays in the garage."

"Oh, I will, for sure, if I have to, but first, I want to check the wardrobe. I might not have to stand guard. I want to prove Uncle

Alfred is innocent. I bet we'll find Aunt Faith has cleaned out her closet."

Linda gave the young man's arm another gentle squeeze. Richie so wanted to believe his aunt was okay. And she so hoped he was right.

Richie stood back, letting Linda enter the bedroom first. She went straight to the old-fashioned armoire and opened the door. Faith's clothes were still hanging in the wardrobe. There wasn't even one empty hanger.

Linda shut the closet door and turned to Richie. "I'm afraid your aunt's clothes are still in the closet." Her jaw dropped. The bedroom door closed, and there was a click of a key turning in the lock.

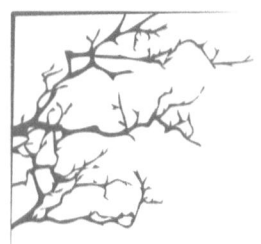

Chapter Nine

M outh agape, Linda stood transfixed, staring at the closed door. "Richie, what the heck?" She sped to the door, gripped the doorknob, and turned, yanking. The door didn't budge. Hammering on the door with her fists, she yelled, "Richie, open this door. Open it right now." She stopped and waited, but there was no answer. She resumed pounding, screaming, "This is stupid. Unlock this damn door."

Her hands numb, Linda pressed her ear to the door, listening. Nothing, not even footsteps. She slumped against the door and slid to the floor, shaking her hands. Beating on the solid oak door was useless. She couldn't beat it down. She was only hurting her hands. Richie wasn't coming back.

Bewildered, Linda rested her head against the closed door. She knew Richie didn't want to believe anything had happened to his aunt. And he certainly didn't want to believe his uncle had anything to do with his aunt's disappearance. But why lock her in the bedroom? Where had he gone? Did he go to the attic to look for his aunt? If he did and he found his aunt tied up, it made sense he'd come back here and let her out. But what if his aunt wasn't tied up in the attic? Would Richie still believe his uncle's version that his aunt had left? Would he come back for her then? And what if he found his aunt dead? Then what? Would he side with his uncle? She didn't think Richie would do that. Linda prided herself on being a good judge of character. He seemed genuinely worried about his aunt. Should she wait for him to return and let her out? Or should she call for help?

Linda's eyes narrowed. Richie Locking her in this bedroom was ridiculous. "To heck with it, I'm not waiting for him to come to his senses." She reached into her jeans pocket for her phone. The phone was gone. Linda's heart lurched. "Damn it," she swore. Richie took her phone when he hugged her. It wasn't a spur-of-the-moment thing with him. Richie had planned it. Was she fooling herself, and Richie was not who she thought he was? Did he lock her in here to protect his uncle? Surely not. Richie told her he loved his aunt.

Now what? Frowning, Linda bit her bottom lip. None of this made sense. How long did Richie plan on keeping her here? Not long, surely.

Her eyes flickered around the room. Would anybody in the town notice that she was missing? Wanda, Mabel's neighbour, might. And she had met some people when Aunt Violet took her to Coffee Row. But those people wouldn't know she was missing. If Aunt Violet were home, she would miss her. But her aunt wouldn't know she was locked in the Hutchins' bedroom. And poor Gertrude, trapped inside the house. Did she have enough food and water? And the kitty litter. Good lord, she needed to get out of here.

Across the room, sunlight streamed through the bedroom window. The window looked out at the backyard. Linda scrambled to her feet and marched to the window. How dare Richie lock her in this room? She'd open the window and call for help. Linda yanked the lace curtains out of her way. The curtain rod snapped, and the curtains slipped on the rod, hanging down. She shoved them to the side, put her hands on either side of the windowpane, and pushed up on the wooden frame. The window remained closed. Coats of white enamel paint had sealed the window shut.

Exasperated, Linda stomped across the room and sank onto the bed. Rubbing her forehead, she looked around at her faded blue wallpaper prison. The room was oppressively hot and had a stale, antiseptic smell. Should she wait? Linda plucked her T-shirt away from her body. She was sweating. But wait for what? What if Richie was a snitch and had gone to alert Alfred? And Alfred was her main concern. The man was a liar. He lied to Richie, or he lied to her and Mary. Why lie if you didn't do anything? Linda licked her dry lips. It would be stupid to wait and take a chance. She needed to get out.

She slapped her knee and strode back to the window. Somehow, she needed to alert someone she was locked up in the bedroom. Linda pressed her forehead against the windowpane and sighed. No one was in the backyard. What did she expect? The yard sale was taking place in front of the house. And the boxwood hedge that lined the yard was high. Anyone walking in the back alley would have to look up at the window. And that was unlikely. Linda bit her bottom lip. Parked in front of the greenhouse was the big silver motorhome. The motorhome that was the bone of contention between Alfred and Faith. Linda stood with both hands on the windowsill, scanning the backyard. A squirrel scampered across the grass. The animal paused in the garden and stood on its hind legs. Its head twitched back and forth, then shot into the hedge.

Then Linda heard a faint tap. Her eyes sparkled with excitement. Across the back alley, on a roof, three men were shingling. The three men were on their knees, their backs toward Linda. "Oh, please turn and look, look over here," she cried, tapping on the window, which she knew was in vain. There was no way they would hear her from across the alley. Linda yanked the curtain off the rod. The curtain rod landed on the floor with a clatter, rolling across the linoleum. Linda jumped up and down, waving with both hands. A tall man with no shirt stood, stretched, and turned. Smiling from ear to ear, she waved frantically. The shirtless man waved back. Linda's spirit soared. The roofer had noticed her. But the man then turned, knelt down, and continued shingling. Linda lowered her arms and leaned against the window ledge. She hunched her shoulders and blew out a long sigh. It was useless. She could probably wave all day, and the man would think she was overly friendly or she was some kind of a nut bar.

Straightening her shoulders, Linda stood, brushing her hands off. There must be a way to escape this overheated room. She looked down at the painted windowsill. A small smile crept across her face. If she could pry the window open, she could cry for help. The men would hear her. Or maybe she could even crawl out. No, there was nothing she could crawl onto, no trees or vines. It was a straight drop down to the ground. She wasn't built for scrambling down the side of a two-story house. But the window seemed like her best chance of escape. She had to alert someone she was trapped inside.

Her eyes lit on the armoire that held Faith's clothes. Wire clothes hangers. Yes, wire hangers, that's the ticket. Excited, Linda sped across the room and ripped open the wardrobe doors. Flinging Faith's dress to the floor, a wire hanger slid across the floor under the bed. She grabbed another hanger from the closet and raced back to the window. Linda scraped at the white paint with the curved neck of the wire hanger.

As Linda clawed at the enamel with the tip of the clothes hanger. Her thoughts returned to Richie. He had deliberately taken her phone and locked her up. An uneasy feeling crawled up her spine. Richie knew something. Something incriminating. Sweat dripped down Linda's back as she chipped feverishly at the white enamel. One small piece flew onto the floor. If Alfred harmed his wife, he would have no qualms about getting rid of her.

She needed to get the window open. With renewed energy, Linda, jaw clenched, pressed down on the hanger. The hanger tip barely made a dent. How many coats of paint were on this stupid window? Linda wiped her sweaty brow and changed hands. Shoulders hunched, she repeatedly scraped on the same spot. Flecks of paint flew onto the floor. "Ha, this is going to work."

Linda froze. She lifted her head, listening. It was the sound of the key turning in the lock.

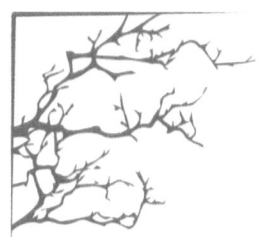

Chapter Ten

L inda sped back to the bed, stuffing the hanger under a pillow. Trembling, she sat on the bed, her sweaty hands clenched. Was it Alfred at the door or Richie? She hoped it was Richie. If it was Richie, there was hope. She bit her lips. But Richie had locked her in this room.

With a sandwich in one hand and a bottle of orange soda pop in the other, Richie entered the bedroom. With a big, broad smile, he set the sandwich and the bottle on the floor beside the bed. "I hope you are making yourself comfortable."

Rubbing her shaking hands on her jeans, Linda took a deep breath, willing herself to calm down. Richie was smiling the same charming smile as when she first met him. He'd made a mistake locking her in the bedroom and had come back for her. But why the sandwich? Linda jumped off the bed. "Locking me in here is ridiculous. What the heck were you thinking?" she asked, striding toward the door.

Chuckling, Richie stepped in front of her. "What's the hurry? Don't you like my hospitality?"

"Did you find your aunt?" Linda asked, her voice quaking, backed up, still eyeing the open door.

"Did you really think I was looking for my dear auntie?" His lips twisted into a crooked smile.

"What did your uncle do to your aunt? Where is she?" Linda's voice rose as she edged away.

"Oh, don't worry about dear Aunt Faith. She's been taken care of," Richie giggled. He grabbed Linda's arm, shoving her back onto the bed.

"What the heck do you think you're going to do? You can't keep me locked in here forever." Linda's voice wavered.

Richie's blue eyes sparkled with amusement. "Now, now, Miss Burton, don't you worry your little head. I'm not going to keep you here forever. It's just until I figure out what to do with you." His lips twitched, and he chuckled softly. "You just be a good girl and eat your lunch. I'm sorry I can't stay and visit. The garage sale is really picking up. And I have to help Uncle Alfred."

Linda's eyes darted to the open doorway and back to the tall, muscular man. Would she be quick enough? Richie was athletic. He would be fast. And she was certainly not athletic, and her legs were much shorter than his. "This is silly. Just let me out. And I'll say nothing about this, this incident." She pinched her quivering lips together.

"No, sorry, I don't think I can do that." Richie sat on the bed beside her, a playful grin on his face.

"You have to. People will miss me. You had better let me go."

"Dear, dear Miss Burton, no one is going to miss you. You told me you are a house sitter from Regina and that you're all alone. No one knows." Richie brushed her hair back from her face, tucking the stray strands behind her ear.

Linda shrank back, glaring at Richie and bunched her small hands into fists. What a fool she'd been. She'd trusted him and blabbed everything.

"Now, that's not very nice, Miss Burton." Richie strode to the window and sat on the ledge. He looked back at Linda and shook his head. "I don't like it when you're disrespectful to me. I was only offering you some comfort. Remember, I'm the well-brought-up boy with excellent manners. My dear old dad taught me well." Laughing bitterly, he began to draw a circle with the toe of his runner. His foot caught on the crumpled lace curtains. He looked at the broken curtain rod. Chuckling, he kicked the curtain rod, sending the rod rolling across the floor. "Temper, temper, Miss Burton. You wrecked dear auntie's precious curtains. Aunt Faith would have a fit if she saw what you have done to them." Richie leaned back on the sill, a hand on either side of his body. His eyes twinkled. A mischievous grin crossed his lips.

Linda watched the big boyish smile spread across his face. Her eyes widened. Richie hadn't threatened her. Her overactive imagination had run away with her. No one had done anything to Faith. Not his uncle, and certainly not Richie. Locking her in this room was nothing more than a silly, annoying prank. It was time to take charge. She'd taught kindergarten and handled many a truculent child. "I'm sorry about the curtains, but it's your fault. You can't expect me to sit here and do nothing. You shouldn't have locked me in. This is stupid." Linda stood, hands on hips, staring defiantly at him. "I'm leaving here right now."

Richie's face flushed. He bared his teeth and snarled, "Stupid! Are you calling me stupid?"

"Now you're being childish. Stop this foolishness and let me go."

Richie grabbed her by the shoulders and slammed her onto the bed. "Childish," he roared. His hands went to her throat, squeezing.

Linda clawed at his hands, her feet kicking. She gasped for air. Her limbs grew numb. Her hands fell to her side, her eyes bulged, and her vision faded. Blood roared in her ears. Darkness descended.

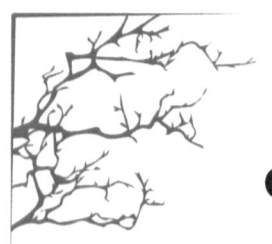

Chapter Eleven

Wheezing and gasping, Linda regained consciousness. *What had happened? Where was she?* Her vision cleared.

Richie glared down at her with disgust. "Look what you made me do," Richie screamed. He stood red-faced, his nostrils flaring and his fists clenched. "The last person who called me childish was my dad." Richie's lips curled in a sneer. "That's when I taught the old bastard some new manners."

Linda's chest heaved as she coughed and wheezed. Her throat burned, and her heart pounded as she gasped for breath. The room was spinning. She closed her eyes. Vertigo was making her nauseous.

Richie strode to the window, his back to her. Taking deep breaths, he turned and snarled, "You're lucky."

"Lucky?" whispered Linda, weakly raising a shaking hand to her neck, wincing.

"It's too soon," answered Richie, looking at the flecks of white paint on the floor. He ran his hand over the divots in the enamel. "Oh, oh, it's not a beautiful day in my neighbourhood," he said in a sing-song voice, striding back to the bed. "You've been a very bad girl." He grabbed Linda by the arm and hauled her up, twisting her arm behind her back.

Linda's stomach churned. She screamed as he pushed her face down to the window ledge.

"Look what you have done to my dear aunt's windowsill."

Linda moaned as her nose brushed the scrapes she had made.

Jerking her upright, his face inches from hers, Richie's eyes bored into Linda's. "What did you use?"

Linda felt his hot breath on her face. She pressed her trembling lips together. She couldn't tell him. The hanger was her way out.

Richie's fingers bit into her arm. Twisting, he yanked her arm upward. Linda shrieked and fell to the floor.

"Tell me." Richie's eyes glinted. His mouth curved into a cruel smile as he applied more pressure. "You know I can make this a lot harder for you. I don't have a lot of time. So, tell me."

White-hot, searing pain coursed through Linda's arm. It felt like her arm was coming out of its socket. "Under the pillows," she whimpered, her voice raspy.

"That's a good girl." Richie patted her on the head. Linda flinched.

"Get up," he ordered, prodding her with his toe.

Clutching the bedcovers, Linda, dizzy and nauseous, attempted to stand. Her hands failed to grip the covers, and she slid back to the floor.

"Oh, for God's sake." Richie grabbed Linda's arm and yanked her to her feet. Linda swayed, putting a hand on the bed for support.

Richie curled his lip in disgust, tossing the pillows to the floor. "I can't call you Miss Burton anymore," he said contemptuously as he picked up the hanger. "You have lost all my respect. Look what you made me do. You made me hurt you. And I hate that."

Tears trickled down Linda's face. She licked her dry, quivering lips. Her legs shaking uncontrollably, she sunk onto the bed. Her arm throbbed. She could still feel his hands on her throat.

Richie, spinning the crook of the clothes hanger on one finger, grinned at Linda. "What should I call you?" he asked as he tramped over Faith's dress to the wardrobe. "Such a naughty thing to do, throwing my aunt's dress on the floor." His eyes twinkled with amusement. "Oh, I know, Naughty Nanny. It fits, don't you think? Or maybe Nosey Nana." He laughed.

His maniacal laughter sent a shiver up Linda's spine.

He turned to look back at Linda crouched on the bed. His lips curled as he shook his head. "You know, you wouldn't be in this...what do we call this? A predicament? You wouldn't be in this predicament if you weren't so nosey. I gave you lots of explanations of where dear old Aunt Faith was. But would you take them? No, not you. You just had to come here and snoop. Yes, your new name is Nosey Nana."

Richie's high-pitched laughter rang out as he opened the closet door. Scooping up his aunt's clothes and the hangers. He threw them to the floor. The hangers clattered as they hit the linoleum. "Tsk, tsk, so many hangers to choose from. We must remedy that, don't you think, Nosey?" he asked.

Linda cringed, wrapping her arms around her trembling body. She rocked back and forth. One minute, he was red hot with rage. The next, he was almost giddy, taunting her.

"Just look at this mess. Aunt Faith would be very upset to see her clothes all over the floor." Richie's eyes glowed with delight as he looked at Linda cowering on the bed.

"Please, come and help me fold my aunt's clothes."

Wiping her nose with the back of her hand, Linda warily eyed Richie.

"Now, Nosey," Richie ordered softly, mockingly.

Linda rose, staggered, slumped back on the bed, then rose again. Holding on to the edge of the bed, she put one foot in front of the other. At the end of the bed, Linda hesitated. The door was open. It was so close. But her shaky legs barely supported her. She would have no chance.

"On your knees, Nosey." Richie put a hand on the top of her head, pressing down. Linda flinched, and he chuckled, shoving her onto the floor.

Keeping her head down, Linda breathed slowly in and out, trying to suppress her fear. She looked at the hangers scattered across the brown linoleum. Maybe she could snag one. Crawling on hands and knees to the pile of clothes strewn on the floor, Linda picked up a dress. Neatly folding it with shaking hands.

"That's what I like to see. Good girl," Richie said, crouching on his haunches. Whistling the tune from Mr. Rogers. '*A beautiful day in the neighbourhood.*' Richie picked up the clothes hangers one by one.

Linda remembered the next line. It was '*A beautiful day for a neighbour. Would you be mine?*' The words '*Would you be mine?*' sent fear coursing through her body. She was his captive. Richie was crazy. He almost choked her to death. And God only knew what he did to his aunt. This psychopath was going to kill her.

Richie took the pile of hangers to the hallway. The hangers rattled and clanged as he set them outside the door. Folding his arms across his chest, Richie leaned against the doorjamb. He continued to whistle as he tapped his toe, waiting for Linda to finish folding his aunt's clothes.

Linda kept her head bent, her mind working feverishly as she neatly folded each garment. Yes, she was scared out of her mind, and she would be a fool not to be. But anger bubbled up inside her. She wasn't the foolish little old woman this maniac thought she was. *Never give up. And never give in.* Linda didn't know where she heard that saying. But now, it would be her mantra. *Bide your time,* she told herself. There had to be a way out of this. And when she did, she'd get back at him if it was the last thing she did. She added the last item of Faith's clothing to the pile and slowly got to her feet.

"Good girl," he said, grinning.

The words, *good girl,* made Linda want to throw up.

Richie picked up the neatly folded clothes. Striding to the doorway, he tossed the garments out the door. Faith's clothes flew across the hallway.

The lunatic was playing a head game with her. Seeing her meekly on her knees folding his aunt's clothes gave him some kind of perverse pleasure. She'd remember that. Know your enemy's weakness.

Linda staggered back to the bed. Her toe hit the curtain rod. The rod rolled under the window. She looked back at Richie. He was kicking Faith's clothes out of the way of the door. Her heart leapt.

If Richie had forgotten about the rod, she could use it to smash the window and yell at the roofers for help. Picking up the soda pop, Linda opened the bottle and put it to her lips, taking big gulps.

Richie sprinted back across the floor and yanked the bottle from her hands. Orange pop spilled onto her T-shirt.

"I don't like to do this, but you know you've been naughty. And you must be taught a lesson. You know you don't deserve any lunch," Richie said, picking up the sandwich. "I want you to sit here and think about what you did. Behave yourself, and I might give you something for your supper."

Linda kept her eyes on Richie as he walked back to the door. Her heart hammered in her chest. He'd forgotten the curtain rod. *Please close the door*, she prayed.

Richie turned at the door and gave her a mischievous, crooked smile. "Oops, I almost forgot the curtain rod. Please bring it to me."

Her heart sank. Another head game. It had been a false hope.

"Now, Nosey, don't make me angry. Don't make me ask you again. You know I don't like it when you make me angry. And you don't like it either. Do you?" he asked. He had a malicious grin on his face as he stood in the doorway, arms folded across his chest.

Linda picked up the rod. If she got close enough, she could hit him in the face and escape. But she would have to be fast. If he saw it coming, she'd have no chance.

Richie stepped back away from the door. Linda bit her trembling bottom lip. The maniac was too far away to get a good shot at him.

"Good girl, Nosey. Now, set it in the hallway. Please don't drop it. Set it down nicely."

Looking longingly at the stairs, she set the curtain rod on the hallway floor.

Richie's eyes twinkled. "Don't even think about it. These stairs are steep. What do you think will happen if you trip? And you know I will make sure you do. You might not die, but I promise you, you won't be tap dancing."

Shoulders drooping, Linda bit her trembling bottom lip, backing into the bedroom. Richie's laughter followed her. Linda remembered how she once liked the sound of his laughter. Now, it made her skin crawl.

"I'll be back when the garage sale is over. Be a good girl, and I might give you supper." Richie shut the door.

Linda's hand went to her throat. Her throat was raw. She tried to swallow, but her mouth was dry. She wrapped her arms around herself, rocking, sobbing softly. Why didn't she realize Richie's boyish charm for what it was? What a dope she'd been. Linda glared at the closed door with tear-filled eyes, remembering his words. *"Oh, I can't do this. Thank you for coming with me. Oh, let's look in the closet,"* she mimicked. The devious psychopath had played her like a fiddle the entire time. Feigning reluctance and obviously feigning worry about his aunt. If only she had left things alone. She was no detective. Richie was right. She was just nosey. Now, she was trapped in the house with a crazed killer and had no one to blame but herself.

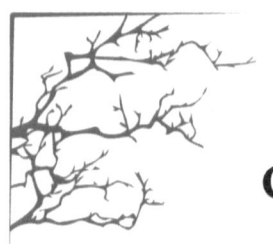

Chapter Twelve

Pressing the palms of her hands to her eyes, Linda took a deep breath. She wiped her eyes and straightened her shoulders. Crying would get her nowhere. She had to be strong. Wiping her nose with the back of her hand, she sniffed. She had to think of something. Linda walked to the window and took off her runner. She banged the shoe on the windowpane. Nothing. The soft sole of the shoe was never going to break the glass. With a bitter smile and a heavy sigh, Linda put her shoe back on.

Rubbing her aching arm, Linda paced the hot, stuffy room. Only stopping to stare out the window. To watch the men roofing the house across the alley, waving any time they looked her way. They either didn't see her, or they were ignoring her.

The light was fading. At first, the time went by slowly. Now, it was moving too fast. Richie would be back.

Linda shuddered. She could feel Richie's hands on her throat, the struggle to breathe, and the darkness closing in. But it hadn't been the broken curtain rod that set him off. It was when she called him childish. She remembered him saying something about his father. What was it? Teach him a lesson? Good Lord, did he kill his dad?

There was no doubt in her mind Richie did something to his aunt. But what? And why? Did Faith call him a derogatory name? Did he lock Faith up somewhere? Or, God forbid, kill his aunt? Did that mean Alfred was covering up for Richie? Why the heck would Alfred do that? Maybe Alfred was the innocent one. When he told Mary and her that Faith was in the attic looking for stuff to sell, maybe Alfred really thought she was. And everything Richie told her was a lie.

Richie was the dangerous one. He almost choked her to death, but he stopped. Why? Why was she still alive? Was he waiting for nightfall? She bit her lips. The sun, now, was low in the west, making its descent behind the houses across the alley.

She had to do something. Linda clenched her small fist. Dare she smash the glass? Could she even break it? And if she did, would she get cut in the process? But did it matter? She'd call out to the roofers. Linda drew back her arm, ready to punch the windowpane. "Here goes," she cried. She dropped her arm. The roofers were packing up. They were leaving. Even if she broke the window now, no one was there to hear her cries. She'd waited too long.

Linda rubbed her temples. *Be a warrior,* Linda told herself, *not a worrier.* Worrying would get her nowhere. *Never give up. Never give in.* There had to be a way out of this mess.

The door opened. Richie, with a broad smile, bounded into the bedroom. "Did you have a nap? I'm told old people need their naps."

Linda swung around, cupping her mouth, suppressing a scream. *Now what?* Shaking inside, she backed away from him to the far side of the bedroom.

"It's only good manners to reply when spoken to."

"I didn't nap," she whispered.

"Come here."

Trembling, Linda remained where she was.

"I'm not going to hurt you. Don't you believe me?" He tilted his head, his eyes twinkling. "You're still alive, aren't you? If I wanted you dead, you would be."

Linda's lips quivered.

"Come here. I have a question for you."

Linda shrank against the wall, shoulders hunched, arms clamped close to her side.

Richie, with a friendly, crooked smile, arched an eyebrow. He waggled his finger. "I'm asking nicely."

Linda knew that smile. It was his signature smile. The handsome blond-haired, blue-eyed, charismatic man across the room from her. Was a psychopathic maniac.

"We can do this the easy way or the hard way." Spreading his hands, he sighed. "It's up to you."

Linda's body shook with fear. *You have to calm down,* she told herself. *You can't think straight if you let him terrify you.* Taking a deep breath, she slowly breathed in and out.

"Are you hungry?" Richie widened his stance and crossed his arms. "If you want something to eat, answer me. I don't have all day. Decide."

Hope surged. Did the offer of food mean he wouldn't kill her? Or was this just another tease? Would he offer food only to take it away? "Yes, I'm hungry," she said weakly.

"I can't hear you," he said in a sing-song tone.

"Yes, please, I'd like something to eat," Linda croaked.

Richie's blue eyes lit up with amusement. "Good girl, I'm glad to hear the magic word."

"Magic word?"

"The please word. Surely your mother taught you please was the magic word." Richie's charming smile gave way to a chilling, malevolent grimace. "My dad drilled that into me." Richie took a step forward.

Linda shrunk back against the wall.

"It's up to you. Do you want supper or not?"

Linda wiped her sweaty palms on her jeans and took a big breath. She let it out and took a tentative step away from the wall. He was offering food. Did that mean he would let her go downstairs? If he let her go downstairs, there might be a chance to escape.

"Poor silly old Nosey. You are a mess. Look what you've done to your T-shirt. You've spilled orange soda pop all over it. Would you like me to take you to the bathroom?"

Linda plucked at the sticky shirt. No way was she going to invite his wrath by blaming the mucky shirt on him. And splashing water on it wouldn't help. But going to the washroom was a good idea. Maybe she could find a tool, a fingernail file. If she could smuggle it back to the bedroom, she would use it to scrape the paint from the sill. "Yes, I would."

"Use your word."

"My word?"

"Dear old Nosey, you think you can play silly games with me?" Richie tilted his head, an amused smile on his face. "I suggest you don't try it. Use your magic word."

"May I please use the washroom?" Linda asked meekly. Richie was taking great delight in belittling her. She hated giving him the satisfaction, but she had to play along. And in truth, it wasn't hard playing the helpless little old lady. At any moment, the psychopath could decide to kill her.

"If you mind your manners, things will go much better for you. And remember, behave yourself. You don't want me standing in there watching you, do you? I certainly don't want to. So don't make me," he warned.

Linda followed Richie down the hallway to the bathroom. It was a small room with an avocado-green pedestal sink and a matching toilet. The toilet sat between the sink and the old-fashioned tub with claw feet. She flushed the toilet and washed her hands. Linda looked into the square mirror of the medicine cabinet. The dark purple and green bruises appearing on her neck were a reminder of Richie's explosive violence. She opened the cabinet door and looked inside and saw bottles of prescription drugs, anti-acids, and a container holding a set of false teeth.

The bathroom door swung open, and Richie entered. He shook his head, and his lips tightened. "Be a good girl and close that cabinet door," he said in a low, ominous voice.

Linda's heart lurched, and she hurriedly complied. Whose teeth were those teeth, Faith's?

"What did you think you would find? A razor blade?"

She looked down at the floor, avoiding his eyes. She couldn't give any answer without bringing his unpredictable rage down on her.

"I'll let it go this time, but next time, if you don't behave yourself. I will have to come in to supervise. And neither one of us will enjoy that, will we?"

"No, of course not," Linda said meekly. He said next time. She hung on to the words *next time*.

"Promise me you'll be a good girl."

"I promise."

"Say it. Say I promise to be a good girl."

"I promise I will be a good girl." Linda choked on the words, *good girl*. She took a deep breath and looked timidly up at his handsome, smiling face. Clenching and unclenching her fists. If only she could punch him in the mouth and wipe that stupid smile off his face.

"There, that wasn't so bad now, was it?" Richie's mouth curved into a smile. His forehead creased, and he shook his head disapprovingly. "Oh, Nosey. You're still a mess. You haven't cleaned yourself up. I wonder if one of Aunt Faith's tops would fit you."

"No!" squeaked Linda. She would not wear the clothes of his aunt, the aunt he probably murdered. She'd just seen a set of false teeth. The hope that Faith was held prisoner somewhere faded.

"Suit yourself. If you insist on looking like a grubby old woman, I can do nothing about that. But." Richie's eyes lit up. "I can tidy you up." He took a comb from a small shelf above the sink, grabbed Linda by her shoulders, and spun her around. He placed a finger under Linda's chin, tipping her head. Grinning, he proceeded to comb her hair.

With every stroke of the comb, Linda flinched.

"There," Richie said, his blue eyes sparkling. He tilted her head one way, then another. "Hum." He brushed a stray lock from her forehead.

Linda swallowed and clamped her lips together. She was going to throw up.

Richie set the comb back on the shelf. "That's much better. I hope you washed your hands. Did you?" he asked, cocking one eyebrow.

Linda, controlling her revulsion, slowly breathed in and out. This was Richie's weakness. It wasn't enough that she was his captive. He needed to humiliate her as well. Richie believed he'd cowered her, and yes, he had. But she wasn't done yet. She'd bide her time. *Never give up. And never give in.* Keep up with the submissiveness he loved so much. He'd let his guard down, and when he did, she'd find a way to escape.

"Yes, I've washed my hands," Linda answered meekly.

Richie held open the bathroom door. "Now that you look almost presentable. You can come downstairs for supper. Uncle Alfred is a good cook."

Linda's heart rose. Why feed her if he planned on killing her? Maybe it was just some sick joke, an elaborate prank. Could she be wrong? And Faith was visiting her sister. No, she'd seen the false teeth. Faith would not go visiting without her teeth. Her hand flew to her throat, remembering his hands squeezing the life out of her. This was no prank. But the good thing was, they were going downstairs. She would try for the front door. It would be her best chance. The door led to the street. Even if Richie chased after her, people would see her running. He couldn't very well grab her and haul her off the street.

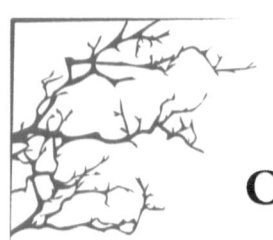

Chapter Thirteen

"**B**e careful going down the stairs," Richie said, a guiding hand under her elbow.

Linda's eyes widened. She cast him an anxious look. Only a few hours ago, Richie was choking her to death and threatening to throw her down the stairs. Now, he was worried she would fall down these steps. Her instinct was to jerk her arm from the unpredictable maniac's grasp. But it was to her advantage that he thought she was a frail old lady. So, Linda steeled herself and let him guide her down the staircase. She'd use his prejudice to her advantage. She would outwit him.

Keeping a firm grip on Linda's arm, Richie ushered her down the hallway into the kitchen. Alfred was wearing a blue and yellow floral apron and taking a pan of spareribs from the oven.

"Hey, Uncle Alfred, look who has come for supper."

Linda's heart sank, and the last tiny ray of hope fell away. Alfred was a part of whatever this was.

Richie's uncle caught her open-mouthed stare. Laughing, he lifted the hem of the apron. "Do you like my apron? It was Faith's favourite."

"Supper smells great," Richie said, prodding Linda to stand beside the table with the white linen lace-trimmed tablecloth that was too large for the small kitchen table. The table, set for two, had matching linen napkins beside each plate. Two bottles of beer were sitting next to empty crystal wine goblets. An ornate crystal swan and two tall, silver candlesticks sat in the middle of the table. Was this a celebration?

"Thanks. I've got oven-baked potatoes, too," Alfred said as he used long metal tongs to transfer the racks of spareribs from the pan to a long oval silver platter.

Linda's eyes darted from man to man. *Remain calm,* she told herself. *And remember your mantra.* Panic clutched her stomach. She felt nauseous. She couldn't remember it.

"I'm sorry our dinner guest's attire is so messy. She's a sloppy old gal." Richie ripped off a length of paper towel. He opened a cupboard door and took out a dinner plate and a blue plastic glass.

"What's the point of feeding her?" Alfred asked as Richie set the glass and the plate on the table.

Linda's heart lurched. Alfred didn't think it was worthwhile feeding her. The faint hope they wouldn't harm her disappeared. Her time was running out.

"Why not? It might be entertaining." Richie placed a fork on the folded paper towel beside the plate.

"Whatever, it's up to you. This one is your problem," Alfred said, putting the platter of spareribs on the table. The tongs slipped off the platter, and barbecue sauce pooled on the white linen tablecloth.

"My problem? I'm the one helping you, remember?"

The stooped man plodded back to the stove. He returned to the table carrying a decorated glass bowl with two foil-wrapped potatoes. "Just get the damn salad."

"Please."

His uncle rolled his eyes. "Okay, please get the damn salad."

Richie chuckled, went to the fridge, and brought a bowl of spinach salad to the table.

"Since you're here, lady, you might as well sit down," Alfred said, pulling out a chair at the head of the small table.

Richie put his hand on Linda's shoulder, drawing her closer to him. "I told you we had a guest. Didn't I tell you who she was?"

Alfred sat down at the table. "You might have; it wasn't important; the important thing was to keep her locked up until we're ready."

Linda trembled; she clenched her fist, her nails biting into the palms of her hands. *Until they were ready?*

"Her name was Miss Burton. Linda Burton. You met her when you sold the wardrobe and bed."

Alfred looked at Linda and scratched his chin. "Yeah, I sold the damn stuff to Mary Woodhouse. I got a damn good price, too."

Giggling, Richie said, "I have a new name for her."

Richie's maniacal high-pitched giggle made Linda's legs weak. She clutched the back of the chair.

"A what?" Alfred, raising his eyebrows, unwrapped his baked potato.

"I've given her a new name."

Alfred picked up the tongs from the table, looked at the stain on the tablecloth, and grinned.

"Her new name is Nosey Nana." Richie snickered. "You like your new name, don't you, Nosey?" His hand tightened on Linda's sore arm.

Pain ripped down her arm. Linda winced and nodded. Richie smiled approvingly and relaxed his hold.

"Nosey Nana?" Richie's uncle took a steak knife and began cutting the ribs on his plate. "Whatever," he said in a disdainful tone.

"You think she's miss-named. Well, my dear uncle. Just a few minutes ago, I caught her snooping in the medicine cabinet."

"Why was she wandering around? I thought you had her safely locked up." Alfred popped the lid off his beer and poured it into the wine goblet.

"Damn it. I didn't let her wander around. What I'm telling you is we have to be more careful. She looked in the medicine cabinet."

Alfred, chewing on a rib, shrugged. "Who cares?" he asked, barbecue sauce dripping down his chin.

"She saw Aunt Faith's false teeth." Richie looked accusingly at Linda. "Didn't you?"

Linda nodded. There was no point in lying.

"See, I told you."

"So?" His uncle ran the back of his hand across his chin, then licked the sauce off his hand.

"What if someone else found them? I could be showing someone this house. What if a buyer found the teeth? What would I have said? You told me you took care of all her stuff. You didn't even take her clothes out of the closet. You have to think of things like that."

"You take care of it. That's why I have you. Now sit down and have some supper before it gets cold."

Linda's eyes had a hopeful gleam as she watched the exchange. These two men were in cahoots. But there was conflict. Could she use that? And who was the boss? But did it matter? She was at their mercy. Remembering her mantra, she squared her shoulders.

Richie's fingers bit into Linda's arm. She gasped. It was the same arm Richie had twisted.

"Sit," he said, his lips drew back into a snarl.

Uttering a small moan, Linda sank onto the chair next to him.

"Yeah, no problem. I'll take care of everything," Richie said, his jaw tightening as he eyed his uncle. He looked down at his plate. When Richie lifted his head, his face had transformed into his crooked smile. "Everything smells great. I can't wait to dig into the ribs. And my favourite, your specialty, homemade bread," Richie praised, helping himself to a slice.

Linda squeezed her eyes shut and bit her bottom lip. What a fool she'd been. The homemade bread she'd seen the first day of the yard sale made her think Faith was alive. But Faith didn't bake it. Where was Faith? The words she heard in the back alley echoed in her mind. *Where am I supposed to hide the body?*

Richie picked up the paper towel from Linda's plate and shook out its folds with a flourish. "It would be a shame to get barbecue sauce on your T-shirt. It wouldn't go well with that orange glob you already have." He laughed as he tucked the paper towel into the collar of Linda's shirt.

Linda flinched. "May I have some water, please?" she asked.

"Of course." Richie poured a glass of water, setting it beside her plate.

Linda grasped the glass, gulping. Richie, snatching it from her hands, spilled water down her shirt. "You didn't say thank you. Magic words, Nosey Nana, magic words."

Linda balled her hands into fists. She looked meekly up at Richie and said, "Thank you."

"Good girl." Chuckling, Richie returned the glass to Linda. "I'm trying to teach this one some manners," he told his uncle.

Linda took the glass, gulping water.

Alfred laughed. Holding a sparerib in one hand, he shook it at his nephew. Barbecue sauce splattered onto the white linen tablecloth. "Good luck trying. She's an old gal. You can't teach an old dog new tricks."

Linda's face flushed. It seemed she looked a lot older than she was. Even the monster's uncle thought she was an oldster. But it didn't matter. It was all another game of Richie's. He enjoyed toying with her, and his uncle was enjoying it too.

Using the tongs, Richie set a rack of ribs on his plate. "The sauce on these delicious ribs is from Uncle Alfred's secret recipe," Richie told Linda. "And they smell great, Uncle Alfred," he said, unrolling a baked potato. Richie folded the tinfoil into a tiny square, set the foil beside his plate, and lavished the potato with butter and sour cream. He looked at Linda as he took a bite of the spareribs. "Delicious," he said, grinning, his mouthful.

Plucking at her dirty T-shirt, Linda looked down at her plate. Her tummy rumbled. She hadn't had anything since breakfast, which seemed like an eon ago. "May I have some?" she asked timidly.

"Are you hungry?" Smiling, Richie arched an eyebrow.

"Yes," Linda replied meekly, eyeing the fork beside her plate. She so wanted to jam it into his smiling face.

"Just sit there like a good girl. You'll get fed if there are any leftovers," he said, spooning salad onto his plate.

Linda drained her glass of water and cautiously poured herself another. Her thoughts churned. What was going to happen after supper? Would they keep her locked up in the house? Panic soared. Why would they? Faith was dead, and she knew it. They couldn't afford to let her go.

The men, chowing down on the food, talked about how the sale went and how much money they'd made.

"To a successful sale," Alfred raised his wineglass, and Richie lifted his. They clinked glasses, downing their beer.

Finally, dabbing his lips, Richie balled his napkin onto his plate. His blue eyes twinkled with amusement. He looked at Linda, and his mouth twitched. "Are you still hungry, Nosey?"

"Yes, I am. The ribs look wonderful," replied Linda. "May I have some?"

"Yes, you may if you use your magic word."

"Please, may I have some?" Her fingers dug into the palms of her hands.

Alfred leaned back in his chair. He stuck a finger into his mouth and picked his front teeth with his fingernail. "I guess you can teach an old dog new tricks."

"Yep," Richie said, picking up a rack of ribs with his fingers. He broke off a section of the spareribs and placed a rib on her plate. "No potato, but there is some salad left. Do you want some?" he asked.

Despite him handling her food, she knew she had to eat. "Yes, please." Her appetite was long gone. But an army moved on its stomach. She'd need her strength.

Richie dipped into the salad bowl and dumped spinach on her plate with his bare hands. Linda's stomach lurched.

Richie took his napkin and wiped his fingers. He looked at her and smiled a sly smile. "You will eat all of what's on your plate," he ordered.

"We must always eat everything on our plates." Richie's taunting tone turned bitter. "My dad always insisted on that, no matter how much there was."

Alfred examined the piece of meat he'd plucked from his teeth, flicked it onto the tablecloth, and laughed. "Your dad was right, boy, waste not, want not."

Richie's eyes narrowed; his jaw clenched. "Yeah, it's a wonder I'm not the size of an elephant." Then, with a crooked smile, Richie joined in his laughter.

Linda detected the scorn in Richie's laugh. There was an animosity toward his father that his uncle did not share. And perhaps the contempt was also directed at his uncle.

Richie had only given her one spare rib, but she had no appetite, so one rib was fine. The rib tasted great, but everything was hard to swallow. Richie had handled all her food. Heeding his warning about cleaning her plate, she shovelled the salad down, thankful she had water to drink.

As Linda struggled to eat the supper, she listened to the men as they continued to talk about the sale. It was like this was a normal day for them. One of them had killed Faith and captured her. And although they didn't say so, she knew she was next. Finished eating, Linda took the paper towel from her neck and laid it on her empty plate.

Richie lifted the towel and looked at her plate. "Good girl, you ate your supper. But you're a very messy eater," he said, picking up the discarded towel, he wiped Linda's cheek. Linda flinched, and he laughed.

His uncle threw back his head and laughed, too. He had barbeque sauce on his chin and down the front of his apron. "I think it's only right you wash the dishes, earn your keep," he said.

"Uncle Alfred's right. Wash the dishes, and don't get any silly ideas. I know how many knives and forks there are. So be a good girl, and don't try anything foolish."

Linda rose and began taking the dishes to the sink. She turned on the hot water, her eyes scanning the room. Okay, she couldn't steal any cutlery. But maybe there was something else.

She still had no idea when she finished drying the dishes. Disheartened, she hung up the tea towel. Hands clasped tightly in front of her, Linda glanced at the door. Could she dart past the maniacs?

Richie grinned at his uncle. "I bet you'd like some ice cream, Uncle Alfred."

His uncle laughed. "That sounds like a grand idea."

"Be a good girl, Nosey Nana, and get the ice cream out of the deep freeze."

Linda wanted to say 'Use your magic word'. But she closed her mouth, went to the deep freezer beside the fridge, opened the lid, and screamed. Inside the freezer, encased in clear plastic wrap. A woman's body.

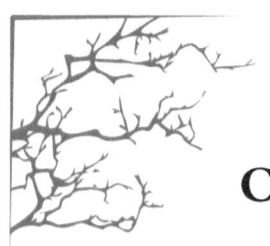

Chapter Fourteen

L inda screamed, clamped a hand over her mouth and sank to the floor. Alfred, guffawing, slapped his knee.

Richie crossed the kitchen and looked in the freezer. "Well, would you look at that?" He hooted with laughter. "Mystery solved. You told me you were a great detective. And you are. You found Aunt Faith."

Linda crouched on the floor, shaking, her hand still over her open mouth, her breath coming in big gulps.

"Yep, you're a lucky woman, Nosey. Do you want to know why?" Richie cocked his head.

Linda stared wide-eyed up at him, speechless.

Richie chuckled. "You don't know why?"

Linda hunched her shoulders, skittering away from him.

"I thought you would have guessed by now," he taunted. "Well, dear Nosey, you're lucky because the freezer is full. There is no room for you."

Alfred roared with laughter.

Linda jumped up, her legs shaking. She backed up against the cupboards. Her body was cold and clammy, and her gut twisted. These monsters had killed Faith and were revelling in it. She should've been prepared. The realization that poor Faith was dead had come to her after she saw the false teeth. But to see Faith wrapped in a plastic bag and stuffed into the freezer made her physically ill. Linda spun around, vomiting into the sink. She was trapped in this house with two homicidal maniacs.

Still hooting with laughter, Alfred wiped the tears from his eyes with his linen napkin and blew his nose.

"I'd better close this lid. We don't want dear Aunt Faith to thaw out now. Do we?" Giggling, Richie closed the freezer lid.

Linda turned on the cold water tap and stuck her head under it, taking big gulps. Wiping her chin with the back of her hand, she took a deep breath and turned to face the men. Her voice trembling, she asked, "Why?"

"Why did we put Aunt Faith in the deep freeze? It's because hiding a body is hard. Someone wouldn't let me plant her in the damn garden," Richie said, scowling at his uncle. "And old Aunt Faith wouldn't last long in this heat."

Alfred nodded and said, "Damn it all to hell, Richie. We had a garage sale. We couldn't let the old bat stink up the place."

"Why on earth did you kill Faith? What possible reason would you have to kill that poor woman?"

"Faith was a nasty old nag. I should have done away with her years ago," roared Alfred. "She was mean, stingy, and mean. We had money. The money she inherited from her great-aunt. But could we spend any of it? Oh no, we mustn't do that. She treated me like a dogsbody. I wasn't good enough for her. Did we ever use the silver she kept on display in that china cabinet? No. But I was good enough to polish this damn stuff." Alfred picked up the silver candlesticks and hurled one after the other.

Linda and Richie ducked as the candlesticks sailed overhead, landing with small clunks on the floor. Baring his teeth, Alfred grabbed the crystal swan off the table and threw the big glass ornament. The swan crashed to the floor and shattered. Glass shards flew. One piece hit Linda in the cheek.

Linda gasped and put her hand to her cheek. She was bleeding.

Richie, chuckling, leaned against the deep freeze. With a lopsided grin, he asked, "Tell us how you really feel, uncle."

Alfred's nostrils flared. He stood and tore the tablecloth off the table, ripping and tearing the linen cloth into shreds. "There," he shouted. "I've wanted to do that for ages. My only regret is that I didn't do it in front of her scraggy face." Breathing heavily, he sat back in his chair.

"I wanted to travel, and she didn't. That was the last straw. I couldn't spend the rest of my days with that useless old hag. Nag, nag, I could never do anything right. The best day of my life was when we offed the old bitch."

Linda ripped off a piece of paper towel and pressed it to her cheek. Her eyes flickered from uncle to nephew. "You said we. Who killed Faith?"

"That miserable old bat took her sweet time dying. That old bitch never made anything easy for me. She even had to drag out dying. She just wouldn't bloody well die. The stupid old cow."

Linda paled, swallowing hard, her eyes wide in disgust.

"Ricin takes time to work," Richie said, "And I don't think you gave her enough of it."

Alfred shrugged. "Could be. It was my first attempt. The cat doesn't count."

Linda, aghast, asked, "You ground up the caster beans from that plant by the front entrance and fed them to your wife?"

"Yep. But I can't take all the credit. It was Richie's idea. He knows stuff. He's university educated."

"Don't sell yourself short, Uncle Alfred. You did it. I just gave the instructions."

"Thanks, but the old witch wouldn't die. She was taking too long. So, in the end, we decided to put the old cow out of her misery. Richie had to lend a hand," Alfred said, howling with laughter. "He choked her. That finally put an end to the old bitch."

"Strong hands," Richie said, joining Alfred's maniacal laughter.

Linda shivered and put her hand to her throat.

"I'd have done it myself, but I'm not as strong as I used to be. My only regret is I should've killed the old bitch years ago." He shrugged.

Linda inhaled a ragged breath. Had they tried to poison her? Maybe it was a good thing she threw up.

A malicious grin grew on Richie's face as he looked at Linda, holding the paper towel to her cheek. "If dear Aunt Faith hadn't been so stingy and bought a bigger freezer. You would be joining her." Snickering, he kicked a shard of glass toward her. "Make yourself useful, and pick up this glass," he ordered.

Taking the towel from her cheek. Linda looked at it. The cut stung, and it was oozing blood. But at least blood wasn't pouring down her face. The cut must be small. She hoped it wasn't deep.

"Hey, are you deaf? Pick up the glass. I won't ask twice."

Shaking, Linda stuck a new piece of paper towel over the cut, hoping to stem the flow. She knelt and began picking up the crystal swan's shattered pieces. One wing had slid to the base of the cupboard. The neck and body lay amid the glass fragments in the middle of the floor. "I need a broom. There are too many small pieces."

As Richie opened a closet door, Linda scooped up the broken wing and stuck it in her pocket. Richie took a broom and dustpan from the closet and handed them to her.

"Better check her pocket," Alfred said with a grim smile.

"Oh, Nosey, you haven't done something bad, have you?" Richie asked in a sing-song voice.

Linda's body went cold with dread. She took the swan's wing from her pocket.

"Naughty, naughty Nosey. And very stupid. You're not very smart, are you?" With a mocking smile, Richie grabbed the broom from Linda's hands and swung the broom handle. Linda, her hands protecting her head, crouched beside the kitchen cupboards.

"Oh, just give her the damn broom. She knows she can't get away with anything. We have more important things to worry about. She's nothing but an extra body to deal with. Now that the garage sale is over. I want to get on the road. It's time we deal with Faith and this one."

The colour drained from Linda's face. Alfred had saved her from Richie's volatile temper, but her time was running out.

Richie handed Linda the broom.

Grasping the broom, Linda began sweeping.

Standing by the fridge, Richie folded his arms across his chest, watching her sweep the shards into a pile. "I know, but the problem is what to do with the bodies. You won't let me put them in the garden."

"The garden is out. Don't even think about it. Whoever buys this place will probably want to plant a garden."

"Yeah, okay, I won't bury them there."

Linda's eyes darted to the hallway. Could she reach the hallway before them? Maybe if she swept in the direction of the kitchen doorway. She could dash out the front door.

Alfred stood and wiped his chin with a remnant of the tablecloth. "There is no use talking about what we can't do. Come up with a plan, boy. That's why I have you."

"No worries." Richie's eyes narrowed. "I'll figure something out." His lips twisted into a crooked smile as he looked over at Linda, sweeping her way toward the hallway. "This is all your fault. You could have just minded your own business. But no, you didn't; you got nosey. Bragging to me about your great detective skills. Well, look where those great detective skills have gotten you. All you accomplished was to make more work for us." Richie sneered.

Chortling, Alfred stepped in front of the doorway. "Little old ladies like you should stick to your knitting."

Linda made a U-turn, sweeping her way back to the cupboards. Fear clawed at her throat as she swept the broken glass into the dustpan and dumped the pan into the garbage bin. She laid the broom against the broom closet and licked her dry lips. "I can't just disappear. People will miss me," she said in a shaky voice.

Alfred looked at Richie, a scowl on his face. "She's right. What's your plan?"

"No one will miss old Nosey. She's house-sitting for Mabel Havelock. She is alone and doesn't even live here. No one will start worrying about her." Richie laughed.

Linda's breath caught in her throat. "That's not true. I have my friends."

"Really," scoffed Richie. "In Regina, maybe. And your friends there know you have gone to house-sit. And no one here will care that you're gone. And when and if they do, we will have covered our tracks by the time they figure it out."

"You said she was house-sitting for Mabel Havelock. She might ask about her," Alfred chimed in.

"This Mabel is in Calgary. She broke her foot. Nosey told me she wouldn't be home. Not for a long time." Richie curled his lip. "That was very helpful of you, Nosey."

Linda's lips and chin trembled. She'd trusted a maniac.

"You'll make her disappear." Alfred's eyes flickered with excitement.

"Yep, dear little Nosey here is going on a trip. How does that line go?" His eyes twinkled. "Gone without a trace."

Linda's face, ashen, clasped her clammy hands. "No, Mabel would know I wouldn't go away and leave Gertrude."

"Who the hell is Gertrude?" asked Alfred.

"A cat. No worries. I'll take care of that damn cat."

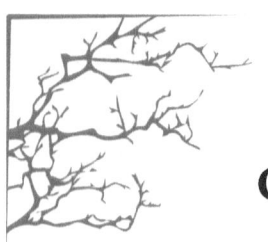

Chapter Fifteen

With a firm grip on Linda's arm, Richie propelled her up the stairs. Terror mounted with every step. What now? Was he leading her to her death? Relief coursed through Linda's body as he opened the door to the master bedroom. Richie was just going to lock her up. He wouldn't take her back to the bedroom to kill her. Would he?

"Make yourself comfortable. Oh, and thanks for reminding me about that cat. Now I have a little errand to run," he said, shoving Linda into the room.

Linda looked pleadingly at Richie as he grinned down at her. "You're...you're not going to hurt Gertrude, are you?" she asked.

"What makes you think I would hurt a defenceless kitty?" Richie laughed. "But if I do, it will be your fault."

Linda sucked in her breath. She desperately wanted to believe Richie wouldn't hurt Gertrude.

He switched on the lights. The frosted globe chandelier flickered momentarily, dimly shining down. Taking Linda by the elbow, he escorted her to the big old four-poster bed, patting it. "There you go, all nice and cozy." Richie gave her a crooked smile. "Tonight, you can have a nice, comfy bed. Aunt Faith loved this bed." His blue eyes sparkled with amusement. "This is the bed she died in."

Linda blanched, turning away. She couldn't bear seeing the look of glee in his eyes.

"I hope you're not squeamish." Pressing on Linda's shoulders until she sat on the bed, he leered into her face. "Enjoy your night's sleep. It could be your last. We'll have to do something with you soon. But first things first. My little errand."

"Please leave Gertrude alone."

"Oh, the poor little kitty will be waiting for you. Probably hungry and thirsty. But don't worry. I'll fix that. We can't let a pet suffer now, can we?"

"Please, please, don't hurt Gertrude. You have nothing to gain by hurting an innocent animal."

Richie chuckled and brushed a stray strand of blond hair off his forehead. "Nothing to be gained? What was it you said? Oh yes, Mabel would not believe you'd leave the cat. So, the cat has to disappear, too. Perhaps you're a cat napper."

"Please," she begged.

Richie put his hand on the doorknob. He turned toward her, giving her a sardonic smile. "Nighty-night. I'm off to take care of a cat."

"Please, don't." The door shut on Linda's plea. Her heart filled with dread. Her shoulders sagged. She crept to the window. The yard was dark, but she could make out the shape of the big motorhome parked by the greenhouse. Linda pressed her forehead against the windowpane. A light suddenly shone from the house, and she could see Richie stride across the yard to the back gate. Her eyes welled up. He was on his way to kill Gertrude.

Tears streamed down Linda's cheeks. "I'm so sorry, Mabel," she moaned aloud. She couldn't save Gertrude. And it was all her fault. If only she hadn't mentioned Gertrude. But maybe Gertrude would hide. The cat didn't like Richie; she had hissed at him.

Was that only this morning? It seemed like a lifetime ago. Now, she was trapped in a madhouse with two psychopaths. They had murdered poor Faith and stuffed her in a freezer. And she was next. Linda grabbed a pillow from the floor and heaved it in the window. The pillow bounced harmlessly off, flying to land beside the bed.

Linda sank onto the floor, buried her head in the pillow, and screamed. She rolled over onto her back and looked up at the ceiling. Screaming into a pillow would solve nothing. Finally, she sat up and kicked the silky pillow. The pillow slid halfway under the bed. She heard a scraping sound.

Lying down on her belly, Linda dragged the pillow out from under the bed. A wire coat hanger had caught the pillow; it was the hanger that had flown under the bed when she had thrown Faith's dress on the floor.

Sitting amidst the pillows, Linda turned the coat hanger in her hands and looked at the windowsill. While the monsters were asleep, she would have time to get that window open. But she knew there was nothing outside to crawl onto. It was a long drop to the ground. But what if she could unwind the hook of the hanger? Maybe it would be sharp enough to stab Richie. She would have to be quick and stab him fatally. The jugular vein in his neck would be best. But he was a man. And she was a small, skinny woman. It was doubtful that would go well. But should she try? It would be better than waiting to die. But to kill someone? Linda bit her lip. Did she have it in her to kill? Probably not.

Running her fingers over the wire hanger, she eyed the big oak door. She jumped up and sped to the door. The hinges. If she broke the hanger, could she push the wire up and pop the hinges off? But would the door fall backward? If it did, it would undoubtedly crush her. No, that wouldn't work. Linda sat on the bed, twiddling the hanger in her hand. Linda's eyes brightened. The door was old, and the key was an old brass key; maybe she could pick the lock if she could break the wire hanger. She'd seen movies where they picked locks. It was an old lock. How hard could it be?

Linda twisted the hanger. The hanger bent but didn't break. She blew out a frustrated breath. Now what? She needed to break it. Twirling the bent hanger in her hands, Linda looked around the room for a clue. There had to be a way to snap the hanger. She grinned, got on her knees, and pulled up the bedspread skirt to reveal the underside of the bed. The four-poster bed made of walnut would be heavy. Could she lift it? Linda nibbled her bottom lip, then nodded. Where there was a will, there was a way. She positioned the coat hanger with her foot. Grasped the corner of the bed and lifted. Her muscles strained, but the bed remained firmly on the floor.

She stood shaking her arms, breathing rapidly in and out. She should join a gym. *And if I get out of here alive, I will,* she vowed. Lift with your legs, not with your arms. Where had she heard that phrase? Taking a deep breath, she gripped the corner of the bed and lifted. The bed rose a tiny bit. Straining, she kept the leg off the floor and kicked the clothes hanger under it. The hanger slid under and encircled the bed leg. With a determined look on her face, Linda again lifted the corner of the bed. With the toe of her shoe, she pulled the hanger back under the leg and let the bed drop. The bed fell on the wire hanger with a thud.

Linda froze. Her eyes went to the door. If Alfred heard the bang, she was done for. She had to be quick. She grabbed the clothes hanger and pried it upward. To her delight, the hanger snapped. She picked up the long, broken end of the wire and kicked the other half of the hanger under the bed. Admiring her handy work, she heard the key in the door turn. Heart pounding, she dropped the broken bit and shoved it under the bed with the rest of the hanger. Her shaking hands clasped in front of her, she waited.

Richie entered. His teeth bared. He stood in the doorway and held up a hand. His arm was scratched and bleeding. His lips curled, and he sneered, "That evil bitch of a cat put up a fight. But you can guess who won. Sleep tight, sweet dreams," he said and slammed the door.

"You evil monster," Linda screamed. She collapsed onto the bed and covered her face with her hands. The small piece of paper towel she'd stuck on the cut on her face came off in her hand. She balled it up and threw it to the floor. Poor Gertrude, it was her fault. She should've never set foot in this yard, let alone the house. Trying to emulate Aunt Violet and Mabel had cost Mabel her cat. Why hadn't she realized Richie for what he was? She thought she was so clever, but she wasn't. She'd fallen for his boyish charm. Linda picked up a pillow. Muffling her sobs, she rocked back and forth. Drained, she lay back on the bed, looking dry-eyed at the rose and gold canopy. Linda shook her fist at the door. "*Never give up. And never give in.* I'll get out of here. And I will get revenge for Faith and Gertrude."

She set her lips in a hard line. Gertrude had put up a fight. The scratches on Richie's arm looked deep. Did he lock the door when he stormed out? Maybe in his anger, he forgot. Linda ran to the door and gripped the doorknob. "Damn it," she swore. He'd locked the door.

She sped back to the bed and laid on her tummy, feeling under the bedspread skirt for the broken coat hanger. She pulled it out, looked at the long piece of wire, and then at the old oak door and grinned. "Time to unlock this damn door." As soon as she was free, she'd alert the police, and they'd find poor Faith in the freezer. She hoped the judge would lock them up and throw away the key. "Mess with Linda to your peril," she muttered.

Kneeling, Linda eyed the keyhole. The wire would have to be bent. She put one foot on the end of the wire and stood, twisting. The wire turned in her hands. Linda grabbed a pillow and shook off the pillowcase. Wrapped the pillowcase around one end of the wire, twisting. Once again, the wire turned.

Exhaling a big breath, Linda stared at the long piece of wire. What now? She paced back and forth around the room, slapping the wire against her thigh. She stopped walking and leaned on the armoire.

Linda's eyes lit up. She tapped on the wardrobe, grinning. They'd made the armoire from the same heavy walnut as the bed. Linda opened the closet door and stuck one end of the broken hanger between the door and the sash. She closed the door, took hold of the other end of the wire, and pried. The hanger broke but did not bend.

A piece of wood from the door chipped off. "Sorry, Mary," Linda said, running her hand over the splintered wood. She looked at the broken wire. There was no point trying to use it to pick the lock. It was too straight. The wire needed to have a curve to fit in the keyhole.

Linda flopped down on the floor by the door. She ran her hand over the small wound on her cheek and then looked at her fingertips. There was hardly any blood. But the cut was the least of her worries. *How do you bend the wire into a hook?* Her eyes widened, and a small smile appeared on her face. The coat hanger under the bed already had a hook. She lay down on her tummy and looked under the bed. The hanger with the crooked part was under the middle of the bed. But the bed was too low for her to crawl under it. She slid her leg under, swishing it back and forth. Nothing. Not even her toe touched the crooked leftover hanger.

Frustrated, she sat back and leaned on a pillow. Her arm slipped off. Yes, the pillows. Linda grabbed a pillow. Laid flat on her tummy and flung the pillow at the broken hanger. The hanger moved. She jumped up and ran to the other side of the bed. Laid back down on her belly and reached, stretching. Her fingertips touched the hanger. She stuck her head sideways under the bed, stretching out her arm. Her fingers clawed, pulling the hanger with the crook from under the bed.

Brushing the dust off her face, she raced to the door and stuck the wire into the keyhole. It didn't fit. Linda raised her eyes to the ceiling, suppressing a scream of frustration. She sat with her back against the door. *Now what?* She took the piece of wire hanger in her hands, turning it over and over. She turned her head, looking longingly at the door hinge. Even if she got the bolt out, and the damn door didn't crush her. The crash of the door would wake the monsters. No, the hinge was out.

But she had to do something. She couldn't just sit on the floor and await whatever fate that lunatic had in store for her. Linda got back on her knees, stuck the hooked part under the door and gently pried up.

She felt the coat hanger bend. She pulled it out from under the door. "Yes," Linda whispered. "This just might work." The hook in the hanger was not as pronounced. She slid the hook into the keyhole and turned. Linda's heart leapt as she felt something catch. She wiggled and jiggled the wire hook one way, then the other, until she heard a click. Holding her breath, Linda tried the doorknob. It turned, and the bedroom door opened.

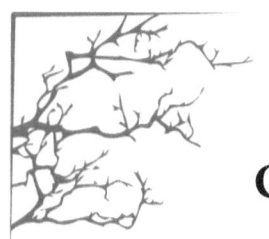

Chapter Sixteen

Linda inched the door wider, peering into the dimly lit hallway. All was quiet. The hallway was empty. She looked at her watch. It was after eleven. Were the men asleep? Her heart pounding, Linda ducked back into the room. She wouldn't take a chance. She'd wait. Closing the door, Linda crept back to the bed.

She rubbed her eyes with the heel of her hands. She was tired, but she needed to stay awake. She could sleep when she was free. And it didn't feel right to sleep on the bed where Faith died. If she got free, should she tell Mary it was Faith's deathbed? *No, not if. When she was free.*

Linda began to pace, the floorboards creaking with every step. She paused. Why hadn't she noticed the creaking before? Sitting on the bed, Linda took off her runners. She had to be stealthy. Linda tiptoed back to the door and listened. Not a sound. Linda didn't want to wait. She wanted out of her prison now.

Cautiously, Linda tiptoed into the hallway, gently closing the door behind her. Sock-footed, she descended the stairs, one step at a time, listening for the slightest creak. At the bottom of the stairs, she froze. There was a light on in the kitchen. Her heart beat wildly in her chest. Should she go back upstairs and wait? The light in the kitchen meant someone was awake. But she was so close to freedom.

Linda cocked her head, listening, then edged to the kitchen doorway. Spread out on the kitchen table were sheets of paper. Line after line of cursive writing filled the page. Holding her breath, Linda inched past the kitchen doorway toward the back door. She paused, turned, snuck back into the kitchen, tiptoed to the table, and looked down at the writing. Page after page was filled with Alfred Hutchins' name. The hair on the back of her neck rose. She shrieked as a hand grabbed her shoulder, spinning her around.

"You are a clever little bird, aren't you?" Richie whispered in Linda's ear as he twisted her arm around her back. "But they do say curiosity kills the cat."

Linda opened her mouth to scream.

"If you make a commotion, I will kill you," Richie hissed, clamping his hand over her mouth. "Do you want to die? It's up to you."

Linda gasped. Her legs felt weak. Trembling, she whimpered and shook her head.

"Are you sure you don't want to die now and get it over with?" Richie tightened his hold, twisting her arm behind her back.

"No," moaned Linda.

Still holding Linda's arm behind her back, Richie frogmarched her to the cupboards. He picked the damp dishcloth from the sink and shoved it into her mouth. Linda gagged. Shoving her up against the kitchen cabinets. He ripped a tea towel off the rack, covering her mouth, and tied it behind her head.

Linda groaned as a sharp corner bit into her back.

"You should have gone out the door when you had the chance. I might have caught you. But then again, I might not have. Now, we'll never know, will we?" He leaned against the fridge and crossed his arms. A lock of blond hair fell on his forehead. Richie brushed it back and shook his head. "But no, you had to look, didn't you? Just like you had to poke your nose into Aunt Faith's disappearance. You really are your own worst enemy."

Linda, having trouble breathing, grasped the tea towel and yanked. The wet dishcloth was disgusting.

"Now, now, Nosey. You know you mustn't do that," Richie said softly. "This dishcloth is keeping you alive." Taking her small hand, he squeezed her fingers together.

Linda flinched. Tears streamed down her cheeks, and her nose began to run.

"Look at you. What a mess." He daintily took the end of the tea towel and attempted to wipe Linda's nose.

Linda turned her head, edging away.

"Well, have it your way. If you want snot running down your face." Giving her a look of disgust, Richie picked up the notepad and the sheets of paper off the table. "As you can see, I have been practicing Uncle Alfred's signature. Any idea why?"

Blinking tears away, Linda wiped her nose with the end of the tea towel and shook her head.

"No? What happened to those famous detective skills you told me about?" he taunted. "Well, dear Nosey, my dear Aunt Faith was worth a good chunk of change. Of course, good old Uncle Alfred is her beneficiary. And the housing market, even in this hick town, is pretty good. So, all I have to do is make out the deed to the house to me and make myself his heir." Richie's eyes burned with anger. "You'd think after all I've done for the old bastard, he'd at least give me some of her money or the deed to the house. He's a selfish old bugger. But he's not as smart as he thinks he is." Richie flashed her a triumphant smile and giggled. "Because, as luck would have it. My dear Uncle Alfred will be met by a tragic accident on his long-awaited road trip. And when they find Aunt Faith's body. And I'm sure they will. They'll blame Uncle Alfred. And rightly so. He ground up the ricin and fed it to the old girl. But by the time they find those old coots, they will both be dead, and I'll be the grieving nephew. What do you think? A good plan?"

The gag in Linda's mouth disguised her disgust at Richie's bragging. His uncle poisoned Faith, but when she took too long to die. Richie choked her to death. And the ruthless psychopath planned to kill again. She and his uncle were the next victims.

Richie, looking at the deep freezer, chuckled. "I guess I'd better get a move on it with my plan before old Aunt Faith gets freezer burn."

He opened the cupboard door above the fridge and wrinkled his nose. "What a bunch of old junk. She never threw anything out. Look at this crap." He took out a handful of half-melted yellowed candles with burnt wicks. And three small white saucers with faded blue trim. A candy dish decorated with reindeer and a small bag of clothespins. Richie stashed the notepad, papers, and pen on the shelf and shut the door. He strode to the kitchen counter. Cringing, Linda sidled toward the kitchen table. He opened the cupboard door under the sink and threw the candles, dishes, and clothespins into the garbage can.

Linda inched farther away from him; her eyes flickered to the door.

Richie's smile broadened. His blue eyes twinkled as he tipped his head toward the door. "Want to give it a try?"

Linda's heart sank. There was no way she could outrun him.

"So now you know. Does this satisfy your curiosity? Was it worth it, dear Nosey? You have to admit, you do bring on these misfortunes yourself." Richie smiled his crooked smile.

Linda's stomach churned with fear and remorse. He was right. Why had she gone back to look at those stupid papers? She could be free.

Richie sighed and shook his head. "You just had to make things complicated for me. What the hell am I going to do with your body?"

Panicked, Linda dashed for the kitchen door.

With two long strides, Richie was at the door, blocking her escape. He grinned his crooked grin and said, "Don't you like our hospitality?"

Linda looked up at Richie's handsome, smiling face, the face she'd trusted. What a fool she'd been. Richie could turn his charm on and off like a light switch.

"We even gave you supper. And my sweet, old Uncle Alfred is kind enough to give up the master bedroom so you could spend your last night in comfort." Richie giggled. "To be honest, that poor old bird hasn't used that bed in years. Aunt Faith locked Uncle Alfred out of that room years ago." Eyeing Linda, Richie's dazzling smile disappeared. "How did you get out of there? Oh, never mind, I'll find out." Richie's eyes became cold and cunning. "But because you escaped from the bedroom, you and I are going up to the attic." He grabbed her by the arm and pushed her toward the stairs. He leaned down and whispered in her ear. "Don't make a sound when we go up those stairs. Uncle Alfred is sleeping."

Linda tripped, stumbling.

Richie righted her. "Careful now, and remember what I just said," he hissed. "There's a good way to die and a not-so-good way. As in die now or die later. You want later, don't you, Nosey? Who knows, maybe you'll find a way to escape. And if you do, my advice is to curb your curiosity." He giggled.

Linda, filled with fear, bobbed her head up and down.

With a hand firmly clamped on Linda's sore arm, Richie strong-armed her up the stairs, past the master bedroom, and down the hallway. The bedroom doors were closed. At the end of the hallway, he reached up and yanked a rope, pulling down a folding wooden ladder. "I'm going to open the attic door. But please, dear Nosey, don't get any ideas. If you make a run for it, we know who will win that race, don't we?"

Run? With the cloth stuffed in her mouth, she could barely breathe, let alone run down the stairs. But maybe she could sneak out of the attic after he left.

Richie smirked, climbed the six wooden steps, drew back a bolt lock, and opened the attic door. He returned down the steps and waved his hand. "After you, dear Nosey."

Linda climbed the steps, ducking through the door into a dark, musty cavern. Richie was a step behind her. She crawled on hands and knees across the dirty, gritty floor.

Richie followed and stood. "There is a lightbulb somewhere up here. It has a string on it if you can find it." He chuckled. "Sorry, there are no windows for you to leap from. And this door, as you can see, has a slide bolt on the outside. I don't think even you can pick that. Was that how you escaped from the bedroom? I do have to give you credit. You're a crafty little bird." He chuckled again. "You may take your gag off when I leave. But don't waste your time hollering. No one will hear you except for Uncle Alfred and me." Richie closed the door, slamming the bolt in place.

Tears poured down Linda's cheeks. Her prison was now this dark, dusty, mildewy attic.

Chapter Seventeen

As soon as the door shut, Linda ripped off her gag and spat. She wiped the tears off her cheeks with the back of her hand and took a deep breath. And immediately began coughing and sneezing. "I'm inhaling dust. And God knows what else," she croaked. Linda stayed motionless in the darkness, waiting for her heart to resume a regular beat. "Alright, Linda Burton," she said, giving herself a pep talk. "Time to stop being afraid. Time to get the hell out of here. First, where the heck is that darn string? The Monster said there was a light."

The attic was pitch black. Raising an arm in the air, Linda waved her hand. A sticky substance wrapped around her hand. "Yuck, spiderwebs," she moaned, wiping her hand on her jeans. "This place is probably crawling with spiders." But spiders were the least of Linda's worries. She needed to find the pull-string and turn on the light. Linda continued to give herself a pep talk. "Never mind the spiders. You can do this. Just put one foot in front of the other."

Linda crossed the dusty plank floor with her arm outstretched, waving it in a circle. "Ouch!" she screeched. She'd stubbed her toe. Hopping on one sock foot, rubbing her injured toe, she stumbled, landing on her bum. "Eww." Something was crawling on her face. What was it? Was it a bat? What did bats feel like when they attacked? "Hold on," she scolded herself. "You are not being attacked. It's a little bug." Linda ran her fingers over her face. The insect, evading her fingers, crawled down her cheek to her chin and onto her neck. Scrunching her lips, she plucked the little bug off her neck and flicked it into the darkness. Her hand returned to the cut on her cheek. Was the cut on her cheek bleeding?

Linda traced the tiny scab that was forming. She hoped it wouldn't get infected, but an infection was the least of her worries. She needed light. The attic was dark, dank, dirty, and crawling with creepy crawlies. Scrambling to her feet, Linda squared her shoulders and waved her hand in the air. Spider or no spider, she would find the lightbulb.

Something brushed her hand. It didn't feel like a spiderweb. Was it the lightbulb cord? She grasped the string and pulled. The light turned on.

Relieved to have light, Linda flopped down on an old, battered steamer trunk. Admiring the dirty, dim light bulb as it swung back and forth. Linda couldn't see into all the dark corners, but what she could see was cobweb-infested. The attic was littered with boxes and discarded pieces of broken chairs. Lamps and pictures and piles of old clothes. It was a wonder she didn't kill herself when she was stumbling around in the darkness.

Exhausted, Linda sighed. Her arm throbbed, and her throat was sore. She shivered, remembering Richie's hands tightening, squeezing. And the darkness that followed.

Linda's eyes welled up. She also remembered the deep scratches on Richie's arm. She hoped the maniac got septicemia. Tears slid down her cheeks. Gertrude had put up a good fight. Sniffing, Linda wiped her cheeks with her dirty hands. She'd been stupid. She'd had her chance to escape and hadn't taken it. Instead, she had exchanged one prison for another. If she got out of this attic, she wouldn't make the same mistake. But how to escape? Her head felt woolly. She was bone tired; she couldn't think.

Linda's eyes widened. She lifted her head. Did she feel a breeze? She tilted her face one way and then the other and waited. "Yes, yes," she squealed gleefully. Linda felt a gentle breeze wafting across her cheek. "Ha, you lunatics, I'm not done yet." She jumped to her feet. There had to be a hole in the roof or the wall, a way to escape. Sock-footed, Linda trod carefully across the dust-covered floorboards. She paused and lifted her chin, waiting to feel the breeze on her face. The tiny wisps of air seemed to be coming from a wall. Linda put her hands on the wall, feeling for the hole. She tripped over a box of Christmas decorations. The box overturned, and bulbs and ornaments spilled out onto the floor. Some broke. Linda curled her toes and looked down at the broken bulbs. Should she wait for the morning? It made sense; in the morning, the light would shine through the hole, and she'd be able to find it.

A little black beetle with bent antennae scurried across the floor and stopped. The bug seemed to be watching her. Linda looked down at the bug. "Oh, no, did I do that? I'm sorry, little guy, I bent your antenna." The beetle looked up at her and wriggled its crooked antennae. "And don't worry," Linda told the little bug. "I'm not here to invade your home. I'm just going to rest a bit. Then I'll make plans. You just go about your buggy business, and I'll go about mine."

She piled old clothes under the lightbulb into a nest. The bug watched her. "Good night, Barry," Linda said to the little black bug. She pulled the string. Shut off the light and lay down on her nest of musty old clothes.

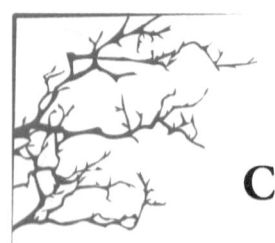

Chapter Eighteen

A scraping sound woke Linda. Her eyes flew open. The room was dark, and what the heck was she lying on? Where was she? Memories flooded back, and with the memories, fear. She sucked in her breath. *Oh God, she was imprisoned by a psychopathic maniac.*

The door opened, and the light shone in from the hallway. Richie entered with a tray in his hand. "Did you sleep well?" he asked in a cheery voice. He set the tray on the trunk and pulled the string to turn on the light. The tray held a mug of coffee and two slices of toast.

Linda jumped up and edged away, tripping over her nest. She stumbled back onto the pile of old clothes. He'd brought her coffee and toast. Why bring her food if he planned on killing her? It didn't make sense. Was this to taunt her? Offer her food and then take it away?

Laughing, Richie reached his hand to her. Linda shrank back, scrambling away, scattering the garments across the floor.

Richie's blue eyes twinkled. "I'm only trying to help you," he said with a mocking smile.

Linda's eyes darted around the attic. Last night, she felt a breeze. Her heart hammered in her chest. There was a gap somewhere in the wall. Would he spot the hole? *Oh, please don't let him see the hole,* she prayed. The opening, however small, could be her escape hatch. "Oh yes, thank you," Linda croaked. She stood; her stomach churned. She wiped her dirty hands on her grubby jeans. Hoping to distract him, she wet her lips and blurted, "You and your uncle are cut from the same cloth."

Richie grinned. Arching an eyebrow, he crossed his arms over his broad chest and leaned against the door frame. "You have deduced that, have you? Because we did away with Aunt Faith? Not a hard deduction there."

"There is that." Linda picked up the coffee mug. Her hand shook. The coffee in the cup sloshed over the rim. "I mean, you both plan to kill the other. I wonder who will succeed first. My money is on your uncle," she said with a burst of bravado.

Richie tilted his head. His brow furrowed, and he shook his head, sneering. "I think you're trying to sow mistrust. Save your breath. Uncle Alfred loves the ground I walk on."

Linda took a swig of coffee, spilling it. The coffee dribbled down her chin. She wiped her chin with the back of her hand and took another sip. This time, Linda was able to drink the cold coffee. If Richie lost his temper like before, he'd probably take the coffee. She needed to keep her fluids up. "You think so, do you? Then why isn't he giving you money or the deed to the house? Have you noticed he still has that caster bean plant?"

Richie gave a contemptuous snort. "There are no beans left on that plant."

"No, I suppose not. But what about ground-up beans? Your uncle does have them. Why else does he still have the mortar and pestle? I washed the pestle and mortar last night when I did the supper dishes. There was residue from something in the mortar. What else would it be?"

"Oh, did you? I never saw anything in the mortar. I think you are lying."

"Why do you think I threw up in the sink? I've seen dead people before," lied Linda. "Finding Faith in the freezer startled me. But her body in the freezer didn't make me sick. I thought your uncle tried to poison me."

Richie uncrossed his arms; his lips curled down, a sneer on his face. "You're lying."

"What do I have to gain by lying? Either you or your uncle intends to kill me. The last one that's still standing is my guess." Linda's voice shook. She set her half-empty coffee cup down and forced herself to take a bite of toast, making herself swallow.

"No worries. I know who will be the last one standing. And we both know it won't be you."

Chapter Nineteen

S haking, Linda sank onto the steamer trunk. Watched the door close. And heard the deadbolt drawn. The coffee in her mug splashed onto the back of her hand. Linda wiped her hand on her T-shirt, willing herself to calm down. Her taunts had done the job. She had distracted Richie from seeing the hole in the attic. Linda's eyes darted around the dirty, dingy, smelly room. If there was a hole? There had to be a hole.

But first, she had to eat. There was no guarantee Richie would bring her food again. Biting down on the dry toast, she made herself swallow, washing the toast down with the cold coffee. Barry, her bug companion, crawled across the tray. "Good morning, Barry," she said. The beetle stopped and waved his crooked antennae in acknowledgment. "Sorry, there are only a few crumbs for you. There was hardly enough for me." The bug wiggled its antennae and continued to creep down the side of the steamer trunk. Linda pulled the cord attached to the lightbulb and shut it off. She scanned the darkened attic for a chink of light. Her heart skipped a beat. The crack in the wall was there. She hadn't imagined it. A ray of sunshine shone through a tiny gap in the old bare boards.

Linda pulled the cord, turning the light back on. "Yes, Barry, I know it's a small crack. But this is an old house. The boards are old. I will make the hole bigger." The little bug paused, looked at her, then resumed its crawl. She grinned. All she needed was something sharp to widen the little opening. And then she could climb through the hole onto the roof. Someone would see her, and she would be free. Shaking her fist at the closed door, Linda screamed, "You think you have me cornered? Well, think again, you scummy piece of garbage."

Stepping over and around the boxes and bins of old clothes and crates of books. Linda made her way to the wall and ran her hand over the bare boards. Her eyes lit up; her fingers found the small break in the weathered wood.

Nearby was a nest of grass and string. Either a bird or a squirrel was using the little hole. Linda grinned and bounced from one sock foot to the other. If a squirrel could gnaw through the wood, it must be rotten. All she needed was a tool to widen the gap.

Linda stuck her fingers into the hole. She heaved a disappointed sigh. The wood felt solid. The board wasn't as rotten as she'd hoped. But if she found the right tool, there was a chance she could make it big enough for her to crawl through. Linda sneezed as she brushed past dirty cardboard boxes to stand in the center of the attic. She sniffed, her eyes searching for anything to dig at the wood.

Despite the sturdiness of the boards, Linda felt giddy with relief; she had a plan. She tramped around the filthy, hot, musty attic, searching in every dirty, dusty corner. Linda looked through boxes of old clothes, books, and old vinyl records. She rummaged through Christmas decorations. Coming up empty-handed, Linda stood, stretching her back. Disheartened, she wiped her sweaty forehead with the back of her hand and sank onto the old steamer trunk. Barry, the bug, perched on an ornate gilded picture frame, was watching. "Okay, Barry, you know this attic. Where will I find a hammer or a screwdriver? Or how about a knife?"

She picked up the mug, downed the last of the cold coffee, and set the cup on the trunk. The coffee mug teetered and slid onto the floor, landing next to a big brass key. Linda scooped it up, raced back to the hole beside the nest, and began digging. As the gap grew, she threw the small bits of wood to the floor. She grinned at the little bug who had skittered over a pile of books to sit, waving his bent antenna at her. "You watch me, Barry. Linda Burton is not done yet. Not by a long shot."

"Ouch, darn, darn," she muttered, shaking her hand. A splinter from the old, worn wood pierced her skin. Linda looked at her hand. Her hand was covered in dirt and grime. She bit on the sliver, pulled it out with her teeth, and spit. Linda sucked on the wound in her hand and spat again. She looked at Barry. "My Aunt Violet would have a bird. She's a bit of a neat freak. And she'd hate this dirty attic. Mind you, Barry. Aunt Violet would never be here at the mercy of those lunatics downstairs. She warned me not to stir up a hornet's nest. If only I listened to her."

Barry waved his antennae in response.

What day was this? She'd lost track of time. She had to think. The garage sale was on Friday. Saturday was the day the maniac locked her in Faith's bedroom. So today had to be Sunday. Would Aunt Violet be home today, or was it tomorrow? Linda was sure her aunt would go to Mabel's house to see how she was doing. And when Aunt Violet did. She would see that she was missing. Would she find poor Gertrude? Or had Richie buried the poor pet in the garden?

Linda exhaled a long breath. She mustn't think about Gertrude. And she mustn't think about poor dead Faith trust-up in plastic and stuffed into the deep freezer. She needed to alert someone she was being held prisoner in this attic. The hole needed to be bigger. Linda turned the old brass key in her hand. She needed something sharper. Linda marched back to the trunk, looked at the key in her hand, inserted the key into the keyhole, and opened the lid.

She wrinkled her nose and sneezed. Stale, musty air wafted from the old wooden chest. The trunk was full of old picture albums and loose photos, some in frames. Linda began to empty the trunk.

Maybe there was something under the pictures she could use. She piled up the albums and photos. One photo caught her eye. It was a picture of a young woman. Linda recognized her as the poor dead woman in the deep freezer. It was a picture of a young Faith in her wedding gown, looking adoringly at Alfred. And he was looking at her with the same loving expression. What had happened to that loving couple? When did love turn to hate? Linda shook her head. There was no time to ponder what happened to the smiling couple in the wedding photo. She needed to get out of the attic before Richie returned.

Linda continued to sift through old pictures and recipe books, their covers torn. At the bottom of the trunk, she picked up an old cigar box and opened the box. A pincushion, hairpins, and buttons spilled onto the floor. A bottle opener and an icepick clanked as they dropped to her feet. Linda picked up the icepick, admiring it. "Look, Barry," she exclaimed. "This is the perfect tool." The little black bug stopped in mid-crawl and wriggled his antennae in response. Linda stepped over Barry and raced back to the crack in the wall.

With a firm grip on the pick, she poked the icepick into the board. She giggled as pieces of wood flew down onto the floor. This was more like it; the hole was getting bigger by the minute. After a few more jabs, Linda paused and peeked out. She could see the street. With renewed vigour, she stuck the icepick into the wood again and again. The hole grew with each stab. Linda paused. Her arm ached. It was the arm Richie had twisted behind her back. She rolled her shoulder to ease the pain. Then, she stuck her hand through the small opening in the boards. It wasn't anywhere big enough to crawl through. She grinned. But soon it would be.

At the sound of a vehicle, Linda pulled her hand back. Pressing her face against the boards, she peered through the hole. A red Ford truck was backing into the driveway. The driver's side door opened. A tall, solid, built man with a baseball cap backward on his head stepped onto the driveway.

"Hello," she hollered.

The passenger side door opened. A short, sandy-haired man climbed out. He held the door open. And a little white terrier dog jumped out. The dog ran around the truck, wagging its tail. The small dog sniffed and lifted his leg at a tire. Then ran to the lawn, sniffed at the grass, rolling on it.

Linda hollered again. "Hello. Help. Please help me. I'm being held prisoner up here in the attic."

The little white terrier squatted, wagged his tail, and looked up at Linda, barking. The men talked to each other as they lowered the truck's tailgate.

"Help, up here. I'm up here. Help, I'm a prisoner."

The terrier kept wagging his tail, looking up and barking excitedly.

Richie came out of the house and bounded up to the men. The little white dog's barking became more intense. The puppy ran around in a circle, only stopping to look up at Linda, yapping feverishly. The sandy-haired man picked up his excited little dog and put him in the truck. The little dog, still barking, pawed at the window.

Linda shouted again, "Up here, I'm in the attic, help! Help me."

The tall, thick-set man with the baseball cap cocked his head. Looking around, he said something to the sandy-haired man. The short man looked up and shrugged.

Linda couldn't hear what they said. If she couldn't hear the men, that meant the men couldn't hear her. She had to holler louder, and she did. "Up here. I'm up here. Help, help," she screamed.

Linda bounced on her toes, giggling with relief. The tall man had looked up. He had heard her cries. She yelled down again. "Up here. I'm up here. Help, help."

Richie looked up at the house, laughed, and slapped the baseball cap man on the back. Alfred came out of the house and down the steps to join the men, beckoning them. The men disappeared from her sight. Did that man hear her? She was sure he did.

Her heart pounding, she paced back and forth, waiting. Barry skittered across the floor and up the side of the trunk. The sound of the bolt sliding back on the door brought Linda to a halt. She was free. The man had heard her calls for help.

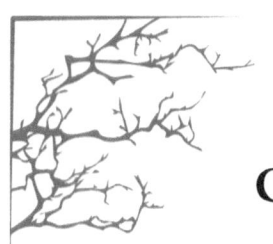

Chapter Twenty

Richie's eyes flashed angrily as he stepped through the door. Slamming it shut behind him. He snarled, "You've been a naughty little girl again."

"That man heard me. He knows I'm up here. You have to let me go," Linda cried, stumbling over cardboard boxes and backing across the attic floor.

"You just never learn, do you?" Richie's nostrils flared. With a cruel smile, he kicked the boxes out of the way, pursuing Linda across the attic.

Linda's back pressed against the wall where she'd been digging. She spread her legs and planted her feet. And crouched in what Linda thought was a knife fighter's stance, waving the icepick at Richie. "I'm warning you, don't come any closer."

Laughing, Richie stood out of Linda's reach. "Really, Nosey? I don't think you have it in you to stab anyone, even if you were quick enough. Which you're not."

"You don't know me. Back up," hissed Linda.

Richie held his hands up, palms facing her, arched an eyebrow, and stepped back. "Well, well, look at you. A lean, mean, little fighting machine." He giggled. "Well, more like a skinny, wizened little elf."

Linda, shoulders back, lifted her chin. She had the icepick. She had the upper hand. Richie stepped back. She jerked her head sharply. "Move." The icepick at the ready, Linda advanced toward the door.

Richie stepped away from the door.

Linda took another careful step forward.

He feigned right, then turned abruptly left, grabbing her arm. He wrenched the icepick from her hand, twisting her arm, bringing her to her knees. "Too slow, Nosey. I did warn you," he jeered.

Linda opened her mouth to scream.

Richie clamped his hand over her mouth, holding the icepick to her throat.

Linda sucked in her breath. She could feel nothing but blind terror. Her bid for freedom was over. She was going to die.

"Be a good girl, and you'll live to fight another day. It's up to you. Die now or die later. I prefer later, don't you? Blood is so messy." Linda sagged in his arms.

Richie took the icepick from her throat and his hand from her mouth. Linda gazed up at him, her face ashen, fear robbing her of speech.

Richie dropped the icepick on the floor and kicked it out of reach. He pulled a roll of duct tape from his jacket pocket. "Better than the dishcloth, don't you think?" he said matter-of-factly. Ripping off a piece of tape, Richie covered her mouth. He secured her hands with a long, white plastic twist tie from another pocket. "Oh, by the way, you are right. The big guy, Hank, did think he'd heard a voice. But we have convinced him what he heard was squirrels. Do you want to know where your saviours are now?" He smirked. "Your saviours are having coffee in the kitchen with Uncle Alfred."

Linda's heart sank. Tears spilled down her cheeks. She'd been so close to freedom.

"As soon as I'm finished with you. Your buddies and I will haul Aunt Faith's old four-poster bed and armoire out to the truck. And I'm warning you. You better not make any sounds, such as stomping on the floor. Do you understand?"

Linda looked meekly up at him and nodded.

"Yeah, I bet. You are a very inventive little gnome. It's too bad your ingenuity will get you nowhere. You just keep making more work for me. This house is on the market. Now, I'll have to patch this damn hole. You are so destructive. First, the windowsill, and now this. Tsk, tsk. What am I going to do with you?" Richie eyed the trunk, smiling his signature crooked grin, he said, "Ah, I have an idea." He opened the steamer trunk and tipped it over, dumping out the last of its contents.

Linda's dread increased as she watched the photos and papers flutter to the floor. She knew what was going to happen.

Richie yanked Linda to her feet. "Either you step inside this trunk, or I throw you in. You pick."

Linda stepped into the trunk. "Sit. No, lie down."

As Linda curled into a ball, Barry, the bug, crawled onto her shoulder. She watched in horror as the lid closed over her. Sick with fear, she listened to the key turn in the lock.

It was dark, cramped, and stifling hot in the small mildew-encrusted trunk. The musty smell was overpowering. Would Richie leave her here in this trunk to suffocate and die? Fear twisted her gut as she struggled to breathe through her nose. *Don't panic, don't panic, don't panic. You can breathe.* Linda told herself. Her body went cold with dread. This could be her coffin. He could leave her in this box until she died of starvation. Linda whimpered. Barry, the bug, nestled in her hair.

Linda elbowed herself to lie on her back. The twist ties were around her wrists, but her fingers were free. Uttering a sharp squeal, she ripped the duct tape off her mouth, coughing and sneezing. Her movements in the small box brought a shower of mildew and dust. She licked her dry lips and concentrated on breathing slowly in and out through her nose.

She felt Barry crawl out of her hair and down her face to sit on her arm. The little bug was her only companion in her dark, musty coffin.

Linda had never thought about death. And certainly not about her own demise. Was this it, then? Was this how she would end her days? She was not leaving much of a mark on the world. Stop it, she told herself. Stop feeling sorry for yourself. She'd had a pretty good life. She'd had good friends. And she had enjoyed teaching kindergarten. A tear trickled down her cheek. Maybe the little people she taught would leave their mark. What would she do differently if she had the chance? She had regrets. She thought about her marriage to Howard. Maybe if she hadn't been such a doormat, Howard would have had more respect for her. It was strange how love could change to dislike. That certainly was the case for Faith and Alfred. Their dislike became hate. And led to death. One thing was for sure: if she could turn back the clock. She would definitely mind her own business.

Things began to get foggy in her mind. Maybe this trunk was airtight? How long had she been in this box? She had no idea of the time. Was there enough oxygen? The little bug Barry ran up her arm and sat on her shoulder. She wouldn't be dying alone. Barry was by her side.

Chapter Twenty-One

The key turned in the lock, and the trunk lid opened. "Come on, old lady, get up."

Linda looked up at Richie's boyish face, smiling down at her, and shut her eyes. She was done. Richie called her an old lady. And she felt like one. She was tired. Tired of being terrorized. She wanted it over.

"Oh, you got the tape off your mouth. I should never underestimate you. Come on, get up. Here, let me help you." He reached down, grabbed Linda by her upper arms, and pulled her up. "Can you stand?" Richie asked. There was a concerned look on his face. "I don't want to have to carry you down the stairs. Uncle Alfred will be no help," he said, helping Linda step out of the trunk. "You look a mess," he added, shutting the lid.

Linda slumped down on the lid of the trunk. Her head hung down. What was the point? Everything she had tried had failed.

Richie took a jackknife from his pocket and flicked open a blade. Linda stared blankly at him. He was going to kill her just like he did his aunt. There was nothing she could do.

"Did you think I was going to cut your throat?" Richie chuckled, slicing through the plastic tie that held her wrists. "That would be a bit messy."

Linda rubbed her wrists and looked up at him. She felt nothing. *Was she dead already?* Richie smiled at her, brushed a lock of blond hair off his forehead, and pocketed the knife.

Barry skittered down her arm and off the trunk, crawling across the floor. Richie screwed up his lips, sniffed, and stepped on the little bug, crushing it. He looked down at the bottom of his shoe, scraping the remains of Barry off on a board.

Linda stood, shaking with rage. He'd killed Barry. "You monster," she screamed. "You kill everything in your path. Poor Barry, he never did anything to you."

Richie looked at Linda and then at the squashed bug. "Who's Barry? I think I left you in that box too long. You're losing your marbles. Pull yourself together, you crazy old lady."

"You are an evil bully. You almost choked me to death. And you locked me up in a box. I'm through being terrorized by you. I've had it up to here!" screamed Linda.

Richie, with a mocking smile on his face, loomed over her. "Oh, nosey little Linda. I would think by now you know what will happen if you make me lose my temper."

"I don't care," she shouted up at him. "You have terrified me enough. You'll never get away with any of this. You killed your aunt. If you kill me, you will have two bodies to get rid of. Your troubles are mounting. Turn yourself in. This is nuts what you and your uncle are doing."

"You're lucky I'm in a good mood. Do you want to know why?" Richie's eyes twinkled as he looked at Linda. He waited, grinned and said, "No? Well, it's because I have figured out what to do with you."

Linda, her energy spent, sank back on the trunk. The familiar feeling of dread replaced her rage.

"You see, you are right. I've no place to put your body. The hard part isn't the killing. That's easy. The hard part of killing is where to put the body."

Linda hung her head; she was numb. He was going to kill her. Nothing she could do or say would help her.

Richie opened a bottle of water and handed it to her.

Why was he giving her water? She didn't care. Closing her eyes, she chugged the water. Who knew how great water could taste?

"Do you want to know what my plan is?" He held her cell phone in his hand. "I have a plan. You are going to love my plan." He chuckled. "Well, maybe not love it."

Linda gulped more water. Her stomach churned. But she was not going to throw up. She was still alive. *Never give in. And never give up.*

"Not curious? You're always such a curious woman." Richie laughed. "I'll tell you, but first, I have a request. Well, maybe not a request. I need you to let someone know you are going away. And the person I have chosen is Mabel, the lady you are house-sitting for. Yes, dear Nosey. You are going to disappear. And there is nothing you can do about it."

Hope returned. Linda's heart leapt. Her mind raced. Somehow, she would tell Mabel she was in trouble.

"Now listen up, Nosey. There are a few rules you need to follow. If you don't, I will take care of Mabel and your aunt, just like I did that cat. You wouldn't want that, would you?" He tipped his head, his signature smile on his face.

Linda meekly shook her head, but her thoughts churned. They were in Calgary. There was nothing he could do to them. Was there?

"Remember this. While you are talking to your friend Mabel, her well-being is totally in your hands," Richie warned.

Linda nodded, her mind racing. What to say? She had to think of something.

He strode across the attic floor and sat on a wooden crate. "Come sit beside me."

Linda stood, her legs shaking; she crossed the floor to sit beside him.

"That's a good girl." Richie patted her knee.

Linda flinched. How was she going to buy time?

Richie screwed up his nose. "You do stink, you know. You've really let yourself go."

Linda ignored his jibe and pressed her lips together. She had to think. The phone call could be her way out. But Mabel was in Calgary. How could she help her? But if she could somehow let Mabel know she was in trouble. Mabel could phone the RCMP. It was a long shot. But it was the only chance she had. But what should she say? She couldn't endanger Mabel or her aunt. But she needed to leave a clue. Linda recalled the stories of how Mabel and her Aunt Violet had solved mysteries. Mabel was smart. She was a master at solving puzzles. But how to let Mabel know she was in the hands of a murderer?

"Yeah, I guess that isn't the best joke," Richie said, giving Linda a sheepish smile. "I guess it's not really your fault you look and smell so yucky."

Linda clenched her hands together. Her anger returned. She so wanted to slap that stupid smile off his face.

"Now for the rules: You will not mention garage sales. Or neighbours. You will tell her that you have to leave." He took Linda's chin in his hand and turned her face so he could look into her eyes. "Remember, I will be listening to everything you say."

Linda looked down at her feet. Richie grabbed her chin and turned her face back toward him. "So do it good. Do I make myself clear?"

It flashed across Linda's mind that her aunt would correct Richie's phrase of speech even in the face of danger. She wasn't that brave. "Yes," she replied meekly. What clue to give to Mabel?

Richie scrolled through the names and pressed Mabel's number. The phone rang, and the voicemail kicked in.

"We're sorry the number you have reached is not available."

Linda's heart sank. She remembered her aunt telling her Mabel was notorious for not turning on her phone and letting her cell phone battery die.

"Well, Plan B will work too." Richie shut off the phone and tossed it into a cardboard box.

Tears slid down Linda's cheeks. Once more, she'd gotten her hopes up only to have them crushed.

Chapter Twenty-Two

Richie grabbed her chin again, making her look up at him. "Look at me," he said, staring into her eyes.

Linda blinked rapidly. Her heart pounded. What now?

"We're going to go down the alley. How you do this is up to you. I can tie your hands and shackle your legs so you can only shuffle. Or you can walk with me down the back alley like a good girl. What's your choice?"

"I'll be good. I won't cause you any trouble." Yes, she was scared to the bone. But she couldn't let fear overpower her. Once she was outside, there was a chance she could escape.

"You better mean what you said. No messing about. Behave yourself. I won't stand for any more disobedience. Do you understand?"

"Yes," whispered Linda. She lifted her dirty hands, wiping the tears off her cheek.

Richie went down the ladder first and waited. Linda's legs quaked as she climbed down the steps. Anticipation coursed through her veins. Soon, she'd be out of this house of horrors.

He ushered Linda down the hallway, past the bedrooms, to the stairs. "Come on, Nosey. Hurry up. We've got places to be." Richie shoved her. His cruel laughter rang out as Linda stumbled down the stairs. She grabbed the banister at the last minute, preventing a fall.

"Hey, hey. Be careful," yelled Alfred from the bottom of the stairs. "Remember, we don't have room to hide her damn body."

"No worries. Nosey and I are taking that ride out into the countryside, just like we planned. Aren't we, Nosey?" Richie grinned.

"Do you remember which road to take?"

"Yeah, yeah. I scouted it out yesterday."

"It's the first turn on your right as you go north out of town, the old Bingo road," Alfred instructed. "No one goes down that road. Years ago, there used to be a Bingo hall there."

"Yeah, yeah. I told you I checked it out. Relax. I got this."

Alfred's eyes narrowed. "Make sure you do, and no fooling around. Phone me when you're on the road."

"No worries, like I said. I've got this."

"My shoes," Linda spoke up. "I left them in the bedroom."

Alfred snorted and gave a harsh laugh. "I threw those damn shoes out with the rest of Faith's crap."

Linda thought of the photo she'd seen in the attic. The loving looks the couple had exchanged on their wedding day. But this was not the time to dwell on what happened to the Hutchins' marriage.

Her brain raced. She had to think of something. Richie was taking her outside and down the back alley. She would feign compliance. And when the monster let his guard down, she'd run for it, slip into someone's yard, and run into their house. Yes, Richie would come after her. But surely, they'd believe her when she told them Richie was after her and wanted to kill her. And even if they doubted her story. They wouldn't turn a woman over to some strange man chasing her. And that was what Richie was. A stranger, he was never the charming, friendly guy she'd trusted. He was a stone-cold killer.

Despite Richie's prodding, Linda paused on the back step, inhaling the fresh air. She wasn't free yet. But it felt like freedom to smell the clean night air. It was raining cats and dogs, and Linda thought it was beautiful.

"Come on," Richie said impatiently, grabbing her upper arm and propelling her into the rain. Linda's socked feet sank into the mud as they crossed the water-soaked garden and out the gate. She felt every rock and stone as they walked down the back alley. Richie loosened his hold on her arm as he pulled up the rain hood on his rain jacket.

It was Linda's chance. She made a run for it. She managed two steps, then slipped face-first onto the muddy gravel laneway. A rock cut into her face, opening the cut from the glass shards.

"Oh, for God's sake, get up. You're only making things worse for yourself," Richie scolded, prodding her with the toe of his rubber boot.

Linda wanted to scream as she struggled to her feet. Once more, her break for freedom had failed. She wiped the filthy, wet grit off her face. Was the cut on her cheek bleeding? Her thin T-shirt was soaked through. Mud and gravel encrusted her shirt and jeans, and her socks were a sopping, muddy mess.

They tramped past the chain-link fence. No black monster dog was there to bark at them. Too wet even for the dog, Linda thought as she stepped into a mud puddle.

"Hey, have you noticed no crazy dog barking? Your trick of tossing a wiener to the stupid dog worked well," Richie said, grinning at her. "I added a special treat."

"It is just a dog barking. It's not harming anyone."

"Thanks to you, that brute won't be barking at anyone anymore. I would never have thought of it but for you."

"What do you mean? What did you do to that dog?" Linda remembered the dog lying panting on the grass, white foam on its muzzle.

"Like I said, I added a special treat to the wiener."

"You killed that poor dog. Just like Gertrude, you killed those innocent animals. Why would you do that?" asked Linda.

"Who cares? They were just animals."

Linda, her head down, slogged down the alley, putting one foot in front of the other. Trying not to think about poor Faith or the dead dog and Gertrude. Rain drummed on the gravelled laneway, and muddy water splashed up. She was drenched.

"Home sweet home," Richie said cheerfully, offering her a hand as they mounted the back steps to the porch.

Shuttering at his touch, Linda shook him off. He lifted the little green and white gnome, removed the house key from under it, opened the back door, and turned on the lights. Linda watched Richie as he pulled off his rubber boots. Why was Richie taking off his boots? He was going to kill her. And yet he was worried about tracking mud on the floor?

"Your car keys, please," requested Richie. "Oh, I see them." Car keys were hanging on a hook just inside the back door.

Linda bit her bottom lip as she stepped over Gertrude's dishes scattered across the kitchen floor. She couldn't think about Gertrude. She had a plan. "Please, may I use the bathroom?"

"Sure, since you used your magic words. I don't want a puddle in the car," he mocked, laughing as he followed her down the hallway. At the bathroom door, he held up his hand. "But first, I'll check it. I can't have you coming out of there with some kind of nasty weapon. You are a crafty old gal." He opened the bathroom door and turned on the light. Richie stood perusing the room. He stepped to the sink, opened the medicine cabinet, searched, looked in the drawers, and took a tube of lipstick, lip gloss, and a fingernail file.

Linda pressed her lips and clenched her fist.

His eyes flickered around the room. "Okay, but be quick. I'll be outside the door."

Linda used the toilet and then looked in the mirror. She had dark rings under her eyes. Her hair was a filthy, matted mess, and a small, jagged red cut ran down her dirty cheek. The scab had ripped off when she fell. Blood was slowly oozing out. Linda opened a drawer, took a Band-Aid, and slapped it over the cut. The Band-Aid didn't stick. Her face was too muddy and wet. She tossed the useless thing in the garbage can. Shivering at the memory, Linda put a grubby hand on her neck. Tracing the black and blue bruises where Richie had choked her.

Linda opened the medicine cabinet and rummaged in the drawers. Her plan to leave a message on the mirror was foiled. Richie had taken the lipstick and the lip gloss. She bit her bottom lip. Richie could open the door at any moment. Was there nothing in this bathroom she could use? Her eyes lit on a tube of toothpaste. Linda picked up the toothpaste and took the cap off. Squeezed the tube and wrote on the mirror. *'Faith deep freezer Alfred Richie'* She added the name *'Hutchan.'* Was that how they spelt their name? She had no time to figure it out. Linda began to write the word help. She wrote *'He.'* She squeezed. Nothing was coming out. She ran her fingers down the tube, squeezing the last bit of toothpaste out of the tube. It formed a small blob with a tail. The toothpaste tube was empty.

Linda opened another drawer. There was no more toothpaste. She spied a nail clipper and stuffed the clipper into the pocket of her wet jeans. If he tied her up again with the twist ties, she could cut them and free herself. Mabel's laundry hamper sat beside the bathtub. Linda opened the lid. She threw dirty garments on the floor as she rummaged in the laundry hamper. Pulled out a sweatshirt and looked at it. The shirt was dirty but dry. She donned the dirty shirt, wiped her bloody cheek and flushed the toilet.

She shut off the light and stepped into the hallway, quickly shutting the door behind her. "Show me your room," Richie said.

Puzzled, Linda led the way and turned the bedroom light on. It seemed like a long time ago since she'd slept in her bed.

Richie followed her to her bedroom. "Time to pack your bag." He opened her closet door.

"Pack my bags?"

"You are going to leave a note telling Mabel you had to leave. So, you have to take your clothes. It would look suspicious if someone discovered you never took anything with you." Richie took a red suitcase from the closet. "Open it," he instructed, tossing the little bag onto her bed.

Linda unzipped the case. Did that mean he would leave her somewhere in a field to be eaten by a bear? Or tied up in a bush to die of exposure? She felt the nail clipper in her pocket. The clipper gave her hope.

Richie yanked her clothes from her closet, tossing them into the case. Linda began to fold a pair of trousers, putting the garment into the bag.

"Stop fooling around. No folding. Stick your stuff in the suitcase." Richie strode over to her dresser and opened a drawer.

Linda blanched. Richie was taking her undies out of the drawer. Good lord, she told herself, *this psychopath is bent on killing you. The least of your worries is that he sees your undergarments.* But still, it gave her the willies.

Richie tossed the garments into the suitcase. He grabbed her purse off the dresser, threw it on her clothes, and zipped up the bag. "Right, just one more little detail."

Linda gasped and put a hand over her mouth. He was going to look in the bathroom! He would see her message.

But Richie strode past the bathroom into the kitchen.

Linda blew out a breath. Someone would read her message. Maybe not soon enough to save her. She'd have to be satisfied knowing the monsters wouldn't get away with murdering her and Faith.

Richie took a notepad from his pocket, ripped out a page, and laid the paper on the table. He felt his pocket. Frowning, Richie picked up the page, strode to the kitchen counter, and grabbed a pen. "Here," he directed. "Write down what I say." He handed the pen to Linda. "Write: Sorry, I have to leave." Richie grinned and snickered. "Write: I'm bored. I can't take this hick town one day longer. Then sign your name."

Linda wrote the note as he directed.

"Good, now put it on the table beside that goofy cat thingy."

Linda complied. Mabel would know she loved Glenhaven. Mabel would know the note was not true. She choked back a sob. But by then, it would be too late.

Richie picked up Gertrude's water and food bowls off the floor. He rinsed Gertrude's dishes and set them in the sink.

Linda wiped her eyes, leaving a dirty, muddy streak. There was no time for tears. *Never give up, never give in.* She'd find a way to escape. She tugged off her dirty, wet socks. Slipped on Mabel's old garden shoes, balled up her wet socks, and dropped the mucky, soppy mess on the shoe mat.

After wiping down the kitchen counter, Richie hung the tea towel on the rack. "There, everything is all neat and tidy. I know you wouldn't leave a mess, just as you would have taken your clothes." Richie flashed his crooked smile at Linda. "So even if someone does miss you, it appears like you left on your own accord."

He took the car keys off the hook by the back door. "Oh, I almost forgot to turn off the kitchen light." Richie's eyes twinkled. "You'd never leave the lights on, would you? Not good for the environment." He flipped the switch and locked the door. "Where do we leave the house key? Oh yeah, we put them under this goofy-looking gnome." Richie picked up the gnome and put the house key under it. "Yep, the perfect crime. Everything will appear normal. And it will be a long while before anyone thinks your disappearance is suspicious. And if, and when, they do find you, well." Richie chuckled. "It will be too late."

Richie stood on the porch looking out at the rain pouring down. He took his phone from his pocket, punched in a number, and held the phone to his ear. "Yeah, it's me. Who else were you expecting?" There was a pause. "Yeah, yeah. Whatever. We will be on the road in a minute or two. Yes." Richie rolled his eyes. "I know which road to take. Don't you be late, I don't want to get wet."

Grinning at Linda, Richie stuck the phone in his pocket. "Look at this beautiful night," he said happily. "It's a great night for a drive in the country. I love a dark rainy night." He giggled. "Nobody around to see you disappear."

Richie hustled Linda down the porch steps. She kicked over the empty plant pots, and he grinned. "Clumsy old Nosey."

Tramping across the yard in his rubber boots, pulling the red suitcase across the damp grass, Richie began to whistle Mr. Roger's theme song: *It's a beautiful day in the neighbourhood.*

Remembering the next line, *'Would you be mine?'* Linda's blood ran cold. If she didn't do something. She would be his next victim.

Richie opened the small door to the garage and pushed Linda inside. His hand found the switch to open the big door. The light came on, and the garage door slowly opened. Richie looked at the old purple Pontiac. "What year is this car? Does this piece of junk even run?"

Linda kept her head down. The monster had just made an error. He had Mabel's car keys. Her key fob was in her purse, which he had thrown into her suitcase. Her car was parked on the street. Richie thought the old car was hers. No one would believe she would take Mabel's car. "Of course, my old purple Pontiac runs," she said.

Richie's hand was firmly on Linda's arm as he forced her to the back of the car and opened the trunk. "In here," he instructed.

"No," protested Linda.

"Oh, Nosey, be a good girl and climb in. Or do you want me to shove you in headfirst? You pick. Because either way, you are going into that trunk."

Her heart pounding, Linda crawled up over the ledge into the trunk.

Richie shoved the little suitcase in after her and slammed the trunk shut.

The trunk of the car was dark and smelly. She smelt the gasoline exhaust as the car began to move. Something dug into Linda's back. She shifted her body, pushing the suitcase away with her foot. Her hand found the object that had been digging into her back. It was a golf club. Linda smiled. When Richie opened the trunk, she would have a surprise for the smiling evil maniac.

RICHIE STARTED THE car and backed out of the garage. "Damn it," he swore. Richie shifted the car into park, and ran back up the driveway to close the garage door. Racing back to the car, he reversed out of the driveway. As he yanked on the steering wheel, he swore again. "Crap, this car doesn't even have power steering. It's like driving a rusty old tank." Richie squinted. The rain was pelting down. The windshield wipers were barely keeping the windscreen clear. "These headlights are a joke." He snorted. "A candle would give more light."

As he sped down the main street of Glenhaven, his mood lightened. It was just as he thought. There were no cars on the street. Richie laughed aloud. The country bumpkins were all huddled in their houses. He turned onto a gravel road. It was the gravel road his uncle had instructed him to take. Richie glanced in the review mirror. No car lights. "Where the hell are you?" The old bird was supposed to be following him. He wasn't going to walk back to town in the damn rain. The car swerved on the wet, slushy gravel. He yanked on the steering wheel. The wheels spun, and gravel and mud shot up. At the last moment, the car straightened. Richie blew out a breath. He'd just managed to avoid the ditch.

Richie eased his foot on the accelerator. But as the car straightened out, he pressed his foot down, increasing the speed. His jaw tightened. Where the hell was his uncle? The car swerved again, and gravel pinged up on the fender wells. He yanked on the steering wheel and grinned. He was getting the hang of driving on the gravel road.

He chuckled. He could hear thumping coming from the back of the car. Old Nosey was trying to break out. The old bird was like a

Houdini, always finding a way to escape. It was time to do away with her. The sooner, the better. Richie tramped down on the accelerator.

The car climbed a hill and spun around a curve, skidding and swerving on the wet, greasy gravel. This time, Richie couldn't control the skid. It fishtailed one way and then the other. The car did a one-eighty. Careening into an embankment, Richie was flung against the steering wheel.

The hood shot up, and steam poured out of the radiator.

Chapter Twenty-Three

Linda was tossed up against the roof of the trunk. She fell back with a thud, smashing her head and back on the floor of the trunk. She rubbed her head. What the heck happened? The car wasn't moving. Ignoring the pain in her back, Linda sat back on her bum and kicked with both feet against the back of the seat. The seat-rest cracked and fell with a thud. She wiggled out of the trunk onto the back seat, feet first. The car was silent. She could hear the rain hammering down on the car's rooftop. Lightning flashed, and thunder rumbled. Linda's eyes widened. Richie was slumped over the steering wheel. Linda reached back in the trunk for the golf club. It was pitch black in the trunk. Linda couldn't feel the club. She needed to get out of the car. Richie might not be unconscious. She grabbed the little suitcase, leaned over the front seat, and smacked Richie on top of his head. Linda dropped the suitcase on the backseat and bit her lip. She'd heard him moan. He wasn't unconscious.

Opening the backseat door, Linda scrambled out. Rain pelted down, and lightning flashed. Richie was sitting up. She dropped to the ground and crawled under the car.

The rain came down in torrents. Linda heard Richie get out of the car. If he looked under the vehicle, he would see her. She crawled on her tummy, curling up by the front wheel on the driver's side. He was so close she could hear him cursing and his feet crunching on the wet gravel. Linda, shivering, pulled her knees up to her chest.

"I'm going to find you, Linda. You're not that fast. I will find you," yelled Richie.

She slunk lower, pressing her face onto the muddy road. Linda lifted her chin, water streaming around her.

Richie's phone rang. "Where the hell are you? You are supposed to be following me. The damn car is in the ditch."

Linda's heart pounded. Richie was standing just inches from her.

"What? I don't care that the power is out. What do you want me to do about it? For God's sake, she won't thaw out that fast."

There was a long silence. Linda lifted her head. Where was Richie?

"I don't give a rat's ass that you've been looking for candles. Forget about the damn candles. I've crashed this damn car. And Linda has gotten away. I've got to find this loopy woman. And I can't see a damn thing in this rain. She is running around somewhere out here in the dark. And it's bloody raining," he raged.

There was a long silence. Linda poked her head out from behind the tire and drew it back quickly. Richie was standing beside the tire. He was holding the phone to his ear, nodding.

"Oh, the papers with your signatures." Richie's voice faltered. "Yeah, yeah. I can explain." There was another pause. "Look, just come out here and get me, and I'll explain," coaxed Richie, his voice pleading. "Like I said, Linda's damn car is in the ditch. Steam is coming out of the motor. The car is hooped. Please come and get me, and I'll explain everything," he cajoled. More silence. "Alright then, have it your way. But I'm coming back to town now. We need to talk. I'm starting to walk back now."

Rain poured down, drumming on the crashed car. A deluge of muddy water coursed under the Pontiac, swirling around Linda. The water was cold. But Linda didn't care. She felt a surge of hope. Richie was leaving.

"No, I'm not worried. Linda won't get far. There are no farm buildings anywhere near here. And seriously, the signatures are nothing to worry about. Please, just come and get me, and I'll explain everything. And it will be easier to find her in the daylight," coaxed

Richie. After another long pause, Richie sighed and said, "Good, I'll meet you. I'll start walking toward town. And you know what? I bet those signatures were —" Richie kicked the side of the car. The car rocked. "Shit, you old bastard. Why hang up? Shit, shit, shit," Richie screamed into the night.

Linda cringed, her head pressed against the car. Richie was pacing back and forth in the rain. Why wouldn't he leave?

He kicked the wheel where Linda was hiding and yelled into the darkness. "Don't worry, Nosey, we'll find you. Hide all you like, but I will find you. And when I do, you'll wish you were dead."

Chapter Twenty-Four

Listening, Linda shivered as the water streamed around her. Mud from the car dripped on her head. His footsteps were receding. But still, she waited. The man could be lurking. Richie took great delight in taunting her. Linda knew she wouldn't get another chance to escape if he found her now. He'd drowned her in the ditch.

Finally, deciding that the only sound she heard was the rain beating down on the car. Linda crawled out from under the car and sat beside the wheel. Arms wrapped around herself, shaking and waiting; Linda didn't dare move. Should she take a chance? She didn't see him or hear anything, but the rain was coming down so hard it was hard to tell. She needed to get far away from the car. Limping, Linda started across the road. One shoe was still under the car, but she wasn't going back for it. The Maniac could return at any minute. The rain continued to pelt down, but it didn't matter. She was already soaking wet, her sweatshirt and jeans caked in mud. Kicking off her other shoe, she ran across the road, feeling the stones as they cut into her cold feet.

Linda shrieked. She tumbled into a ditch. Clamping her mouth shut, Linda waded through the rushing water. The cold, muddy water coursed around her, sweeping her off her feet. Regaining her footing, Linda splashed her way to the side of the ditch and clawed at the weeds. She had to get out of the ditch. If she didn't, she could drown and save Richie the trouble. Her hand grabbed hold of a clump of weedy grass, and she pulled herself up. The weeds pulled out from the ground, and Linda fell back into the rushing water. She surfaced, shook her head, coughed, spitting out muddy water, and struggled back to the side of the ditch. This time, digging her toes into the muddy ditch, she grasped the ropy weeds and clung. The weeds held, and Linda pulled herself out of the ditch. Crawling up the ridge and spitting out the foul-tasting water, she lay in the tall grass. Coughing, Linda pushed herself to her feet. She had to stay clear of the road. Alfred and Richie could return any minute. Their car lights would spot her. She had to move.

Linda plodded away from the road with her head bent against the pouring rain. She was freezing, her legs trembling as she struggled through the tall, wet grass. Tramping through the weedy grass, Linda came up against a barbed wire fence. Down on her knees, she crawled under it. Standing on the other side, Linda shivered, hugging herself for warmth. If she didn't find somewhere dry, she could perish from hypothermia. Linda trudged onward, the wind whipping rain into her face. One step at a time, she told herself. Never give up. Never give in. But she was starving. When was the last time she ate? Toast and a cold cup of coffee. Her feet were numb, and so were her hands. Lightning flashed, lighting up the dark sky. Linda felt the ground shake. She threw herself flat on the grass. She was in a pasture. You were never supposed to be in an open field with lightning. Lifting her head, she scanned the heavens. Was it safe to stand? Her mouth tasted like she'd licked the bottom of old boots. She so needed to brush her teeth. Linda laughed aloud as she regained her feet, stumbling over a rock. Cold, tired, and running for her life in an open field where she could get struck by lightning at any moment. *And she wanted to brush her teeth?*

Stumbling over rocks and around bushes, Linda tramped on. Sheet lightning flashed, and she saw a signpost. Linda leaned against the post. She was so tired. The sign on the post read Brown Wolf School. The established dates had faded. She couldn't read the numbers, and she didn't care. Linda trudged up the rickety steps of the abandoned old building. The windows were boarded up, but the door was open. Dripping wet, Linda stood in the doorway of the dilapidated old schoolhouse. Jagged fork lightning lit up the night sky. Thunder roared, the ground vibrated, and Linda leapt into the building.

Linda grabbed the doorknob and yanked, trying to close it. But the door didn't budge. The door hung open on one hinge. She moved further into the dingy schoolroom. A tin can rolled across the floor. The can rolled up, clanking against a metal rod. Lying beside the thin rod was an old canvas lawn chair. As her eyes adjusted to the dark, she saw an assortment of old lawn chairs, empty beer bottles, and cans scattered across the floor. The old, abandoned schoolhouse appeared to be a hang-out for teenage beer parties.

She vigorously rubbed her arms, trying to warm herself. She was freezing. Should she take off her wet clothes? It probably wouldn't help. She'd be even colder. And, if the maniacs, God forbid, found her, she did not want to be captured unclothed.

Linda tramped around the old schoolroom. The small room smelled of stale beer and cigarettes. But at least the musty old place was dry, and the roof wasn't leaking. She spotted two old torn window blinds lying on the floor. Her eyes lit up. She'd make a tent.

Dragging the rickety chairs away from the open door, Linda piled the lawn chairs in a small circle. She draped the blinds over the chairs. Satisfied that she was shielded from the draft from the door, Linda crawled under her makeshift tent and lay down on the dirty, old wooden floor.

She'd wait until the storm passed and then strike out across the field. She knew the monsters would be back looking for her. But she needed to warm up. Walking back out into the dark, rainy night was not an option. She could get hit by lightning or die of hypothermia. She'd rest here until the storm stopped. There was no danger of her falling asleep; the floor was hard. She curled up in the fetal position, hugging herself for warmth. Linda fell asleep.

Chapter Twenty-Five

The rain lashed down as Violet pulled into her driveway. She smiled. The car lights lit up her neat, cream-coloured house with its brown shutters. It was nice to visit her family, but it was also nice to be home. She enjoyed visiting with her daughter and grandchildren. But she was ready to kick her shoes off and enjoy some peace and quiet. City life was fine, but she'd take small-town living over it any day. Shutting off her car, she looked out the windshield at the pouring rain. There was nothing for it. She would have to make a mad dash through the rain to her house.

Violet, a tall, thin woman, was drenched when she reached the door. She shook her short, wet, red hair, fished in her purse for her keys, opened the door, and dropped her purse inside. She pulled her jacket over her head and sprinted back to her car to fetch her suitcase. Luggage in hand, Violet stepped into her house. Her coat was soaking wet. She rolled her eyes, shook the water droplets off her jacket, and draped it over the back of a chair. She should have waited for the morning to get her bag from her car.

Violet, obsessed with neatness and order, sorted through her clothes. Putting her dirty laundry into the laundry basket. She refolded her clean clothes and put them into drawers. Violet looked at her watch. It was late. She picked up her phone. Should she call Linda?

She'd called Linda before she left Calgary and again when she stopped for lunch. But Linda had not picked up. Her phone had gone to voice mail. This was not like her niece, Linda, always answered. Violet punched in Linda's number and got a *the person you have called is unavailable right now* message. "Linda, where the heck are you?" It had been two days since she'd heard from her. But then Linda might have gone off with friends somewhere and forgotten her phone. It was totally unlike her niece. But that was most likely what happened. Violet smiled; she was glad Linda had made new friends. And it was late, and she was tired. She'd try Linda in the morning.

LINDA MOANED; SOMETHING was poking her in the ribs. She rolled away, every part of her body protesting.

"Wake up, sleepyhead."

Linda's eyes flew open. Daylight shone through the open door. Richie's blond hair glowed like a halo. He stood over her, grinning his crooked grin. "Rise and shine. It's morning. The rain has stopped."

Her mouth fell open. Fear clawed at her throat. Linda could feel nothing but blind terror. Heart hammering in her chest, she struggled to sit upright.

"Here, I'll help you." Richie reached a hand down to Linda.

Linda shook off the grimy old canvas blinds. Shuddering, she crawled on her hands and knees, cowering beside the wall, putting her hands over her face.

"Don't be silly, Linda. You're just delaying the inevitable." Richie smiled. He hunched down beside her, sitting on his heels. "I do have to give it to you. You have put up a good fight, but it's over." He chuckled. "And lucky for me, you chose this old schoolhouse to hide in. I knew you couldn't get far. Not at your age and in that rainstorm. This was a no-brainer."

Linda scuttled away. Backing up to a wall near the door, she pushed herself up. Her legs shook. She was weak from cold, hunger, and fear. Linda wanted to run, but her legs wouldn't obey.

Richie rose and sauntered over to her. He put a hand under her elbow. "Come on, Linda, one foot in front of the other. I'll help you. It's not far."

Linda wanted to scream and beat her fists into his smiling face. But her arms hung limp, quivering, and her mouth was dry. She licked her lips. Tears dribbled down her cheeks. Richie put his other arm around her shoulders and helped her out the door. Outside, it was damp. A misty fog lay over the green countryside. Linda took a deep breath. Would this be the last time she'd see the sun as it began to break through the early morning mist? Her bare feet slipped on the wet, dew-covered grass, and she fell to her knees sobbing.

Richie smiled down at her and helped her to her feet. "Poor little Nosey. Crying won't help. I learned that lesson at my father's knee." He gave her shoulders a gentle squeeze. "You did put up a good fight. Remember that." He escorted her to the back of the schoolhouse, parked in the weeds, the silver motorhome. Richie opened the door of the campervan. "Come on, Linda, lift your foot; you can do it," he encouraged.

Trembling, Linda did as he said, grasping the side of the door to pull herself inside. She immediately felt the welcome warmth. The motorhome had a new car smell. Fake wood panels covered the walls. The driver and passenger's padded chairs were covered in white vinyl. A woman's bicycle lay on the floor behind the seats. Linda stumbled and sagged onto a padded bench at a little table across from the small kitchen counter.

"Be a good girl and sit still," Richie ordered. Picking up the bicycle, he opened the door and set the bike on the ground. Grinning, he stood in the doorway, dusting off his hands. "You have to hand it to Uncle Alfred. The old bird bought the best. Just look at this kitchen. It has everything: a stove and an under-the-counter fridge. This camper even has a little bathroom, complete with a shower. And look," Richie said with a wave of his hand. "Look there, hanging on the wall, a TV."

Dull-eyed, Linda watched Richie bound about the camper. He was so hyper. It was like he was a salesman pointing out to her the amenities of the campervan.

Richie's eyes danced. "This wall the TV is hanging on separates the bedroom from the living area. Well, the bedroom is really just a bed. Come have a look."

Linda looked numbly up at him. "Why?" she croaked.

"Aha, she speaks," chortled Richie. He grabbed her arm and propelled her toward the partition.

Linda hobbled weakly across the small space to the wall. She looked behind the wall and screamed.

Richie shrieked with laughter.

Lying on the bed was Faith's frozen corpse. Stretched out beside her was Alfred. Alfred's face was yellow. His eyes rolled back in his head, his mouth hung open, his chest heaving, his breath coming in ragged gulps.

Linda collapsed onto the floor, crawling away from the horror bed.

With a bounce in his stride, Richie strutted to the small kitchen counter. He leaned against it and folded his arms across his chest. He had a playful smile on his face as he sighed. "Good old ricin. It takes a while to die, as we found out with Aunt Faith. I could put the old guy out of his misery. And choke him like Aunt Faith. But he did remind me about handprints. And he's probably right. I can still see my handprints on your neck."

Backing up toward the driver's seat at the front of the campervan, Linda's hand went to her throat. "What have you done?" she cried.

"Oh, Nosey, you know darn well what I have done. Last night, during the storm, lightning hit something, and the power went out. Uncle Alfred went looking for candles. The candles I threw out. Anyway, he found my practice sheets. You know, the sheets of paper I was practicing signing his name on."

Richie's lips twitched. "You did tell me he would try to poison me, and you were right. I have to thank you for the warning." His smile widened as he looked down at her. "The old bird did come to the road to pick me up. And on the drive back to town, I tried to convince the old guy that it was Aunt Faith's writing. He let me believe that he believed me. But after, we carried Aunt Faith out to the motorhome. Uncle Alfred suggested we have a cup of tea. He made the tea and poured us each a cup." Richie guffawed. "But my dear old uncle was easy to distract. I switched cups, and there you have it."

Richie chuckled. "You should have seen his face when he figured out I changed cups. And it got even more hilarious when I helped the old boy into his wonderful dream home. And made him lie beside old Aunt Faith. I totally lost it." Giggling, Richie gasped for breath, shook his head and continued. "Now, the old bird is going to meet his dear wife on the other side of the great beyond. It will be hell for each of them, not as they will go to hell. Although they might. No, they made a living hell for each other while they were alive. I see no change now that soon they both will be dead."

"You're a monster," moaned Linda. "You killed your aunt and uncle. How could you do that?"

"I'm a monster?" Richie curled his lip. "Hey, Uncle Alfred started it. He poisoned Aunt Faith. I only helped her on her way. And he was going to poison me. He got what he deserved. And you. If you had minded your own business, you wouldn't be here either."

"You won't get away with this. I will be missed," Linda said in a trembling voice. She licked her dry lips and added, "As will your aunt and uncle. Your days are numbered."

"No, my dear little Nosey Linda. No one is going to miss anyone. It's simple. My aunt and uncle were going on a road trip. Everyone in town knows that. And you, you were getting the hell out of Glenhaven. You left a note. Of course, eventually, they will find where you crashed your car." He giggled. "Things just keep going my way."

"Yes, they will find the car. And they will look for me," Linda said, her hopes soaring.

"Yeah, probably. But they won't find you, not for a long time. And when they do, it will look like Uncle Alfred stopped and kidnapped you."

Hunched by the driver's seat, Linda shook her head.

Richie brushed a lock of blond hair off his forehead and smiled mockingly at Linda. "You look puzzled. Don't be. When the cops or whoever finds this campervan. Which, by the way, will be a long time from now." His blue eyes sparkled as he waved a hand toward the front of the RV. "Because just at the back of this property, there is a really deep ravine. I'm going to drive this RV to the edge of the ravine, put it in gear, and you all will go over the edge. Never to be seen." Richie smiled his trademark boyish smile and added. "Well, at least not for a long while. I trekked down there a few days ago. The gully is perfect. It's deep, and there are lots and lots of brush and trees in that ravine. It will be ages before anyone spots this camper. By then, Aunt Faith will be thawed out. Uncle Alfred will be dead. And so will you. The best part is." Richie giggled. "Even if they suspect foul play, they'll blame it on Uncle Alfred."

"Your plan won't work. Your poor aunt and uncle are lying on a bed," rasped Linda.

"Oh, it will work," bragged Richie. "I'm not going to leave them both in that bed. I'll drag old Uncle Alfred up and prop him in the driver's seat. But you know he doesn't even have to be in the seat. I'll leave him on the floor. It will look like he fell off the seat when the RV went over the edge. He's old. They will probably think he had a heart attack."

"Linda's stomach twisted with dread. This was how she was going to end her days. Trapped in this campervan with two dead people. And it was her own fault. If only she had ignored the voice. She hadn't saved

Faith. The poor woman was already dead. And she hadn't saved Alfred. Everything she did was pointless."

"And now, my dear little Nosey. I'm going to tie you up with plastic tie wraps. Again!" He looked at Linda with admiration. "You are like a Houdini." Richie took plastic ties from his back pocket. "But this time, you will stay put. Put your hands behind your back."

Linda, struggling to stand, pushed herself up to the driver's seat. The campervan key was in the ignition, but the door was her best bet. The door was open. If her shaky legs cooperated, she'd be free. If she could get to the door before Richie, she would lock him in the camper with his victims. The bike was outside. This might be her last and only chance to escape. Linda looked at him, then darted toward the door.

"Oh, Linda, you do make things difficult." Richie grabbed Linda and thrust her to the floor. "Well, not for me. But for you. I'd like to stay and chat, but I've got a long bike ride back to town." Twisting her hands behind her back, he zipped and tied her wrists. He looked at her feet. "And just to make sure your Houdini days are over. I have another tie for your feet." He grabbed her feet and fastened the plastic ties around her ankles. He rolled Linda over. Brushing a lock of his curly blond hair off his brow, he stood, looking down at her, smiling his big, wide, crooked smile.

Linda recalled her first meeting with the charismatic blond-haired boy. He'd bounded across the front lawn of his aunt and uncle's house, his friendly blue eyes twinkling. With his perfect manners, Richie greeted them with a happy, charming smile. What a fool she'd been. Richie was an evil psychopath. And now she was going to pay with her life for her foolishness.

"I don't think even you can unlock this camper door now that you are..." He paused as though he was searching for the right word. "Hum, what is the word I'm thinking of? Oh, yeah, I know, hogtied." Richie chuckled. "I'll leave you here to spend some quality time with my aunt and uncle."

"You will be found out. You will be punished!" Linda screamed, tears streaming down her cheeks.

Richie shook his head, smiling down at Linda. He took out a roll of duct tape from his jacket pocket, knelt and taped it over a struggling Linda's mouth. "You should be thankful I haven't taped over your nose too. But then maybe not. Dying of starvation probably isn't the most pleasant of deaths." He shrugged. "And it's not going to smell too pretty in here, is it? But remember, this is all your fault. You didn't have to be here. But you are. Because you are nosey. Oh well, it is what it is." Whistling A Beautiful Day in the Neighbourhood. Richie closed and locked the motorhome door.

Chapter Twenty-Six

Violet dried the last of her breakfast dishes. She shut the cupboard door and thought about her daughter's home in Calgary. Marylou's home was a sleek, modern, open-plan house. But Violet loved her cheerful kitchen with its yellow walls and white cupboards. She folded her tea towel and hung it on the towel rod. Her phone lay on the gray granite countertop, charging.

She grinned. Linda probably forgot to charge her phone. It was unlike Linda to forget. But it could happen. Violet tried Linda's phone again and got the same voice message as before. "Really, Linda, why don't you answer your phone?" she muttered. Violet dialled Mabel's landline. And waited, but again, no answer. She looked at the little green and yellow stuffed dinosaur she'd bought as a joke gift for Linda. She debated. Should she pop over to Mabel's place now or wait? Yes, her lawn needed mowing, and her flower beds needed tidying. No, to heck with her yard. Something might be amiss. Almost every day, Linda touched base by text or phone. And she hadn't heard from her since Saturday. Maybe Linda was sick. Violet picked up the gift bag and walked to Mabel's house to see what was what.

VIOLET KNOCKED ON THE door and tried the doorknob. The door was locked. "Linda," she called. "Are you home?" Violet waited, but there was no answer. She peeked in the kitchen window. No Linda. Was Linda sick? Was that why she didn't answer her phone or Mabel's landline? Violet picked up the Rider gnome, reached under, took out Mabel's house key, and unlocked the door. The kitchen was empty. "Linda, are you alright? Are you sick?" Violet tiptoed down the hallway toward the bedrooms. She screwed up her lips at the muddy sock footprints on the floor. Linda had to be sick to have left mud on the floor. Violet looked in the guest bedroom. The bed was made, and the bedroom light was on.

Violet frowned. It was morning. She shrugged, shut off the light, and poked her head into Mabel's room. She tiptoed around the muddy footprints and looked in the living room. There was no sign of her niece anywhere.

She circled back to the kitchen. Sitting on the table, a small plate with toast crumbs. Gertrude's feeding dishes were in the sink. What the heck? Where was Linda? Violet set the gift bag on the counter and folded her arms. The last time they talked, Linda said she was going to the town-wide garage sale. And Linda must have gone because a blue bud vase and a cat ornament were sitting on the kitchen table. It was an ornament she'd never seen before, and she was as familiar with Mabel's house as she was her own. So, Linda must have bought it.

When was that town-wide garage sale? A couple of days ago? Yes, the garage sale was on Friday. But it rained last night, and there was mud on the floor. Of course, it could have rained on the day of the garage sales. But why would Linda leave mud on the floor? And why was Gertrude's water and feeding bowl in the sink? Where was Gertrude? Violet went out to the back porch, stood on the back step, and called, "Kitty, kitty." She waited, no Gertrude. The cat was usually in the yard, stretched out on the railing, or perched on the back steps.

Violet spotted a coffee mug on the railing and picked up the cup. It was filled with water. She dumped the cup and set it back down. Rainwater? It rained last night. The coffee mug must have been left out there all day. Why? Of course, Linda might have just forgotten about it. But where was Linda? Where did she go? And Linda always had her phone with her. So why didn't she answer it? Something wasn't right.

At the bottom of the porch steps, empty plant pots sprawled across the lawn. Violet couldn't abide anything untidy. She shook her head and strode down the stairs. A flip-flop lay beside the pots. Violet picked up the pots, piling them neatly against the wall. She looked around, only one sandal. Where was the other one? Violet shrugged. She guessed it didn't matter. What mattered was where Linda was. Was Gertrude lost, and was Linda out looking for the errant cat? Should she phone Mabel to see if she heard from Linda? Or was she getting worried about nothing? Linda probably went somewhere.

Violet's eyes grew thoughtful. But that somewhere had to be where there was no cell phone coverage. When did Linda leave? There was a plate with toast crumbs but no sign of lunch or supper dishes. So, did Linda leave in the morning? But the bedroom light was on. Violet pressed her lips together. It couldn't have been this morning. It wasn't coffee in the cup. It was rainwater. So when? Obviously, after the garage sale, the ornaments were on the kitchen table.

Violet rubbed her forehead and closed her eyes, remembering their conversation. Linda had said she'd overheard somebody talking about hiding a body. Or was it where to hide the body? She couldn't remember Linda's exact words, but it was something weird like that. And Linda thought it was a neighbour or someone in the neighbourhood.

She took out her phone, looking at the last text Linda had sent her. Violet read, *'Hope you are having fun.'* An icon with fingers crossed. *'I may have a lead.'*

Okay, so Linda had a lead. A lead on what? Or who? Violet jammed her phone back into her pocket. Linda said she was going garage sale shopping mainly to look for clues. Linda was going to be on the lookout for someone missing. The text was sent on Saturday morning. So, was it at the garage sale where she picked up the lead?

Violet shook her head and clenched her jaw. What had Linda gotten herself mixed up in?

Violet hurried down the sidewalk to the street. She thought of Coffee Row. Coffee Row was a group of citizens from the town of Glenhaven. They gathered each morning for coffee at Pam & Ally's café. The seniors were like the village bulletin board. They always seemed to know what was happening in their town. Last summer, she took her niece there when she was visiting. Yes, she'd go to Coffee Row. Someone there might know where Linda was.

"Hi," greeted a friendly voice. It was her friend Fred Granger, walking his little dog Poky. The sandy-haired man grinned. He tugged on the leash as the little white terrier tried to run up to a leafy green shrub in Mabel's front yard.

"Hi, Fred. Have you seen Linda around?"

"Linda? I'm afraid I don't know who that is. Is she new in town?"

"No, Linda is my niece; she is house-sitting for Mabel. Linda's a slim woman about five feet tall. She has red hair and a freckled face."

"No, sorry, I haven't seen her."

Violet furrowed her forehead. "As I said, she's house-sitting for Mabel. I was just there. Linda is not home. And she is not answering her cell phone. I'm kind of worried about her."

Gertrude, meowing, appeared from behind the shrub. Poky backed up, barking. Gertrude ignored the little white terrier and scurried over to Violet, rubbing her furry body against her leg.

"There you are." Violet smiled as she picked up the orange tabby cat. Gertrude purred loudly, rubbing her head against Violet's chin as Poky continued to bark madly.

"Hi, guys. Great morning," greeted a blond-haired man. He was riding a woman's bike. He stopped and put his feet on either side of the bike. Resting his forearms on the handlebars. A blue nylon jacket was balled up in the bicycle basket. He wiped his sweaty brow with the back of his hand, damp patches on his T-shirt. "I've been out in the country for a morning bike ride. I guess I'm a little out of shape." He chuckled, smiling sheepishly. "Great morning for a ride. Nice and sunny. That was quite the rain we had last night."

"I haven't looked at my rain gauge, but I bet we had two or three inches," replied Fred.

Gertrude leaped out of Violet's arms, hissing and spitting, her hair standing on end. The cat arched its back, crouched. Then sped off across the street and down the sidewalk, disappearing into a yard.

Fred grinned. "Gertrude and Poky don't always seem to get along." Poky, wagging his tail, yapped.

The young man, smiling a big, broad, crooked smile, laughed. "Cats and dogs. They are like oil and water. They just don't mix." He flicked a lock of blond hair off his sweaty forehead.

Violet liked the sound of the friendly young man's good-natured laughter.

"This nice young man is Richie Hutchins," introduced Fred. "He's Alfred and Faith's nephew. He came out here all the way from Toronto. And this lovely lady is my good friend, Violet Ficher."

"Nice to meet you." Richie's eyes narrowed, and he arched his eyebrows. Then, he smiled a crooked grin and took Violet's hand, giving her hand a gentle shake.

"And nice to meet you," Violet said. "Are you staying long?"

"I'm just visiting. I've been helping my aunt and uncle get ready." He gave her a winsome smile.

"Ready for what?" Violet asked. She liked his smile. Maybe they could convince him to stick around. He was a gentleman. Not many young people shook hands anymore.

"Get ready to move. I helped my aunt and uncle with their two-day garage sale. They got rid of a bunch of stuff and sold a lot of their furniture." He turned to Fred. "You and your buddy moved Aunt Faith's old four-poster bed and wardrobe."

"Yep, that was heavy stuff. Me and Hank delivered the furniture to Mary's bed-and-breakfast." Fred tugged on Poky's leash. The little dog was attempting to follow Gertrude across the street.

"Alfred and Faith are moving?"

"Yep, Aunt Faith and Uncle Alfred are selling their house and moving. And when I say moving, I mean really moving. They bought a motorhome. They are going to travel across Canada and winter in Texas."

"Wow." Violet shook her head and smiled. "They really are pulling up stakes. I'll have to stop by before your aunt and uncle leave and say goodbye."

"Oh, sorry, they already left. But I'm staying on for a while. Uncle Alfred doesn't want to go through an agency. So, I'm going to get the house ready for sale. And hopefully, sell it for them."

"It's nice they can spend this time together travelling and doing what they like," Fred said.

Richie's blue eyes gleamed. "Yep. Uncle Alfred and Aunt Faith are spending quality time together." Grinning, he said, "They deserve everything that's coming to them." Using his forearm, he wiped his sweaty forehead.

"I can't help but notice that you have some really deep scratches on your arm. They look suspicious."

"Pardon me?" Richie gave Violet a worried look.

"Those scratches look nasty. You'd better get them looked at. They could be infected," advised Violet.

Richie grinned sheepishly. "Nah, it's nothing. I was helping Uncle Alfred move some stuff, and I scratched myself on something. It looks worse than it is."

"Those scratches look deep, and your arm looks a little puffy. At least get some antibiotic cream for them."

Richie looked at the angry-looking scratches on his arm. "Yeah, thanks, I will."

"You mentioned your aunt and uncle had a garage sale. Did you happen to see my niece, Linda?" Violet asked, giving him the same description of Linda as she'd given to Fred.

Richie gave her a lopsided smile and shrugged. "Sorry, I don't know. I could have. But I couldn't say for sure. We had such a good turnout. Uncle Alfred said half the town came."

Chapter Twenty-Seven

Violet paused in the doorway of Pam & Ally's café. The café's décor was from the seventies, with two rows of dark green Formica tables and matching chairs set in the middle of the café. A row of booths lined one wall, with two more tables set up by the front windows. Violet's friends were sitting at the tables by the windows. The men sat at one table, and the women sat at another. It wasn't a rule, but it seemed to work out that way. Today, only five seniors were sitting at the tables. Violet poured herself a cup of coffee and dropped a toonie into a dish beside the coffeepot. Coffee in the morning at the café operated on the honour system. And if the pot ran dry, the patrons made more.

Helen Graham, Mary Woodhouse, and Alice Woodstock sat at the women's table. Mary's husband, Alvin, and Helen's husband, Mike, were at the men's table.

Mary, the friendly, plump-faced woman with salt-and-pepper hair, moved her chair to make room for Violet.

"Good morning, everyone," Violet said.

The women answered with good mornings of their own.

With a smug knowing look, Alice asked, "Did any of you hear about the Carberry's dog?"

Violet, lifting her coffee mug to take a sip, replied, "No, what about their dog?"

Alice, the tiny bird-like woman with frizzy orange hair, liked to be the first with any news, good or bad. She was the town gossip. And not everything Alice said could be taken at face value.

Alice pursed her lips and said, "Someone poisoned their dog."

A chair from the next table screeched on the linoleum floor as Alvin turned to face the women. The plump man asked, "Poisoned? Are you sure?"

"Yes, of course I am." Alice lifted her chin. "I heard that the Vet said the dog was poisoned."

"Heard? You're probably full of hot air," scoffed Alvin.

"I am not."

"Alvin, don't be rude," scolded his wife. Alvin shrugged.

Violet set her cup down and drummed her fingers on her coffee mug. Sad as it might be, she wasn't interested in the Carberry's dog.

"That dog was a brute," snorted Mike. The sloped-shouldered man added, "The dog probably died from meanness."

"That's a silly thing to say." Helen, a fidgety woman with tightly permed iron-gray hair, shook her head.

Mike shrugged his round shoulders. "Sorry, dear, but that dog was a mean-tempered dog."

"Brute or not, someone poisoned him," snapped Alice.

"Let's talk about something else," intervened Mary. "Welcome home, Violet. Did you have a nice holiday visiting your daughter and grandchildren?"

"Yes, I did. I enjoyed it very much. It's nice to go, but nice to come home again, too," Violet said, sipping her coffee.

"Where's Mabel? You two are almost joined at the hip. Did you have a falling out?" asked Alice. Her eyes flashed in anticipation.

Helen's brow wrinkled. "Alice, why would you say such a thing? Mabel and Violet are best friends. You should mind what you say."

Alice shrugged and picked up her coffee mug. "I'm just asking."

"No, Alice, we haven't had a falling out. Mabel is still in Calgary."

"Who's feeding her cat?" asked Helen. "Wanda?"

"No, my niece Linda. She's house-sitting for Mabel. You met her last summer when she was visiting me."

"Oh, yes, nice girl." Helen nodded.

"I got home last night. And I popped over to see her this morning. But she's not home. Have any of you seen her?"

The women shook their heads. "Mike, have you seen Linda today?" asked Helen.

"Linda?"

"Linda, remember, she is Violet's niece. She's that friendly little freckle-faced redhead girl. You met her last summer."

"Oh yeah, but nope, I haven't seen her. Why? Is she missing in action?" Mike chuckled, and Alvin joined in.

"The last time I saw Linda was when we went garage sale shopping," Mary said.

"Was it raining the day of the garage sale? Or was it a nice day?" Violet asked. "I hope you had a good day for it."

"It was a beautiful day, and Linda and I did very well. I do like it when Glenhaven has a town-wide one. So many bargains."

Chuckling, Alvin leaned back in his chair and winked at Mike. "Junk more like," he said.

"Alvin, you know that's not true. I got that wonderful four-poster bed and that lovely walnut wardrobe." Mary smiled. "Antique and in perfect shape. Well, the armoire had a small chip on the door. Still, it was a real bargain."

"Yeah, if you ask me, you paid enough. Not such a bargain."

Mary turned to the women at her table. "Don't pay attention to Alvin. When he opens his wallet, moths fly out." The women giggled.

Alvin shrugged and rolled his eyes, grinning. "Someone in the family has to hold the purse strings."

Mary smiled at him and shook her head.

"Where did you pick that up? Imagine finding antique furniture," marvelled Helen.

"It was at Hutchins' garage sale. They were selling everything."

Alice leaned forward, her arms on the table. "The Hutchins are moving. Selling out. I heard they bought a big motorhome. And they're going to live on the road. If you ask me, it's pure foolishness." She chortled. "Those two will soon tire of being cramped up in that motorhome. They're always bickering. It will be hell on wheels if you ask me."

Violet raised her eyebrows. Alice always thought the worst. Ignoring Alice, Violet turned to Mary and asked, "Was Linda with you all day?"

"Most of the day. Linda and I had a great time looking for deals. She was with me when I bought the bedroom suite at the Hutchins. I remember she bought bedding plants. I think it foolish of Faith to start all those bedding plants. It makes me wonder if she is as keen as Alfred on this lifestyle change."

Violet's thoughts returned to the stack of pots at Mabel's house. "Did you ask Faith why she started those plants?"

"No, we didn't see her. Alfred took us up to see the bedroom furniture. Richie, Alfred's nephew, was going to, but Alfred took charge." Mary giggled. "It was probably the first time Alfred ever took charge of anything. Faith wears the pants in that family."

Violet suddenly thought of Linda's car. "Did Linda drive her car?" she asked.

"No, I took mine, and it's a good thing, too. I bought way more stuff than Linda. But we had fun."

"So, the last time you saw Linda was the garage sale day?"

"Yes, it was. Why?"

"I'm a little worried about her. She wasn't at Mabel's this morning, and she's not answering her phone."

"I'm sure everything is fine. Linda is a grown woman. And she's here in Glenhaven. What on earth could happen to her here? You know, maybe Mabel's mother knows. You could ask her," suggested Mary.

VIOLET HURRIED DOWN the sidewalk; she waved to a friend coming down the post office steps. But Violet didn't stop to visit. She was probably worrying about nothing, but it wouldn't hurt to phone Sophie. She knew Linda had taken a fancy to Mabel's feisty little mother. Mary could be right. Sophie might know where Linda was. She punched in Sophie's number.

"Hello, who is this?" Sophie's brittle voice crackled.

"Hi, Sophie, it's me, Violet."

"Oh, are you and Mabel back home? Mabel hasn't called me. But I'm always the last one to hear from her."

Violet resisted the urge to sigh aloud. Sophie liked to play the martyr. Not only was Mabel a good daughter. She catered to her mother. "No, Mabel is still in Calgary."

"I tried phoning Mabel. But of course, her blame phone was off. I don't know why she even has one if she's going to shut it off. At least on a landline, you don't shut it off," complained Sophie.

Violet continued at a brisk pace down the sidewalk. She could sympathize with Mabel's mother. Mabel was notorious for shutting her phone off, but Linda wasn't.

"I did talk to my granddaughter Melina. She's going to get Mabel in to see an orthopedic surgeon." Sophie chuckled. "Melina said her mother wasn't happy about that. Mabel can be so stubborn. She must have got that from her father."

Violet grinned. She wanted to say no. She got it from you. But instead said, "That's why I'm home, and Mabel isn't."

"Oh yes, of course. By the way, when you talk to that niece of yours. Tell her I've got a bone to pick with her."

Violet slowed her steps as she approached Mabel's house. "Why?"

"Well, Mabel told me Linda would take me to bingo. And she didn't. I waited and waited, and she didn't show up. I even phoned her cell phone. And, like Mabel, the girl must have had it off. So, I phoned the house. And she wasn't there. That girl was off- gadding about and not thinking about me. I can tell you I was quite upset. But then I thought of Sandra, a friend of mine. I knew Sandra was going to bingo, so I got a ride with her. But really, when you agree to something, you should follow through. Or at least she should have the good manners to let me know if she wasn't taking me to bingo. And to top it off. Linda has never phoned to apologize."

Violet stood still, biting her bottom lip. Linda was not like that. She was a very kind and considerate person. Why had Linda stood-up Mabel's mother? "I'm sorry, Sophie. I'll tell her when I see her. When was bingo?"

"Saturday."

"Right."

"I have to go, Violet. My oven timer is beeping. My cookies are ready to come out of the oven."

"Sure, no problem." Violet ended the call and put her phone in her pocket. She stopped and stared. Nothing made sense. Parked in front of Mabel's house was Linda's Volkswagen Jetta. Had the car been there this morning? Or had Linda come home?

Violet sped up the sidewalk and entered the kitchen without knocking. "Linda?" There was no answer. She called again, and again there was no answer. Linda was not in the house. Violet leaned against the kitchen counter, closed her eyes, and pinched the bridge of her nose. How on earth did she not spot Linda's car this morning? "Stupid, stupid," Violet muttered, sagging onto a kitchen chair.

Shoulders slumped and brow furrowed, Violet despondently picked up the blue vase, turning it in her hand. She sighed, set the vase back on the table, and ran a finger over the orange ceramic cat. A piece of notepaper was sticking out from under the cat ornament. She pulled out the note and unfolded it. Unnoticed by Violet, her arm brushed another sheet of paper; the paper fluttered to the floor and floated under the table. Violet's eyes widened in puzzlement as she read. 'Sorry I have to leave. I'm bored. I can't take this hick town one day longer.' Linda had signed the note with her full name.

Shaking her head, Violet stared at the note. So, on the spur of the moment, Linda decided to leave. But how? Her car was still parked in front of Mabel's house. And why leave a note? Why didn't she call Mabel to let her know she was leaving town? Violet bit her bottom lip and rubbed her forehead. She'd stopped by Mabel's daughters to say goodbye, and Mabel didn't say anything about Linda leaving. Of course, Linda might have tried to phone Mabel. Mabel probably didn't have her phone on.

Violet picked up the note and reread it. 'I can't take this hick town one day longer.' She thought Linda loved Glenhaven. Linda even talked about moving to the little town. Violet slumped back in the chair. Nothing made sense. Linda went to the garage sales on Friday. But missed the bingo appointment on Saturday. And then, all of a sudden, she got bored and took off out of town. And without her car?

And what about the dried-up muddy footprints on the floor? And they were not just footprints. They were muddy sock footprints. The rainstorm was last night. Who else but Linda would be in Mabel's house to leave those tracks? The house was locked. So where had Linda been to get her socks covered in mud? And why socks? And not shoes? And the note. It was odd that Linda signed it with her full name. What the heck was going on? The niece she knew would never leave Gertrude on her own. Unless she asked Wanda next door to look after the cat? Maybe Wanda knew what was going on?

Chapter Twenty-Eight

Violet tapped on Wanda's door and waited. Was she being a Nervous Nelly? Linda was a grown woman. She wasn't some teenager who had run away.

Wanda, a stout, attractive woman, opened the door. Leaning a mop handle against the doorjamb, she wiped her hands on her jeans. "Hi, Violet. You've caught me mopping my floor," she said.

"Oh, sorry." Violet pasted a cheerful smile on her face and asked, "I just wanted to know if Linda said where she was going?"

"Going?"

"Did Linda mention where she was going?" Violet asked, trying to sound nonchalant.

"I didn't know Linda was going anywhere. Isn't she home? I mean at Mabel's. I thought Linda was house-sitting.

"She is, or she was. Linda isn't at Mabel's. Did she ask you to check on Gertrude?"

"Nope. I would have if Linda asked. I don't mind. Gertrude and I are good buds. I sometimes look after her for Mabel. When did Linda leave? Did she go home?"

"I don't think so." Violet furrowed her brow. "No, I'm sure she didn't go home. And you haven't seen her around?"

"No, the last time I saw Linda was the morning of the town-wide garage sale."

"Not since then?"

"No, I haven't seen Linda, just Gertrude. She's been in and out of my yard these past two days. I don't mind. As I say, we are buds. She keeps the mice away."

"Oh, oh, okay. Thanks," Violet stuttered. "I'll let you get back to your mopping."

"No problem. And hey, when you catch up with Linda, bring her over for coffee. I think she is thinking of moving. I want to extol the virtues of Glenhaven."

"Yes, I will," Violet said. She stood for a moment, staring at the closed door. No one had seen Linda since Friday.

Violet strode back to Mabel's yard, her eyes thoughtful. Of course, most people in Glenhaven wouldn't know Linda. But Coffee Row knew Linda, and they hadn't seen her.

"Oh, dear. Gertrude, you've been up to your old tricks." The plastic plant pots had fallen on the ground. "Kitty, kitty," Violet called. She gathered up the pots, carrying them to the garage. She opened the small side door of the garage and dropped the pots. Mabel's car was gone. Violet blinked. She stood staring at the empty garage. Why would Linda take Mabel's old Pontiac and leave her Volkswagen Jetta?

Gertrude circled her ankles, meowing. Violet closed the garage door and followed the cat up the porch steps to the house. Gertrude beat her to the door. Violet stood inside the door, staring into space. What the heck was going on? Gertrude, meowing pitifully, brought her back with a start. She took Gertrude's cat dishes from the sink. Poured water into the empty bowl and dumped dry cat food into another. Violet pressed her lips, worry gnawing at her insides. Her mind churned as she watched the cat gobbling the food. Gertrude was sure hungry. Why would Linda go away and leave Mabel's pet to fend for itself? Violet pursed her lips. She had no answers.

Sighing, Violet spied Linda's dirty socks rolled up into a ball. "Oh, Linda, where the heck are you?" she asked, picking the dirty socks off the floor. She stepped around Gertrude, chowing down on the dry cat food. "You keep eating, Gertrude. I'll just put these dirty socks in the laundry hamper. Then I'll look for some wet cat food for you. And figure out what the heck is going on."

Violet's forehead furrowed. She followed the dried footprints to the bathroom. Towels and clothes were strewn across the bathroom floor. Tisking, Violet picked up the dirty clothes and put everything in the hamper. She turned to the sink to wash her hands and froze. Unmindful of her dirty hands, she covered her mouth. Her stomach dropped, and cold sweat crept over her body.

She read the toothpaste message written on the mirror. Faith Deepfreeze Alfred Richie and a scrawly word slanted downward. Another name? Did it say Hutchan? The name Hutchan was followed by another letter, An 'h' or maybe an 'e.' Then, a round blob with a tail. An empty toothpaste tube lay in the sink.

Shaking, Violet grasped hold of the sink. "Linda, Linda, what have you gotten yourself into?" She took her phone from her pocket and punched in the RCMP number. What was Linda drawing, and more importantly, why?

Chapter Twenty-Nine

Violet stood on the front steps of Mabel's house. Her stomach was churning. Where were the police? She looked at her watch. Okay, it hadn't been that long since she phoned. But where were they? She clasped her hands.

Relief coursed through her veins. An RCMP car pulled up and parked in front of the house. A tall, broad-shouldered RCMP officer climbed out of the cruiser.

Violet rushed down the steps to greet the officer. "Thank you for coming," she said.

"You have a missing person to report?" the young officer asked.

"Yes, I do. Please come into the house."

The officer followed Violet up the front steps into Mabel's house. "I'm Constable Gatineau," he said, taking a notepad from his pocket.

Violet detected a French accent. "Please come into the kitchen. Or maybe I should show you the bathroom."

"The bathroom?"

"Yes, that's where Linda left the message. That's why I called you. Oh, sorry, my name is Violet Ficher. It's my niece, Linda Burton, who is missing. Please come with me." Violet hurried down the hallway. "In here, look at the mirror." Violet stepped back from the door, allowing the tall officer to enter the bathroom.

Using his phone, the constable took pictures of the toothpaste message on the mirror. He put the phone in his pocket and turned back to Violet. "What do these names mean to you?"

"I'm not sure, but the names written in toothpaste are very disturbing. Something is wrong."

"Does Linda have dementia? Or Alzheimer's?"

"Linda does not have dementia of any kind," Violet said hotly. "She is missing. Please come to the kitchen, and oh, mind the muddy footprints. They could be evidence."

Constable Gatineau raised his eyebrows, stepped around the footprints, and followed Violet to the kitchen.

"Please sit down." Violet pulled out a chair for him.

"Why do you think your friend Linda Burton is missing?"

"She's not my friend. She is my niece. And she is missing."

The constable sat, his eyes watching Violet as she sat across from him. "How long has Linda been missing?"

"I don't know?"

"You don't know?"

"No. I don't know for sure how long Linda has been missing. I can make a guess."

"I see. A guess." He made a notation in his notebook.

"Well, yes. I think the last time anyone saw Linda was the day of the town-wide garage sale."

"When was that?"

"It was Friday. And I know she went because of the blue vase and the cat ornament."

"Blue vase and cat ornament?"

"Well, they aren't Mabel's. I'd never seen them before."

"Right." The constable puckered his forehead.

"This is Mabel's house. And I know her house as well as my own. The vase and cat ornament are not Mabel's."

"You keep saying Mabel, but you said Linda Burton is the missing person."

"Yes, Linda is missing. I'm very worried."

Constable Gatineau scrutinized Violet. "Right. So, your niece Linda lives with Mabel."

"No, my friend Mabel Havelock is in Calgary."

The constable tapped his notepad with his pen. "Linda Burton lives in Mabel Havelock's house, who lives in Calgary."

"No." Violet closed her eyes, took a deep breath, exhaled, and opened her eyes. "Linda is house-sitting for Mabel, who has a broken foot and is visiting her daughter in Calgary. I was in Calgary, too. I came home last night."

"Okay," he said, nodding his head. "What do the blue vase and the cat ornament have to do with Linda Burton's disappearance?"

"I don't know. Except. I talked to Linda on Friday morning. And she said she was going to the garage sales. And this vase and the cat indicate that she did."

"You talked to her but didn't see her?"

"No, I was in Calgary visiting my daughter."

"Where Mabel is."

"Yes, I told you Mabel has a broken foot." Violet blew out a long breath.

"Yes, you did."

"So, she couldn't drive, I did."

"Right." The constable's eyebrows arched again. "Back to your missing niece."

"Yes, good idea. I don't know why you keep asking about Mabel and Calgary?"

Constable Gatineau's lips formed a thin line. He looked up at the ceiling, then back at Violet. "The thing is, you were not here. And you don't know when your friend, sorry, your niece, went missing."

"That's true, but the thing is. Linda is missing."

"I understand you are worried."

"Worried? That's an understatement. Just look at this silly note Linda left." Violet picked up the note, waving it.

The constable's eyes narrowed as he took the note and read it. "Mrs. Ficher, this note is very clear. Your niece just got tired of this town. She called it a hick town. I believe that is a derogatory term. Why are you worried?"

"For God's sake. Look at the muddy sock prints. And the kicker, the toothpaste message on the mirror."

"And what does that message mean to you?"

"I told you, I'm not sure. I don't know what it means?"

"Who are these people written in toothpaste?"

"There, you have it written in toothpaste!"

"Yes?"

"No one writes in toothpaste."

"Perhaps a joke?"

"Seriously, who is Linda pulling this prank on? No. She wrote the note because it was the only thing she could lay her hands on. And, writing it on the bathroom mirror means to me that she was hiding from someone."

"Is there any sign of a disturbance?"

"No."

"Besides the toothpaste names on the mirror. Is there any other reason why you think Linda is missing?"

"For one thing, she didn't take Sophie, Mabel's Mother, to bingo."

Constable Gatineau's eyebrows flew up again, and he stared at Violet.

Violet took a deep breath. She could see why he dismissed the bingo. He didn't know Linda. But she had to make him listen. They had to find Linda. "And Linda left Gertrude alone, and she said she had a lead. And the muddy prints. And well, you saw the mirror."

"She left Gertrude. I want to speak to her. Where is she?"

"Over by the counter eating."

The constable looked at Gertrude and then at Violet. Sighed and said, "Okay, Linda left her cat, and there are muddy footprints on the floor. This does not leave me to believe we have a missing person." He tapped his closed notebook with his pen.

"Gertrude isn't Linda's cat."

The constable eyed Violet. "Let me guess. The cat is Mabel's."

"Yes, but Linda wouldn't leave Gertrude to fend for herself. That is not like Linda. And she would not leave mud on the floor. Furthermore, it's just not mud. They are muddy footprints. Muddy sock prints and those footprints lead to the bathroom, where you saw that message written on the mirror." Violet, chin high, her eyes flashing in anger, sat back in her chair, her arms folded across her chest.

"I think you are worried needlessly. Your niece Linda left a note telling you, or this Mabel, she was leaving."

"Linda told me she loves Glenhaven. In the note, she calls it a hick town. Why the sudden change? And why did she leave so suddenly?"

"People say what they think other people want to hear. It's your town. She didn't want to insult you. She was house-sitting and found out she didn't love this town. You read the note. She wrote she was bored."

Violet sighed. That could be true. "But Linda signed it with her full signature. That was weird."

"Force of habit?"

"Maybe."

Constable Gatineau sighed. "Mrs. Ficher, did you look to see if she packed a bag?"

"No."

"Would you know from looking in her closet if she did?"

"Yes, I would."

"Then please go and have a look. You can rest your mind if your niece has packed her suitcase."

As Violet hurried down the hallway to Linda's bedroom, the constable checked his phone for messages.

Violet returned; her forehead was creased. "The dresser drawers are empty, and Linda's suitcase is gone."

"There, all is well. You have nothing to worry about. Your niece Linda isn't missing. She went home."

"No, she didn't," protested Violet. "I've phoned her cell, time and time again. She never answers. If Linda were home, she would answer. And Linda always has her phone on. And..." Violet tapped her lips with a finger. "And what about the message on the mirror?"

Constable Gatineau rose from his chair. "I'm sorry you are worried. But —"

"No, wait, the day before the garage sales, Linda told me she overheard someone, a man, and this man said he had to hide a body."

The constable, raising his eyebrows, sat. He rubbed his forehead and said in a stern voice, "You should have told me this at the outset."

"Yes, sorry, I should have. I'm so worried. I can't think straight."

"Never mind. Tell me about this conversation regarding hiding a body." He opened his notebook.

"Yes, of course. In the back alley, Linda overheard a man say it was hard to hide a body." Violet's eyes widened as her voice rose. "What if that man was in the house?" Violet pounded the table with her fist. "Yes, that's why Linda wrote down the names on the mirror in toothpaste. She had to do it secretly."

"In secret."

"Yes, of course, so he wouldn't know she knew," Violet said, bubbling excitedly.

"Knew what?"

"I don't know." Violet shrugged her shoulders, then slapped the table with her hand again. "The body, or bodies. Where he hid them."

The constable flipped through messages on his phone. "A body or bodies?"

Violet squeezed her eyes shut, opened them, and said, "It was something about hiding a body or bodies."

"We've received a complaint about a poisoned dog."

"Yes, Alice told me there was a dog poisoned."

"Alice?"

"Alice from Coffee Row. She said a dog had been poisoned."

The constable looked down at his notepad and pinched the bridge of his nose.

Violet's eyes flickered with excitement. "The letters under those names! Maybe the man Linda heard talking was talking about hiding a dog's body. A dog he poisoned. Linda was trying to spell out the names of the dogs. And she ran out of toothpaste. So, Linda made that little blob with the tail. Linda was a kindergarten teacher. Maybe that's how she draws dogs?"

The RCMP officer rolled his eyes. "I'm not going to ask about Alice or Coffee Row. Or the kindergarten teaching. Back to the message. Linda wrote the word deep freezer along with the names." He looked at his phone and read. "Faith, Alfred, Richie, and someone called Hutchan?"

"I think Linda misspelled Hutchan. The name is Hutchins. And the people's names she wrote on the mirror are Faith and Alfred Hutchins, and Richie is their nephew." Violet leaned across the table and grabbed the constable's hand. "Now, you believe me."

Constable Gatineau, looking uncomfortable, removed his hand from Violet's grasp.

Undeterred, Violet continued, "Maybe more dogs have been poisoned, and Linda found out who is doing it. Namely Faith, Alfred, and Richie Hutchins. And they are hiding their dastardly deeds. The poor dead dogs are in their deep freezer."

"You are jumping to conclusions."

"But what if they have done something to Linda?"

"There is no reason to suspect the Hutchins or anyone else of harming your niece. Or committing a crime."

"Please. Couldn't you go and take a look? Linda might be there."

The constable was quiet. He closed his eyes, opened them, shrugged his big shoulders, and said, "It's a long shot. But I'll check these people out. Where do Faith, Alfred, and Richie live?" he asked.

"Faith and Alfred have left town. But Richie is here. Maybe he's the dog poisoner. I'll take you." Violet jumped up and rushed to the door.

"No. You will stay here. I'll let you know what I find. Just give me the address, please."

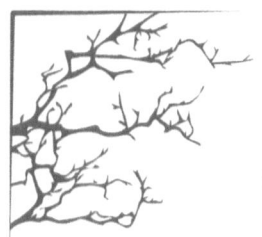

Chapter Thirty

Constable Gatineau parked his cruiser by the curb. He looked at the Hutchins' two-story house. A sign *'For sale by owner'* was on the front lawn. He hesitated for a moment before putting his hand on the door handle. He doubted these people had anything to do with Linda Burton leaving town. The note was blunt. She was tired of Glenhaven, packed her bag, and went home. And for some reason, she was ignoring her aunt's calls. Perhaps some misunderstanding between them. His concern was the report of a poisoned dog. The message on the mirror could be referring to the Hutchins. And then again, it could just be some prank message the girl put on the mirror before she left. But maybe it was a message about dogs. He had to investigate. This was a long shot. But on the off chance that the lady was right, these people might have hurt or killed dogs. In his opinion, anyone hurting an animal could also harm a person. He opened the car door. It wouldn't hurt to do a little investigating.

The tall, broad-shouldered officer climbed the steps and knocked on the door. He waited, knocked again, and said, "RCMP."

A tall, blond-haired man opened the door. The young man smiled lopsidedly and said, "Sorry, I was in the kitchen washing dishes." A tea towel hung down from his shoulder.

"I'd like to have a look around your house."

"Is there a problem, officer?"

"I saw the for-sale sign and thought I'd have a look."

"Oh, it's not my house. It's Uncle Alfred and Aunt Faith's. I'm their nephew Richie Hutchins." He stretched out his hand.

The constable shook it. "I'm Constable Gatineau. As I said, I'd like to look around. Are your aunt and uncle home?"

"No, sorry. They left on a road trip." Richie grinned. "My aunt and uncle bought a big motorhome and have decided to tour Canada and the USA." He laughed good-naturedly. "Not a midlife crisis, more of I'm retired, and I want to take it easy." Richie stepped into the doorway and shrugged. "I'm not sure driving a motorhome across Canada is easy. But that's what they want, so why not?"

Constable Gatineau stepped forward. "So, they left you in charge of selling their home."

Richie backed up a step and giggled. "Yeah, I don't mind. It makes me happy to think of those two together in that camper." The corners of Richie's eyes crinkled. "The camper is a dream for Uncle Alfred, oh and, of course, Aunt Faith. They deserve it. Neither one is getting any younger." He chuckled again. "Time is running out for those two."

The constable frowned. "So, can I come in and have a look around?"

"Oh, yeah, sure, sorry. Come on in. We sold most of the furniture before Uncle Alfred and Aunt Faith left, so the place has a hollow feel. Are you posted here?"

Constable Gatineau followed Richie into the hallway. "Yes, in Kipling."

"And you want to live in Glenhaven?"

"I just want to see what the options are."

"Okay, sure. Where do you want to start?"

"Why not upstairs? We can work our way down."

"Yeah, sure, follow me."

The constable followed Richie up the stairs. Richie opened a bedroom door. The room was empty. "Nice size room," commented Constable Gatineau.

"It was their bedroom. The main suite, I guess you could say. The windowsill is on my to-do list. A little bit of paint has chipped off the sill. They used to have a dog." Richie smiled a crooked smile and closed the door. "But not anymore."

"What happened to the dog?" asked the constable.

"Oh, it was an old dog. We had to put it down."

"That's too bad. When was that?"

Richie frowned. "A while ago. Here is another bedroom." He opened the door.

Constable Gatineau saw a small bed that looked like it had recently been slept in, on a chair, an open suitcase, clothes spilling out of it.

"This is where I sleep. As you can see, I'm not as neat as I should be." Richie flashed the constable a sheepish smile. "But I guess I'd better get neater if I'm going to show this house."

The next bedroom also had a small bed, but this bed had been stripped of bedclothes.

"Do you want to look around downstairs? I'm afraid there is only one bathroom. It's kind of quaint. There is an old-fashioned claw-foot tub."

Constable Gatineau opened the door and took a look. "Yeah, quaint." He looked down the hallway and saw a small folding ladder. "Where does that go?" he asked.

"The attic, but not much to see up there except junk."

"Why don't we have a look, anyway?"

"Yeah, sure, if you want."

The constable mounted the narrow wooden steps and opened the small door. He ducked his head and went in. The attic was full of old junk, just like the young man said. "You have squirrels," commented the big officer. "They've made quite a hole."

"Yeah, it was a nasty little thing. But I took care of it. The crafty little devil won't be causing me any more trouble." Richie chuckled. "I should say the house any more trouble."

They descended the stairs and did a quick tour of the living room and dining room, ending in the kitchen.

"There is no dishwasher. I'm afraid Aunt Faith liked to wash dishes by hand. And as you can see, the kitchen appliances are old. But they have been well taken care of. There were only the two of them, rambling around in this big old house." Richie dropped his dishtowel on the counter.

"I see they have a deep freezer." Constable Gatineau walked past Richie and opened the freezer.

"Yeah. It's not a big one, but it's a good size. And there is a microwave. It's like new. Aunt Faith hardly used it. But she did get a lot of use out of the deep freezer," Richie said. He tilted his head, a big, wide grin on his face.

Chapter Thirty-One

Violet rushed out the door and down the sidewalk. Grabbing Constable Gatineau's arm as he climbed out of his car.

"What did you find? Did you find Linda?"

"No. I'll explain. We should go inside."

Violet's face crumpled. "Oh, no, is she hurt?" She led the way into the house, her legs shaking. Was Linda dead? Gertrude met them on the step. Brushing against the constable's legs, the cat followed them back into the kitchen.

"Sit down, please, Mrs. Ficher. I'm sorry, but I didn't find your niece, Linda."

"Okay, then that means Linda is okay, and she's not. Well...you know." Violet gulped. "I thought you were going to tell me she was—"

"No, no. And there is no reason to believe any harm has come to your niece."

"No reason?" shrieked Violet. "You saw the message. Did you look in the deep freezer?"

Constable Gatineau sighed and gently said, "I searched the house and looked in the deep freezer. There was no dog and nothing in the deep freezer except a lot of frozen food. And the only person at the Hutchins' house was the nephew, Richie Hutchins."

Violet clasped and unclasped her hands. "The message on the mirror. In toothpaste, of all things! Their names and the word '*deep freezer*.' It has to mean something. It has to be about the dog. You had a report that a dog was poisoned. Any sign of a dog?"

"Mrs. Ficher, I said there was nothing in the deep freezer. Richie did say they had put a dog down. And there were dog scratches on a windowsill."

"There you have it," Violet said, her chin up; she folded her arms across her chest.

"I don't have anything. The Hutchins owned a dog. That doesn't mean they killed the neighbour's dog. In fact, that strange message on the mirror doesn't say anything about dogs."

"But the message means something. And Linda is missing," Violet's voice rose. "And so are the Hutchins."

"The Hutchins are not missing, Mrs. Ficher. You were the one who told me they were not home. And their nephew Richie confirmed it. He told me his aunt and uncle left on an across Canada camping trip."

"Maybe they have gone to bury the dogs somewhere in the country. And Linda is following them. To catch them in the act."

"There is a report of one dog poisoned. Not dogs."

"Yes, but something happened. You can't ignore the message Linda left written on the mirror. Or the fact that she is missing. Remember what Linda overheard?"

The constable sighed and flipped open his notebook. "Right. What precisely did your niece tell you she heard?"

"I remember Linda saying the voice was a man's voice. She told me she heard some guy complaining about digging a grave."

"First, you said a man wanted to hide a body. Now you are telling me this man was digging a grave?"

"Well, no, oh, maybe. I'm not sure of the precise words. But Linda thought someone had killed someone and wanted to hide a body." Darn, why couldn't she remember Linda's exact words?

"So, your niece didn't think this man was burying a dog? She thought there was a murder victim?"

"Well, yes, she did. You were the one who suggested it was a dog."

The constable's eyebrows lifted, and his eyes widened. "Me?"

"Yes, you. The poisoned dog, remember?"

The RCMP officer inhaled a big breath, let it out slowly, and glared at Violet. "Forget about the dog," he said in a harsh, booming voice.

Violet flinched.

"The issue is." Constable Gatineau's eyes bored into Violet's. "Linda thought there had been a murder and didn't report it."

"Yes, well, she wasn't sure. Linda didn't want to get someone in trouble if she was wrong. About digging the grave, I mean. But she definitely heard the man behind a hedge in the back alley. And before you ask me why she was in the back alley. I'll tell you, she was looking for Gertrude."

"Gertrude, the cat." His mouth set in a hard line.

"Yes."

"Right, looking for a cat." Constable Gatineau rolled his eyes. "So, this voice your niece overheard was on this block? A neighbour?"

"Yes, that's why she went to the garage sales." Violet leaned forward with her hands clasped on the table. At last, he was taking her seriously.

The constable tilted his head and eyeballed the ceiling. He exhaled and tapped his pen on his notebook. "You're saying Linda went to garage sales to find a killer?"

"Or a would-be killer."

"I see. A would-be killer." Constable Gatineau closed his notebook.

"Well, maybe not looking for a killer. Linda wasn't sure if anyone was dead. That's why she didn't report it. She thought maybe you would think she was a loon." Violet's lower lips trembled as she looked worriedly at the constable. He was standing and putting his notebook and pen in his pocket.

"Right."

"Linda was on a mission. She was going to find out if someone was missing. You know, ask around. Stuff like that."

"Right. Stuff like that."

Violet bit her bottom lip. What she was saying was falling on deaf ears. He was not going to do anything.

"I'm sure everything is fine," Constable Gatineau said. "Linda left you a note telling you she was going to leave. She packed her suitcase and drove home. I know she didn't answer your call. But that doesn't mean she didn't go home."

"But her car is parked outside."

"Her car is parked outside! I wish you had told me that earlier."

"Sorry, as I said, I'm a bit discombobulated."

"This sheds new light on your niece's disappearance. Linda packed her suitcase and left on foot. We will look into this." He brought out his notepad.

"And she took that old beater of Mabel's."

"You mean Mrs. Havelock's car."

"Yes."

He gave Violet a stern look. "Linda Burton, your niece took Mabel Havelock's car. Are you reporting this car as stolen?"

"Oh, no, of course not. Mabel wouldn't care that she borrowed her car. But seriously, Linda drives a Jetta. And Mabel's car is an old, beat-up purple Pontiac. Which would you drive if you had the choice?"

Constable Gatineau's eyes flickered, and he nodded. "But what I would drive, or what you would drive, is not the point. Do you want us to put out a stolen car bulletin?

Violet twisted her hands and sighed. If that was what it took to get the police looking for Linda. "Yes," she said.

"Would you perhaps know the licence plate number of Mabel Havelock's car?"

"Of course I do." As Violet rattled off the information, it crossed her mind that Mabel probably wouldn't know hers.

The constable finished writing the details and looked up from his notepad. "Thank you. We will put out a BOLO."

"A BOLO? What is that? How will this BOLO help find Mabel's car? What about an APB?"

"Don't worry, we will find the car. A BOLO means 'Be on the lookout.' Please try not to worry. And if anything else comes up, please call. I'm sure there is a simple explanation for your niece's disappearance." Constable Gatineau smiled kindly back at Violet and closed the door.

Violet went to the window and watched as the police cruiser pulled away. She was sure the young officer thought she was a nut bar. She knew the only reason the police were looking for Linda was her false accusation of a stolen car. Violet dropped the curtain and returned to the kitchen, her shoulders sagging. Where did Linda go? Violet plopped down on a chair, covering her face with her hands. It made no sense for Linda to take Mabel's old car.

She sat up with a start and drummed her fingers on the table. And what on earth did the message on the mirror mean? *Alfred, Faith, Richie, deep freezer* written in toothpaste on the mirror. Were the Hutchins really dog nappers? What did she know about the Hutchins? They did keep themselves to themselves. And they were not real community people. But dog nappers? And the nephew Richie? She'd only met him this morning. He seemed like a nice young man with a bright, winsome smile. But she didn't know anything about him besides his good manners. It did seem unlikely that these people were dog nappers. The constable had certainly dismissed that theory. Violet stopped drumming, her eyes pensive. But what if they were? And Linda was hot on their trail.

Chapter Thirty-Two

Gertrude meowed, looking intently up at Violet. "I wish Mabel was here," Violet said to the cat. "Your mistress would have handled that constable better. Sometimes, I'm just a scatterbrain," she said, smacking her hand on the table. Gertrude scooted under it. Violet crouched and looked under the table. "Oh, Gertrude, I scared you. I know you've had a few bad days. But I'll make sure you're taken care of now." The cat was sitting on a piece of notepaper, switching her tail. "Sorry, Gertrude," Violet said, shooing the cat off the sheet of paper. She picked it up. The paper differed from the small, lined paper on which Linda's goodbye note was written.

Violet brushed off the sheet of creamed-coloured paper. The notepaper had a small cluster of grapes in the corner. The sheet of paper was from Mabel's notepad on the counter. This notepaper was what Mabel wrote her grocery list on. But this was not a grocery list. Written in big block letters, was the word *BINGO?* She stared at the words in puzzlement. Bingo?

Gertrude came out from under the table and stared at her, her tail switching back and forth. "I bet bingo is a clue," she told the cat. The tabby cat jumped up on her lap. Absently, Violet began to pet her. "When Linda went looking for you, she heard a man say he had to hide a body. At least, that's what I think she said." The orange tabby cat meowed a reply. Violet continued to voice her ideas aloud as she stroked the cat. "It makes sense, Gertrude. Somehow, Linda found out the Hutchins poisoned the dog. The dog was in the freezer because they didn't know where to hide it. Mary said Linda was in their house at the garage sale. Linda looked in the freezer for some reason and found a dog." Purring, Gertrude snuggled down on Violet's lap.

Violet stopped petting Gertrude, raised her hand, and rubbed her forehead. Yes, that irritating constable had gone to the house and saw no signs of a dead dog. Violet slapped the kitchen table with the flat of her hand again and said, "Of course, the dog isn't in the freezer now! Because the Hutchins took the dead dog on their cross-Canada camping trip. They plan on burying the dog at the old Bingo Hall. It makes sense. Linda took Mabel's car to follow the Hutchins' camper down Bingo Road. Judging by the muddy socks, it was raining, so she took Mabel's car, not wanting to get her Jetta dirty."

Gertrude stopped purring, glaring reproachfully at Violet. Violet's eyes flashed. She smiled knowingly. "Linda is following them. And she has had car trouble. That car is so old I'm surprised it even works. She's out on Bingo Road. There must be no cell coverage there. That's why she hasn't called or answered her texts." Violet pushed the thought of the suitcase out of her mind. It didn't fit her scenario. "Bingo is the clue. I'm sure of it." Violet jumped up, and Gertrude fell to the floor.

VIOLET SPED OUT OF town. The Subaru shimmied back and forth before gaining traction, churning down the rutted gravel road. "No wonder Linda didn't want to use her Jetta," muttered Violet. "Bingo, bingo," she sang, tapping her fingers on her steering wheel. It had to be the clue Linda had left for her. The road was called Bingo Road because an old one-room schoolhouse had been used as an old Bingo Hall. The building was abandoned. But the name stuck. But why leave a clue? And why write on the mirror? In toothpaste, of all things. Maybe it wasn't a dog's body. Perhaps it was a person. "Oh, Linda, what is going on?"

Slowing her Subaru, Violet brought the car to a halt. "This bingo clue is garbage," Violet shouted, slamming her fist on the steering wheel. She was on a wild goose chase.

Laying her head back on the seat rest, Violet squeezed her eyes shut. She blew out a breath. "Linda wouldn't even know this road was called Bingo Road," she moaned. And Linda wouldn't camp overnight on the road because of a stalled car.

She sat up, her jaw clenched. What an idiot she'd been. Why would Linda pack a suitcase to follow the Hutchins? And how would Linda know in advance that the Hutchins would go to the old Bingo Hall? A hall she didn't even know existed. It was all false deductions. The Hutchins, wherever they were, were not dog nappers. She always accused her friend Mabel of jumping to conclusions. She hadn't just jumped. She had leaped. The bingo clue was a dud. She had to go back to town and wait for news of Linda. The police would track down Mabel's car. Disheartened, Violet started her car; she needed to find an approach to turn around.

She drove over the hill and slammed on her brakes. Her car swerved as it skidded on the gravel. Across the road, Mabel's muddy purple Pontiac was rammed against an embankment. The car's hood was up, and the back and driver's side doors were open.

Her heart beating wildly, Violet was out of her car in seconds. She ran to the crashed vehicle and stuck her head inside the car. A red suitcase lay on its side, clothes spilling out. She breathed a sigh of relief. There was no Linda trapped inside.

Stepping back from the car, she looked around at the empty countryside. In the distance, the old schoolhouse. Linda had lost control of her car and went for help. Her cell phone wasn't charged, or she would have called for assistance. "The old Bingo Hall," Violet yelled, sprinting back to her car. The hall wasn't that far away. Linda must have gone there for shelter in the rain.

Violet gunned the motor; mud and rocks flew, pinging on the fender wells. "I'm coming, Linda," she shouted as she sped down the road. She had to slow her car down as she turned off the grid road onto the weed-infested lane. The Subaru jolted and rocked in the deep ruts, grinding to a halt in front of the old schoolhouse.

Slamming her car door, Violet raced into the abandoned Bingo Hall. The small, dark schoolroom smelt of dirt and mold. Coughing and sneezing, she kicked an empty beer bottle. The bottle rolled over cigarette butts that littered the floor, coming to rest beside a pile of broken plastic webbed lawn chairs. A dirty canvas blind hung off of one old chair. Her heart sank. Linda was not inside. Stepping on a small nail clipper, she kicked the clippers across the floor.

"Where are you, Linda?" Violet moaned, wrinkling her brow and biting her bottom lip. Her eyes darted around the small room. Spotting profanity written on the blackboard. She pursed her lips, marched over to the board, and tried erasing the words with the flat of her hands. But the words weren't in chalk. Violet turned her back on the blackboard and wiped her hands on her jeans. She sighed. Profanity was the least of her worries. Where was Linda? She wasn't in the crashed car.

Hurrying out the door, Violet stood on the rickety steps surveying the countryside. A flock of crows cawed as they circled in the clear blue sky. The warm spring breeze rustled the long grass and bushes. In the distance, a herd of cows grazed in a lush green pasture. Everything looked so peaceful.

Violet fought a rising sense of panic. Linda could be lying out in the field, injured.

Chapter Thirty-Three

She'd phone the police and organize a search party. As she reached into her back pocket for her phone, Violet heard the sounds of muffled thumps. She stood still, cocked her head, listening. She waited and heard another faint thud. At the sound of the next bang, Violet turned and raced around the side of the old schoolhouse. She stopped in her tracks. A big silver motorhome was parked behind the school. Was this the Hutchins? If it was, they hadn't gone far. Had last night's rain stopped them? Maybe Linda was with them, or they'd seen her?

Violet knocked on the door and waited. "Hello, anyone home?" She heard another thud, and the door vibrated. "Hello, can I come in?" The banging increased.

Violet tried the door. The door was locked. "Hello, it's me, Violet Ficher. May I come in?" she asked. A rapid tattoo of banging followed her request. Violet put her hands on her hips. Someone or an animal, perhaps a dog, was locked inside. She hurried to the front of the motorhome and climbed up on the bumper, clambering over the hood. She put one hand on either side of her face and peered through the windshield. An old, ragged tramp lay tied up on the floor. The old tramp raised his head, duct tape over his mouth. The little tramp looked pleadingly up at Violet.

"Oh, my God!" Violet shrieked. It wasn't a tramp. It was Linda, her hands tied behind her back and her ankles shackled. "I'm coming, Linda," she yelled, jumping off the bumper. She ran back to the door, yanking on the handle, trying in vain to open it. "Wait, I'll get something," she shouted.

She sprinted back to her car and opened the trunk. What to use? There was a tire wrench. But would that work? She needed a pry bar or something. It would have to do. She grabbed the tire iron and raced back to the van. She banged on the latch. The latch bent. If the handle broke off, she wouldn't be able to open the door.

Where were the Hutchins? Were they really the dog nappers? And if they were, why did they tie up Linda? But she had no time to puzzle that out. She had to get Linda out of there. And she needed to hurry. These people were obviously deranged. They could be back at any moment. Violet ran to the front of the campervan and looked up at the windshield. Could she break the windshield? Violet climbed back up on the bumper, crawled across the hood, knelt, and swung the tire iron with one hand. The tire iron bounced off the windshield. The recoil sent Violet sliding down the hood to the bumper. She scrambled back. Kneeling on the hood, Violet lifted the tire iron over her head. With both hands tightly clenching the wrench, she swung the tire iron. The windshield cracked. She beat at the windshield again and again.

The glass shattered but didn't break. A thin film was holding most of the broken glass in one piece. Violet swung the iron again and made a hole. She reached her hand into the hole, grabbed the jagged piece of glass, and pulled. The chunk of glass stubbornly stayed put, lacerating her fingers. She peered through the hole in the windscreen. Linda's eyes were pleading. Violet slid back on the hood, away from the windshield. Sat on her bum, leaned back and planted both hands firmly on the hood. She reared up and slammed her feet against the cracked windshield. The windscreen shattered; chunks of glass fell out.

Unnoticed by Violet, her phone popped out of her pocket. The phone slid down the hood, bouncing off the bumper and landing on the grass.

Violet's heart hammered frantically as she chipped away at the hole with the tire iron. Fragments of glass flew. The hole grew bigger. She knelt. Was the hole big enough? It would have to do. The Hutchins might return before she freed Linda. Headfirst, Violet crawled through the shattered windscreen onto the dashboard. Dropped the tire iron on the driver's seat, slid to the floor, and sped over to Linda.

Violet's eyes were wide with shock. Linda's clothes were ragged and caked in dry mud. Her hair was dirty and matted. She sucked in her breath. Linda's bare feet were bloody, a jagged cut on her cheek, and her neck had big ugly bruises. Good god. The Hutchins were monsters. Violet knelt. "Oh my God, oh my God, oh my God. Linda, what have they done to you?"

Lying on her side, Linda looked up at her aunt, tears welling in her eyes.

"It's okay. You're okay. I'm getting you out of here. I'm going to pull this tape off. It will hurt, but I think fast is better. Don't you?"

Tears shimmered in Linda's eyes as she nodded weakly. Violet ripped the tape from Linda's mouth.

Linda flinched. Blood trickled down her cheek. She squeezed her eyes shut but didn't make a sound.

Violet wrapped her arms around her niece, hugging her. Linda buried her face in Violet's shoulder. Violet stroked Linda's hair, leaving bloody streaks. She pulled Linda closer, hugging her harder.

"You should go. Go now while you can. Phone the police," whispered Linda hoarsely.

"These people are monsters. What the hell have they done to you?"

Linda licked her cracked, dry lips and croaked, "Never mind, go. Get out of here and phone the police."

"I'm not leaving you here all alone." Violet threw the crumpled duct tape on the floor, rushed to the cupboard, and opened a drawer in the cabinet. She pawed through the utensils. Grabbed a handful of knives and forks and tossed them onto the counter. Grasping a steak knife, she hurried back to Linda and began sawing the plastic tie wrap on her wrists.

"I'm so glad you found me," Linda rasped. "I thought I was going to die."

"I found you. Thanks to your clues." Violet pressed on the steak knife.

"The clues? The mirror?"

"In part. That told me something was desperately wrong. But what brought me here was because I thought bingo was a clue." Violet threw down the steak knife and returned to the cutlery drawer.

"Bingo?" Linda licked her dry, bruised lips.

"Yes, bingo. I saw your note with bingo written on it and thought it meant Bingo Road." Violet clawed through the pile of knives and forks, sending the items into the sink. "Aha," she said. Picking up a paring knife, she returned to Linda.

"I don't know what you mean. I don't know where Bingo Road is," croaked Linda.

"Yes, I know," Violet said, kneeling, she attacked the plastic tie strap on Linda's wrists. "I made a major leap, as in jumping to conclusions. But it's a good thing I did. If I hadn't, I wouldn't have found the car. And I wouldn't have found you."

"Thank you," whispered Linda. "He left me here to die."

Violet sliced through the restraints on her wrist. "The Hutchins have to be insane. What is it about them and dogs?"

"Dogs?"

Violet grimaced; the dog theory was wrong, just like the bingo clue. But it didn't matter; first things first. Free Linda. Linda could explain later. "Never mind. Let's get you out of here. These people are evil. I can't understand why they did this to you."

"Whatever you do, do not go to the bedroom," whispered Linda.

"I don't know what you mean? A constable looked in their house," Violet said, slicing the plastic tie strap on Linda's ankles. "He would have looked in their bedrooms."

"Not the house, I mean here," Linda said, struggling to stand.

Puzzled, Violet stood and strode to the partition.

"No, don't go there," Linda said, her voice breaking; she sank back onto the floor.

Violet poked her head around the wall. On the bed was Faith's corpse, wrapped in plastic. Lying beside her was Alfred. His mouth hung open, his eyes gazing sightlessly up at the ceiling. "Oh, my God!" screamed Violet. Stunned, she turned and rushed back to Linda.

"Richie. Richie killed them. He locked me in here with these dead people. He wanted me to slowly starve to death."

"Richie locked you in here, with these corpses, to starve to death!" Violet crouched down and swept Linda into an embrace. "Oh, Linda, my dear." She stroked Linda's hair and said, "It's okay. You're safe now. I'm getting you the hell out of here."

Chapter Thirty-Four

The door to the motorhome swung open, and Richie stepped in. Arms folded across his chest, he stood in the doorway with a big, broad smile. "Well, well, it looks like we have company."

Violet, heart pounding, stood; she snatched the paring knife off the floor and stepped between Richie and Linda. Waving the knife in front of her, she yelled, "Don't come any closer."

Richie darted forward and grabbed Violet's hand, twisting her arm. Violet dropped the paring knife and backed away. Grinning, Richie kicked the small knife, sending it across to land beside the cupboard.

Glancing down at Linda crouched on the floor, Richie curled his lips and sneered, "Ah, dear old Nosey, curled up on the floor like a good puppy dog. That's a good girl, you stay down." His blue eyes sparkled with amusement as he looked at Violet cowering by the white vinyl driver's seat.

"Now, what am I to do with the two of you?" Richie asked. He took a jackknife from his pocket. Opening the blade slowly, he said, "I guess this is the answer. Knife wounds won't show on a decomposed body." He looked down at Linda. "An RCMP officer came by the house. The cop said he was looking to buy the house. I didn't buy that. How did he know to come looking for you, I wonder? And why did he look in the deep freeze? I confess I underestimated you. I don't know how you did it. I have to give it to you. You were a crafty little devil." He gave her a broad smile. "But it was all for naught. Right, Nosey?"

Linda, cringing on the floor, curled up into a ball.

Richie giggled. "I see you finally learned your lesson, Nosey. All the fight seems to have gone out of you. There's not much left of your feisty little self now. And this one." Richie looked at Violet. "You don't have any fight in you at all." He glanced at the windscreen and shook his head. "You made a nasty mess of the windshield. Uncle Alfred would have been livid. But that doesn't matter. What does matter is that damn cop snooping around. Now I have to speed things up."

Jackknife in hand, Richie moved toward a recoiling Violet. "You can be first. I'm not picking favourites. I have no hard feelings against you. It's because I want Nosey to watch you die." He giggled.

Linda stabbed him in the ankle with the steak knife, and Richie's high-pitched laughter turned into a scream. He spun around, hopping on one foot, and stared down in surprise at Linda. Violet grabbed the tire iron from the driver's seat and slammed it on Richie's head. He stumbled but didn't go down. Violet hit him again. She was about to hit him one more time for good measure. But Richie stayed down. Crouching, he put his hands over his head. Violet lowered the tire iron and picked up his knife, tossing it onto the driver's seat.

Wide-eyed in disbelief, Richie looked up at Violet. Blood from the wound on his head ran down the side of his face. "Please don't hit me again," he pleaded. His voice shook, and his body trembled.

"I won't if you stay down," Violet said coldly, reaching into her back pocket for her phone. Her hand came up empty. She looked at Linda, who was struggling to get to her feet. "I've lost my phone, or it's in the car. We need to call the RCMP."

"Don't go," rasped Linda, licking her dry, cracked lips. "Don't leave me here with this monster."

Violet eyed the man cowering on the floor. "Don't worry, I won't leave you. But we need to call the police, and I don't have my phone."

Leaving bloody handprints on the floor, Richie pushed himself back to the kitchen cabinet.

"Richie has a phone." Tottering on weak legs, Linda slowly advanced toward Richie, her hand outstretched. "Give me your phone."

Richie, his back against the cabinet, wiped his hand on the knee of his jeans. Reaching into his pocket, he produced his phone. "It's not locked," he said.

As Linda stooped to take the phone from his hand, Richie dropped it and seized her, pulling her onto the floor beside him. Holding the paring knife in his other hand, he pressed it to her throat.

"Good try, ladies." Richie's blue eyes glinted. A sneer on his face. "But your old lady dynamic dual act is over." He stood, pulling Linda up with him.

Linda grabbed Richie's arm, digging her fingers into the angry red slashes that Gertrude had made. Howling in pain, Richie jerked away. "Now," screamed Linda.

Violet swung the tire iron. Linda ducked. The tire iron clipped Richie square on the side of his head. He dropped to the floor. And Linda scrambled away.

The women looked at each other and then down at Richie, who lay face down on the floor. White-faced and gasping, Linda picked up his phone and handed it to Violet.

Violet took the phone and said, "That should put a stop to this despicable, evil man."

Linda, eyes wide, her arms hanging limply by her side, looked at her aunt. "Oh, Aunt Violet, I can never thank you enough for coming to my rescue," she said in a thin, hoarse voice.

Violet looked down at Richie. He lay motionless on the floor. Blood was seeping from the wound on the side of his face. She put her arm around Linda and hugged her. Her lips curled in a sneer. "His biggest mistake was underestimating women."

"I've got to get out of here. I've been trapped here with these two dead people. I can't stand it another minute." Linda opened the motorhome door and stepped out into the bright sunshine, breathing big gulps of fresh air.

Violet looked at the partition. Richie's dead aunt and uncle lay on the other side of the wall. And the evil psychopath wanted to make Linda the next victim. Her fingers tightened on the tire iron. Violet stepped toward him and paused, hovering over him with the iron raised. Compressing her lips, Violet turned and followed Linda out of the RV, closing the door behind her.

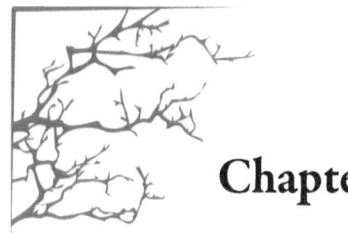

Chapter Thirty-Five

Linda staggered to the bike lying against the old schoolhouse wall. A water bottle lay in the bottom of the bike's wire basket. She picked up the sealed bottle and unscrewed the top, swallowing big gulps of water. She sank beside the bike and leaned against the wall. Tilting her head back, she felt the sun's warmth and the fresh air wafting across her face.

Violet dropped the tire iron into the bicycle basket, leaned against the RV door, and tapped on the phone. "He lied. His darn phone is locked." She bit her bottom lip, her eyes thoughtful. "You know, I think I had my phone in my back pocket when I climbed on the hood of this camper." Violet tossed Richie's phone into the wire basket and ran to the front of the motorhome.

Linda looked up at the cloudless blue sky, breathing deeply, and smiled. In a cluster of wild yellow clover, the bees hummed. A blue jay flew down to sit on the schoolhouse roof. The bird cocked its head and chirped. A gopher sat up on its hind legs, looking at her, then scurried away into the tall grass. Off in the distance, a goose honked. Linda sighed a contented sigh.

"Yes, my phone is here," Violet called.

The sound of the campervan motor revving brought Linda to her feet. The motorhome crept forward.

She tossed the bottle of water into the basket and sprinted to the front of the camper. "Run," she screamed at Violet.

Violet jumped out of the motorhome's path. Holding onto her phone, she rolled on the grass.

Linda raced alongside the RV. Sitting at the wheel was Richie, blood running down his face. He flashed her a big, broad, eerie smile.

"You're not getting away, you bastard," screamed Linda. The Campervan sped past her, mowing down an old page wire fence, careening across the prairie grass.

Jumping up, waving her phone, Violet yelled, "I'm calling the RCMP! He won't get far."

Linda sprinted back to the bicycle. She grabbed it and jumped on, peddling after the motorhome as it bounced across the open field.

"Linda, don't. Stop. Stay here. I'm calling the police."

Linda kept peddling. The peddles dug into her bare feet, and her leg muscles screamed in protest. The campervan was far ahead, but Linda had no trouble following it. Dust flew up in the wake of the motorhome carrying its macabre cargo. It bumped and churned through the weed-infested grass. The camper was going faster now. Intent on Richie and the motorhome, Linda peddled faster.

But the motorhome was speeding. She was going to lose sight of it in a minute. And then, it was gone.

The sound of metal grinding, glass shattering, and rocks falling filled the air. Followed by a thundering thud. A cloud of dirt spiralled up into the sky.

Linda, panting, leg muscles burning, peddled on. She came to the edge of a ravine. It was the ravine; Richie said he was going to push them off. Linda threw the bike down on the ground. The tire iron, phone and water bottle flew out of the basket. The bottle bounced and soared over the edge into the gully. In the steep rocky gorge below, the campervan. The camper had hit an enormous boulder and flipped over onto the roof. Unlike in the movies, the RV didn't burst into flames. Instead, the silver motorhome's body lay squashed amid a swirling cloud of dust and dirt. The only sound was of grinding. The motorhome's wheels were turning in the air.

Linda grabbed the tire iron off the ground and began her barefoot trek down the unstable slope of the gorge. One hand holding on to the tall weeds to help her descend, the other clutching the tire iron. Stones dug into her feet, and thorns pierced her legs and hands. She slid on her bum the last few feet to the campervan.

She thought of poor Faith trussed up like a chicken and her evil husband, Alfred. Where were their bodies? But more importantly, where was Richie? Surely, he couldn't have survived the crash. Did he have a seat belt buckled up when he made his bid to escape? Linda hefted the tire iron. She crept over rocks and the ripped up bushes and stones to the front of the motorhome. There was no windshield, and the driver's chair was empty. Linda whirled around. She sunk down on the boulder and dropped the tire iron.

Laying a few feet away was Richie. His body twisted, his head crushed. Her tormenter was dead.

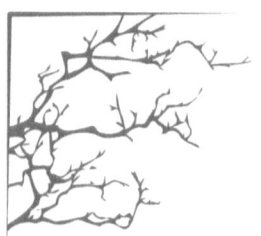

Epilogue

Pink and purple hues of the setting sun filter through the leafy green trees. Mabel plopped down onto her favourite faded red Adirondack chair and sighed happily. Her foot was healing nicely. She was home, and it was a beautiful July evening. Gertrude mewed and jumped from the porch railing to leap on Mabel's lap. The tabby cat purred as her mistress scratched behind her ear.

"Good evening."

Mabel turned to see her friend Violet and Violet's niece Linda mount the steps. She bit her lip. Linda was willow thin, and she had a slight limp. There was a faint scar on her cheek. And her red hair was streaked with gray.

Gertrude hopped off her lap and scampered to Linda, circling and brushing against the younger woman's legs.

"My cat is very fickle, but she has good taste," Mabel said, chuckling.

Linda knelt, rubbing the orange tabby cat's belly. "I've missed you," she said to the cat.

"This is a nice surprise. Come and sit."

Linda, followed by Gertrude, crossed the porch. Linda bent to place a kiss on Mabel's cheek. "Thank you. You look comfortable."

"I am. It's a beautiful evening. And now it's even better because you girls are here to enjoy it with me."

Violet set a bottle of champagne on a small, round, red plastic table. "We are celebrating tonight. I'll pop into the kitchen and get glasses. If that's okay with you, Mabel?"

"Oh, for sure. You know my kitchen as well as you know your own."

"I could go and get them," Linda said.

"No, let me. We are celebrating, remember?" Violet said over her shoulder as she entered Mabel's house.

Linda arranged two more chairs beside Mabel. "Your garden looks wonderful."

"Thanks. And thank goodness my friend Fred came to weed. I was laid up with my broken foot. But I'm right as rain now." Mabel held up her foot, rotating it. "You're looking rested."

"I am. I feel fine; no, I feel great." The tiny, thin woman said as she sat on a deck chair. Gertrude jumped on her lap, rubbing her furry head against Linda's chin.

"You should get a cat. I can tell you're a real cat person."

"I will, but first, I'm getting a dog."

"A puppy. What breed? Or is it a Heintz puppy?"

"No, not a puppy. I'm getting a fully trained dog."

"A fully trained dog, that does make it easier. So not a Heintz then?"

Linda tugged her multi-coloured T-shirt out of the band of her blue jean shorts. "No, a rottweiler."

Mabel arched an eyebrow. Linda wasn't quite as fine as she said.

"I've already met with the kennel people. They match the dogs up with the owners. My dog's name is Bernie. As soon as I'm settled, I can bring him home." She grinned. "Do you want to know what we are celebrating?"

"I might have a clue. I hope I'm right."

"I purchased a house."

"Great. The rumour mill said you were buying Mrs. Pinquist's house. Am I right?"

Linda giggled. "Yes, you are."

Violet came out of the house carrying a tray of champagne glasses. "Linda signed the papers today. She is now officially a Glenhaven resident," she said, setting the tray on the small table.

"Congratulations. This is fantastic news."

"Yes, it was a private sale, the papers are signed, and the next step is to give the house a proper clean and then move in."

"I'm so glad you are moving to Glenhaven. I was afraid after your nightmare experience with the Hutchins. You would be put off of our little town."

"Linda is made of good stuff," Violet said, popping the top off the bottle of champagne. "But I was afraid, too."

"It wasn't Glenhaven's fault what happened," Linda said.

"After your horrible ordeal. I wouldn't have blamed you if you never set foot in Glenhaven again," Violet said, pouring the champagne into the glasses.

"I admit I had a very naïve view of small-town Saskatchewan. I found out there are evil people everywhere, not just in the cities."

"You are a very resilient girl." Marvelled Mabel, accepting a glass of champagne from Violet.

"You think so?" Linda smiled. "I know I never gave up. Well, except when I was locked in the trunk in the attic."

As Violet handed Linda a glass of champagne, she exchanged a look of concern with Mabel.

"But it's over. And I do realize how lucky I am. Aunt Violet saved me from certain death. I was a naïve person. But not anymore. I always thought people underestimated me. And I guess I underestimated myself, too. But I learnt a lot about myself."

"You are a strong, determined woman. I can tell you no one here underestimates you." Violet poured herself a glass of champagne.

"Thanks. I'm not as trusting as I once was. But that's okay. I learnt it's okay to be scared." Linda's fingers lingered on her neck. "It's our intuition's way of warning us of danger and evil. But fear is not going to rule my life. I won't let that happen. Richie wins if I cringe and cower and run back to the city. I love Glenhaven. And that evil man can't take my love of life away from me." She smiled. "Oh, and one more reason to celebrate. I've got a part-time job at the library. I will be doing story time with the youngsters, among other duties."

"Here's to a new bright future," Violet said. The women held up their glasses in a salute.

"Yes, and all is right with my world," Linda said, clinking glasses with Mabel and Violet. Her eyes darted to the darkening alley. She was safe. She had to stop imagining someone was watching her. She didn't believe in ghosts.

The End

Don't miss out!

Visit the website below and you can sign up to receive emails whenever Joan Havelange publishes a new book. There's no charge and no obligation.

https://books2read.com/r/B-A-CCKUC-FUKUF

BOOKS 2 READ

Connecting independent readers to independent writers.

Did you love *Moving is Murder*? Then you should read *Murder Exit Stage Right*[1] by Joan Havelange!

Murder is a hard act to follow. The only thing Mabel knows for sure is that the butler didn't do it.

All the drama doesn't take place on the stage at the Glenhaven Drama Festival. A collection of amateur actors, with big egos, land in Mabel Havelock's hometown. A cast member of the Glenhaven Players is dead. An accident or murder?

Mabel has been railroaded into taking a role in the play. As the drama festival progresses, mysterious accidents and sabotage are happening on and off stage. Then the adjudicator becomes the prime target.

---

1. https://books2read.com/u/b6XKY6

2. https://books2read.com/u/b6XKY6

Was Mabel's brush with death an accident, or attempted murder? Mabel and her best friend, Violet Ficher, are determined to ferret out the culprit. The problem is why? Who has anything to gain and why did Sherman have to die?

Also by Joan Havelange

Mabel and Violet Mysteries
Wayward Shot
Death and Denial
The Trouble with Funerals
The Suspects
Murder Exit Stage Right

Standalone
Moving is Murder